MAGIC
BOX
MURDER

MAGIC BOX MURDER

A DARCY GAUGHAN MYSTERY

J.C. KENNEY

LEVEL
BEST BOOKS

First published by Level Best Books 2024

Copyright © 2024 by J.C. Kenney

This novel is entirely a work of fiction. The names, characters and incidents portrayed in it are the work of the author's imagination. Any resemblance to actual persons, living or dead, events or localities is entirely coincidental.

J.C. Kenney asserts the moral right to be identified as the author of this work.

First edition

ISBN: 978-1-68512-587-5

Cover art by Level Best Designs

This book was professionally typeset on Reedsy.
Find out more at reedsy.com

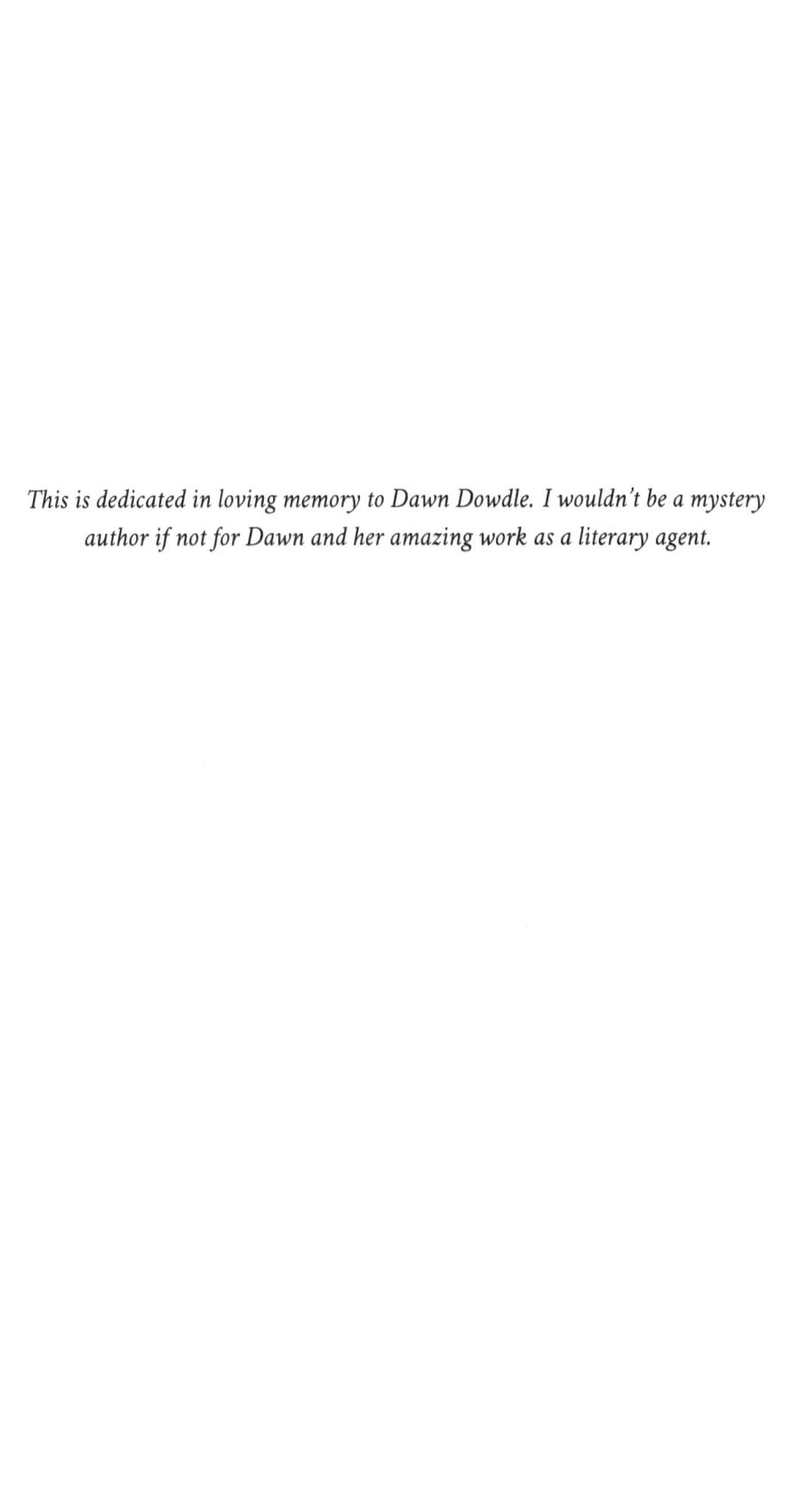

This is dedicated in loving memory to Dawn Dowdle. I wouldn't be a mystery author if not for Dawn and her amazing work as a literary agent.

Chapter One

Darcy Gaughan loved her life. She had a job that rocked. She had friends she'd do anything for and who'd do anything for Darcy. Her family, from her parents to her cat, loved her. She was happy. Life was good.

Darcy hated snow, though. It wasn't that she had anything in particular against the form of precipitation. The last time she consumed alcohol, she'd left a bar, slipped on a snow-covered sidewalk, and fallen into a gutter. Too drunk to extricate herself from the predicament and too depressed to care about what happened to her, she lay there until she passed out. The next thing Darcy remembered, she was being lifted out of the snow and bundled into a warm car by her friend Jenna Washburn and her mentor Eddie Maxwell, may God rest his soul.

Eddie and Jenna saved Darcy's life that night.

To this day, six years on from that regrettable episode, heavy snow left her on edge. She told people her aversion to it was because she didn't like driving in the hazardous conditions that often came with the wintery precipitation.

The real reason was that she couldn't escape the memory of the worst night of her life. And the role snow had played in it.

"You never forget rock bottom." Darcy shivered and crossed her arms as she watched big, fat flakes fall from the impenetrable, dark sky.

"You doing okay?" Charlotte Ryan, the general manager of Marysburg Music, joined Darcy at the store's front window to watch the snow fall. With no customers in the store at the moment, the only sound came from the rush of air through the HVAC system. It was as if the environment indoors

1

was attempting to match the serene conditions outdoors. Even the George Winston album that was playing on the turntable had ended.

Darcy shrugged. "I dunno. It's been a lifetime ago, and when I see weather like this, I still go right back to that night. The rock gods know there are plenty of nights I don't remember. If there's one night in my life I wish I could forget, it's that one."

Charlotte put her arm around the record store owner. "I can't pretend to know what you went through back then. What I do know is how far you've come since then. I know Jenna's proud of how far you've come and everything you've accomplished. I'm sure Eddie is, too."

"Stop it. You're going to make me cry." Darcy wiped a tear from the corner of her eye as she hugged Charlotte back.

"And all of us here at good old Marysburg Music are proud to call you Boss."

"Seriously?" Darcy sniffed and wiped her eyes with her sleeve. "One more word out of you, and I'm going to melt into a puddle right here on the floor, just like the Wicked Witch of the West."

"Who, you may recall from when we went to see *Wicked* at the Civic Theater, didn't really die. And, I believe, lived happily ever after."

Darcy glanced at Char out of the corner of her eye. Her friend had raised her eyebrows, as if she was waiting for Darcy to challenge her. One didn't challenge Char when it came to musical theater.

"She did rise from the dead, kind of. Didn't she?"

Charlotte broke out in a wide grin. "Not unlike someone else I know. She even got the guy, too."

"Let's not get ahead of ourselves, girl," Darcy said with a laugh. "Just because I'm finally comfortable calling Liam my boyfriend doesn't mean we have anything permanent."

"Uh-huh." Char gave a slow nod. "Whatever you say, Elphaba."

Their back and forth was interrupted when someone entered the store, bringing a gust of frigid air with them.

"Welcome to Marysburg Music." Charlotte stepped toward the customer, who was brushing snow off their shoulders. "Frightful conditions out there.

2

Can I get you a cup of tea?"

"That would be nice." The customer removed an Indianapolis Colts stocking cap that had been pulled down low over his head. It was Sean O'Sullivan, known to one and all in Marysburg as the Hobbit.

"What's up, Sean." Darcy took a tentative step toward the man and held out her hands. "Can I take your coat?"

"Oh, uh, sure. Thanks." His awkward response had been as uncertain as Darcy's greeting.

The two of them had a strained relationship. The man had been holding onto a grudge against her for almost a year now. On three different occasions, she'd offered a heartfelt apology for the way she roped him into her investigation of Eddie's murder.

His acceptance of the apology had been slow in coming and had been eventually verbalized with a begrudging "Whatever."

"What brings you by? Haven't seen you here in ages." Darcy knew for a fact that the Hobbit had been avoiding her by visiting the stores on Tuesday, her day off.

"Need to pick up the prize for the Magic Box Marathon." With a small smile, he accepted the cup of steaming coffee Charlotte offered him.

"Right." Darcy glanced over his shoulder so she could read a flyer posted on the bulletin board. It wasn't difficult to do since he was maybe five feet, five inches tall. She had at least three inches on the guy.

The Magic Box Marathon was a gaming tournament, twenty-four-hours in duration, that the Hobbit started a decade ago. Over the years, it had grown into one of the community's biggest annual events. Players came from all over the Midwest to compete for bragging rights and prizes in three different divisions—board games, card games, and video games.

Since the tournament was celebrating its tenth anniversary, the Hobbit had been hitting up every business in town to ask for donations to take the event to another level. The buzz around town was that, for the first time, a large cash prize was going to be awarded to the overall winner of the event. How that was going to be determined was a closely guarded secret.

And was generating a ton of excitement in the gaming community.

Charlotte had promised to contribute a twenty-five-dollar Marysburg Music gift card as one of the prizes. She was no dummy, so taking no chances that she'd be overruled due to her boss' frosty relationship with the man, she told Darcy after making the pledge.

"The gift card. Char told me about that." Darcy shot her general manager a quick look. "Ten years is kind of a big deal. Instead of one gift card, how about we make it two? What do you think?"

"That would be cool, Darc. And make us look good, too. Be back with them in a minute."

"That's very kind of you." The Hobbit kept his gaze on Charlotte for a while before turning it toward Darcy. "Any particular reason why? I mean, it's not like we're friends or anything."

Darcy barked out a laugh. The man wasn't wrong. She took a moment to refold a Marysburg Music T-shirt that a customer had left askew while she figured out how, exactly, she wanted to respond.

"We may not be buddies, but there's no reason we can't be allies. We're both local business owners. We ought to stick together. You know, look out for each other and help when we can."

"Hear, hear." Charlotte gave her a thumbs-up.

"The store had a good holiday season. This gives us a chance to extend those good vibes for a while." She took a glance out the store's front picture window. It was still snowing. "Beats thinking about the weather. Ugh."

"Well, thanks. Thanks a lot. I appreciate it." He chuckled as he ran his beefy fingers through his shaggy hair. "Normally, I love winter. Not right now, though. I hope the snow doesn't lead to any last-minute cancellations for the tournament."

"I don't think you'll have to worry about that, Sean," Charlotte said as she handed him the gift cards. "If the chatter I've heard in the store is any indication, people aren't going to let a few inches of snow stop them. That's a whopper of a grand prize you got this year."

It was common knowledge within the walls of Marysburg Music that Darcy didn't keep up with local goings on very well. It had been understandable in the years before she inherited the store. In those days, she was focused on her own health. As it should have been.

Now, though, she owned the place. There were certain expectations regarding her engagement with the Marysburg, Indiana business community. She was trying, but still had a way to go before she became someone who was truly in the know.

In light of that, she relied on Charlotte to keep her up to date.

"Yeah, five hundred bucks. That's a sweet chunk of change." She looked at Charlotte and raised her eyebrows in a silent gesture of thank you.

The Hobbit slid the gift cards into a pocket. "The business community you were just talking about really came through. It took a few years for everyone to see the economic impact the event produced. Now everyone gets it. Shoot, even the Marysburg House is booked full this weekend."

Darcy let out a low whistle. Normally, late February was a slow time for the town's local bed & breakfast. Selling out its rooms was great news.

"That'll be some nice bank for them." Darcy gave the Hobbit a light punch to his upper arm. "Good on ya, man."

"It's a labor of love." He looked at his watch. It was a massive luxury model that looked like it probably weighed five pounds. "And along that line, I have a couple more stops, and then I need to get back to the store. Play kicks off in an hour."

"If there's anything I can do to help, let me know." Darcy's cheeks got hot. She wasn't used to offering to help someone outside of her small circle of friends. Her hope was that, in time, she'd get over her embarrassment when making such an offer and simply enjoy the good feeling it produced.

"You know what?" He slurped the last of the coffee down. "There is something. Do you want to present your gift cards to the contestant that wins them? Some of the folks in town making donations are doing that. It'd be even more publicity for you."

"Yeah, totally." Darcy checked the poster. "I should be there at six tomorrow night, right?"

"Yep. The games end at six, and the awards ceremony starts at a quarter after."

"I'll be there. Sounds like it ought to be a memorable evening."

Darcy had no idea how prophetic her statement would turn out to be.

Chapter Two

"I can't believe it's still coming down." Darcy mumbled a few curse words under her breath. The three inches of snow that accumulated through the night, on top of the two inches from the previous day, was enough to make getting around a challenge. Even in her old but trustworthy jeep named Rusty, she'd had a few white-knuckle moments on the drive to work, thanks to slick roads and yet-to-be-paved streets.

"Ahem." Peter Douglas, one of her two high school-aged employees, had a glass jar in his hand. "I believe that's three dollars for the cuss jar." He held out the jug and gave it a little shake. The change rattled around among the bills that had accumulated over the past few months.

Darcy's shoulders drooped. "Come on, man. Cut a girl some slack. You know how much I hate this weather."

"We may have heard a rumor." Ace, one of the store's regular customers, came alongside Peter. He was grinning. He also had two Leon Bridges albums under his arm. "Pay up. I want to get home ASAP and listen to these."

"When you put it that way." Darcy dropped a five-dollar bill into the jar. "Keep the change, Peter. I may have a few more choice words if the snow doesn't stop soon."

The group shared a good-natured chuckle as Darcy rang up the sale. A lot of snow had fallen since the first of the year, and most folks around the Marysburg, Indiana, area were ready for a bump in the temperature that would lead to the snow melting.

Ace thanked Peter as he slipped the purchase into the customer's canvas bag, then wished him well and said goodbye.

A few other customers had queued up to pay for purchases. She stayed at the cash register. The focus required to ring the items up provided a welcome alternative to her whining about the conditions outdoors. Instead, she got to spend the next fifteen minutes chatting with fellow music lovers about their choices while also getting to thank them for their support.

It wasn't a surprise that traffic in the store slowed around five o'clock. It was the beginning of the dinner period. Given the weather conditions, things would likely stay quiet until six-thirty or so. Then Darcy's team would be busy until closing time at eight.

Which meant it was the perfect time to head out so she could catch the end of the tournament at the Magic Box. With a quick pit stop at Selena's for a snack.

"Okay, y'all, I'm heading out. Promise to be back no later than seven."

Hank Greenbaum, the second of Darcy's full-time employees, emerged from the office. He dropped a napkin in the trash can behind the sales counter, then smoothed his gray hair while he inspected his sweater vest for any stray crumbs.

"I will never get tired of Little Sicily's New York-style pizza. It's even better cold the next day." He flicked his fingers in Darcy's direction. "Peter and I have things covered. Have fun."

The young man fetched her coat and helped her into it. "What Hank said. And be careful. Not everyone's cleared their sidewalk as well as ours."

Darcy patted him on the arm. "You did a chart-topping job with it. I appreciate it. I'm sure the good folks of Marysburg appreciate it, too."

When the weather was pleasant, it often took Darcy ten or fifteen minutes to walk to Selena's Mexican Cantina, her favorite restaurant in the world. That was because she took time to revel in the sights and sounds of downtown Marysburg. It was the kind of area the travel blogs liked to call quaint.

Darcy preferred the term authentic. The businesses were owned by folks like her. Members of the community who truly did care about each other, both on a professional level as well as a personal one.

On this day, Darcy arrived at Selena's in five minutes. The snow and cold had spurred her long legs into quick, purposeful strides. It wasn't like any of the storefronts had changed in the past few days, after all.

After taking a moment to stamp the snow from her combat boots in Selena's foyer, she made her way to her good friend Thea, who was behind the bar. While there was a line to get into the dining area, the bar area wasn't busy. Local real estate magnate Todd Meadows was at a table with his current girlfriend, Jasmine Longoria. A few other tables were occupied with groups of three or four.

"What'll it be, Ms. Gaughan?" With a wide smile, Thea placed a glass of lemonade on the bar in front of Darcy.

"Supreme nachos, please, my dear." She pointed over her shoulder with her thumb. "Dining room's packed tonight. Yet another reason I prefer to hang out with you."

The bartender laughed. "You're too kind. People have learned that when the Hobbit's tournament ends, a lot of them come here to either celebrate or to drown their sorrows. They want to be long gone before a crowd of nerds who haven't showered in over twenty-four hours arrives."

"Ouch." Darcy took a sip of her lemonade. "It's not that bad, is it?"

"No." Thea shook her head. "I like the gamer crowd. Sure, some of them might be a little odd, but who doesn't have their quirks? On the whole, it's a friendly group that tips well and says, 'Thank you.' That's all a regular human bartender like me or the legendary Jackie Daytona can ask."

A few moments later, Thea placed the nachos in front of Darcy. While she munched on the crispy chips laden with aromatic salsa and spicy chicken, she considered Thea's words. The woman's description of the gaming community reminded her a lot of the music lovers who congregated at Marysburg Music.

She sat on her stool a little straighter as she recalled the previous day's exchange with the Hobbit. It would have been easy to give him the gift card Charlotte promised and be done with it. That would have been totally fine. Instead, though, she made the decision to make the donation out of a sense of solidarity and togetherness.

Darcy Gaughan and Sean O'Sullivan might not ever become best of buddies. She could make the effort for them to become allies, though. After all, they were in the same proverbial lifeboat. It wasn't easy being a small business owner in a small town. Being there for each other was truly one of the ways to help them all survive.

It was one of the lessons Eddie Maxwell, Darcy's mentor and hero, had spoken about often. The realization that his words on the topic hadn't fallen on deaf ears warmed Darcy's insides more than the nachos.

Before she knew it, the only thing left on her plate was a stray dollop of nacho cheese and a tiny chunk of tomato. She used her index finger to finish them off.

"What?" Darcy shrugged in response to Thea's smirk. "These nachos were as smooth as Marvin Gaye singing 'Let's Get It On.' Wasting even the tiniest amount would be a crime against humanity."

"Whatever, girl." Thea let out a chuckle as she put Darcy's bill on the bar top. "Back to work, I take it?"

Darcy dropped a twenty on top of the strip of paper. "Actually, I'm off to the Magic Box. O'Sullivan asked if I wanted to present the prize the store donated to the winner. I figured, why not."

"Sweet." Thea put Darcy's plate and cup in a tub behind the bar. "Do yourself a favor. Be sure to get a few pictures of you with your prize winner. When you get back to the record store, post them on social media. Boom! Free advertising."

"I'll do that. Thanks, girlfriend." They exchanged a fist bump and Darcy made for the exit. She hadn't thought about taking any pictures. As she stepped back into the wintry conditions, she laughed. Everyone seemed to be in Help Darcy Promote Marysburg Music Mode. She'd take all the help she could get.

It came from a sense of companionship. Friends were looking out for her. With the sensation keeping her mood good, she hummed Jimmy Buffett's "Boat Drinks" on the walk to the Hobbit's store. If she couldn't enjoy the tropics in reality, why not enjoy them in her imagination? It would definitely help keep her warm.

By the time Darcy got within three blocks of The Magic Box, every one of the diagonal parking spots along the streets was occupied. The lot behind tournament central and its neighboring businesses was full, too. Despite what everyone had told her, until that moment, Darcy had harbored doubts about the tournament's popularity.

"My bad, Sean." She shook her head as her hand gripped the store's entrance handle. "This is a big deal. Good on ya."

The transition from the frigid outdoors to the warm and noisy indoors was as stark as the difference between an Alice Cooper album and an Amy Grant recording.

A wall of voice-filled sound smacked her in the face when she stepped inside. The cacophony was accompanied by a wave of climate-controlled heat that had her sweating within seconds. To top the assault off, the less than pleasant stench of people who'd been competing for almost twenty-four without showering was unavoidable.

As she shrugged out of her coat, Darcy reminded herself the visit wasn't about her. It was about supporting another Marysburg business. She'd spent the early tours with her old band, Pixie Dust, stuffed inside an old cargo van with her bandmates and a single technician for hours at a time. She'd been confronted with worse smells in the past.

And had been the source of some nasty ones, too.

"Darcy." The Hobbit himself, Sean O'Sullivan, approached her with a wide smile, and his hands extended toward her in a welcoming gesture. "I'm really glad you could make it. We'll be wrapping up in a few minutes. Why don't you wander around a bit, take in the scene."

She handed her coat to him and grinned. Dozens of people with dark circles under their eyes, no doubt due to sleep deprivation, were milling about. They were grinning, too, though. Tired, yes. But not unhappy. That was pretty cool.

Two card tables were occupied. At one of them, four contestants were playing a card game. A sign hanging from the ceiling above them indicated they were playing "Magic, the Gathering." Two women and one man were seated at the other table under a sign with a single word on it: "Catan."

A massive flat-screen television took up a good portion of one wall. Two people were seated in folding camp chairs. They were each holding a game controller and were focused on the screen. Some sort of battle was being waged in a game that was called "League of Legends."

Darcy let out a little gasp when she recognized one of the two video gamers. It was Rafe Majors. Darcy had known Rafe for years. Eddie's stepson had gone through a lot of changes since the man's murder. The town's foremost slacker when Eddie was alive, Rafe had been putting in more hours at his job at the Marysburg Public Library. He's also been working hard, learning how to take care of himself.

Darcy was proud of the positive changes the man had made in his life. She wasn't surprised to see he was still gaming, though. It was one of the few things he'd always been passionate about. Since he was still playing and the event was almost over, he was presumably good at it.

Well, Darcy could respect someone who spent enough time at something to become an expert. Even if she had absolutely no idea what was happening on the screen.

Her meandering around the store ended when the Hobbit started counting down the seconds until the tournament ended. When he reached zero, he let out a quick blast from an air horn. The sudden sound made Darcy cringe. At least the man had covered the horn with a hand towel to muffle it. Instead of ear-splitting, it was merely nerve-rattling.

It accomplished its task, though, as all players stopped, and the attending crowd grew quiet.

The man hoisted his bowling ball-like frame up to the top of a step stool. Even with the assistance from the platform, his head still barely rose above the crowd.

"The tenth annual Magic Box Marathon has ended. Let's give a big round of applause to all of our contestants. Without them, none of this would be possible." He put his hands together as the gathering broke into a cacophony of hooting, hollering, clapping, and stomping.

"This year, we have a new overall champion to crown. While the overall scores are being tabulated, it's my pleasure to announce our division champions."

The din dissipated as one of O'Sullivan's employees handed him a piece of paper.

"The winner of the Electronic Division, who totally kicked butt and took names while playing 'League of Legends' is, for the second year in a row, Rafe Majors."

Amid repeated chants of "Rafe, Rafe, Rafe," the man waltzed through the crowd. He stopped to exchange high-fives with a few folks. With a glittering smile, he stood next to the Hobbit, holding a prize package that included a gift certificate to the Magic Box, discount cards to a handful of local restaurants, and one hundred dollars cash.

"Not a bad haul for a day's work, huh?" With his hands full, Rafe extended his elbow so Darcy could bump it, while she got her camera ready to take a selfie with him.

"Great job, man. I'm happy for you." She truly was. The scowling, surly Rafe Majors of the past was nowhere to be seen. This happy version of him was a good look.

Their conversation was interrupted when the Hobbit announced the winner of the card game division.

"This year, we played 'Magic, the Gathering,' and nobody did it better than Jesse Dugan. Come on up here, Jess."

Rafe leaned close to Darcy as Dugan went to get their prizes. "I know Jesse. They're good, but I didn't expect them to win. Kind of cool."

"And, last but not least, the winner of this year's board game, which was Catan, Angelica Stipe." The applause was not as enthusiastic as it was for the other two winners. Even Sean, who had been all smiles with Rafe and Jesse, looked like he'd just bitten into a lemon when Darcy presented a young, blond-haired woman with her prize package.

A moment after the Catan champion took her place next to the other winners, the Hobbit's smile returned, as if a dark cloud that blocked the sun for a moment had moved on.

"And now, the moment we've been twenty-four hours for. For the first time in history, the crowning of the overall winner of the Magic Box Marathon." The Hobbit held his tongue for a moment, relishing the palpable tension in the room. "To present the Grand Champion prize of five hundred dollars cash and other assorted goodies, please welcome Marysburg's favorite realtor and the creator of our new scoring system, Todd Meadows."

Setting aside her dislike for the man, Darcy clapped along with everyone else as he took his place between the Hobbit and the division champions. His dark suit and purple tie provided a stark contrast to the rest of the T-shirt and jeans-clad gathering.

A store employee gave the Hobbit a folded piece of paper. He studied it for a moment, then slipped the refolded sheet into his back pocket. With a wink at the crowd, he took hold of a two-foot-high trophy that had been standing on the sales counter, then gave Todd a thick envelope.

"The calculations have been completed and verified. It went down to the wire. The overall champion of the tenth annual Magic Box Marathon is...Angelica Stipe. Congratulations, Angelica!"

Another round of applause filled the room as the winner accepted her prizes and posed for photos. While Jesse was all smiles as friends snapped pictures of the trio of champions, Rafe was scowling.

The first chance he got, Rafe stomped away from the center of the celebration to join a group of friends.

"That's total b.s." Rafe's venom-filled voice carried throughout the entire store. "I know I had enough points to win. O'Sullivan must have rigged the whole thing so she'd win."

"Come on, man," one of Rafe's friends said. "Take a breath. We'll find out what the deal is."

Rafe's outburst was the strongest show of emotion the man had ever displayed. Uncertain whether it was simply a matter of him being a sore loser or something else going on, Darcy weaved her way through the crowd toward him. On her way, a few other comments caught her attention.

"Look at that smile on her face. How fake is that after she spent the whole tourney complaining," a young man in a Legend of Zelda shirt and ballcap said to a companion.

"Gotta give the Hobbit props for playing nice," the man's friend said. "A couple of hours ago, I heard him say he was going to strangle her if she didn't stop her whining."

Darcy didn't know the young men, so it was impossible to know what to make of the comments. Rafe's scowl as she joined his group left no doubt about how he felt about the developments.

"You okay, buddy?" She put her hand on his upper arm. It was a gesture she learned from Eddie. Whenever he did it to her, Darcy's heart rate slowed.

Rafe jerked away.

"No, I'm not okay." He blew out a long breath. "There's no way she won. I dominated my division. She must have cheated big time."

"If you want, I can go and talk to the Hobbit about it." Darcy was no diplomat, but the last thing anyone in the store needed was Rafe confronting the tournament director. It would be too easy for harsh words to escalate into a thrown punch. Nobody seemed able to talk through conflict anymore.

A fight wouldn't do anybody any good.

He opened and closed his fists as he seemed to debate his next more. After a minute, he shoved his prize package at one of his friends, then stormed out of the store, dropping a few curse words in the Hobbit and Angelica's direction.

Once he was gone, Darcy turned to Rafe's friends. "Is anyone going to go after him? You know, make sure he doesn't do anything he'll regret?"

Between the shrugs and headshakes, it was clear that Rafe was on his own. Well, he was a big boy, and Darcy had a record store to run. She'd check in on him later. After he had a chance to cool down. She wasn't his mother, after all.

The Hobbit was busy chatting with a reporter from the Muncie Star Press, so Darcy gave him a quick tap on the shoulder and a wave as she made her exit. A gust of wind took her breath away the moment she was back outdoors. She buried her gloved hands into her coat pockets and double-timed it to the record store.

Her breath condensed into small clouds with each breath she took. Hopefully, the conditions hadn't worsened inside the Magic Box after her departure. Nothing was more toxic than a brew of heightened, negative emotions and money.

"Note to self. If anyone suggests Marysburg Music hold a battle of the bands or some other music competition, tell them no way." The open mic nights were huge successes, full of positive energy. There would be no messing with that success.

A while later, Darcy was hard at work returning misplaced records to their homes when the clock struck eight.

"Closing time, Boss." With no customers in the store, Peter locked the door and turned off the red neon "Open" sign. The young man seemed to be in a hurry to get going.

"What's the rush, young man? Got a hot date?" Hank chuckled and began working on the night deposit.

"Yeah, with my bass. My audition at IU is next Saturday. I need all the practice time I can get."

"Then get going." Darcy flicked her wrist toward the door. "Practice makes perfect, not that you need it."

Peter didn't need to be told twice. The young man's dream of studying at Indiana University's Jacobs School of Music was getting closer to reality every day. The in-person audition was the final hurdle. After that, it was all up to the admissions team.

Darcy had done all she could to help Peter make sure it was going to be an easy decision in Peter's favor. She'd thrived in her time as a music student at Ball State. She had no doubt Peter would do the same at IU.

She was humming Bobby McFerrin's hit from the eighties, "Don't Worry, Be Happy," as she swept the floor when her phone buzzed. It was the Hobbit. The man dispensed with pleasantries when she answered.

"I need your help, Gaughan. Angelica Stipe is dead."

Chapter Three

Darcy tapped the side of her head with a knuckle to make sure she wasn't imagining things. She'd survived a few hallucination-filled episodes when her drinking was at its worst. Not a drop of alcohol had entered her system in almost six years, though.

Sean O'Sullivan's call for help was real.

"What you mean she's dead?" Darcy glanced at a Harry Styles clock on the wall. It was a little after eight. Fewer than ninety minutes had passed since Darcy left the Magic Box.

"Who's dead," Hank asked.

She shushed her co-worker but put the phone on speaker as she walked toward the cash register. It couldn't hurt to have a second set of ears listening in.

"I was taking the trash out. On my way to the dumpster, it's behind the store, I saw something. It was on the ground, next to a car. It was too big to be someone's backpack, so I went to see what it was. Figured I'd that whatever it was inside and wait for a call from someone to claim it."

Darcy shook her head. The Hobbit was beginning to ramble. He was probably in shock. Still, she needed the man to focus.

"Sean. What did you find?"

"It was a body. Face down." He sniffed. "At first, I thought maybe one of the players who went out early had gotten drunk and passed out, so turned the body over. That's when I saw it was Angelica."

"And then what?"

"I shook her arm to wake her up. Thought maybe she slipped on an ice patch and hit her head. When she didn't move, I tried to find a pulse. When I couldn't find one, I called you."

Darcy looked at Hank. His eyes were wide, and his mouth was hanging open. She had no doubt her expression was similar. He mouthed the word "police." It got her back on track.

"Okay. Don't try to move the body or anything like that. Have you called the cops?"

"No."

"Oh, my goodness. Here we go." Hank tossed his head back as he put his palms together in praying fashion.

Darcy turned away from him. She didn't need him adding to the drama coming from the person on the other side of the phone call.

"Why haven't you called the cops?" Cold tendrils of dread began to clutch at her heart. In all honesty, she really didn't want to know the answer. Had the Hobbit accidentally killed Angelica?

"Because yesterday, you said we gotta stick together. Help each other out. Well, right now, I need your help. I need you to figure out who murdered her."

A drumbeat had started banging against the inside of Darcy's skull. The stress headache wasn't a good sign. She ran a record store, not a private detective agency.

Yes, she'd solved two murders in her town recently. That didn't make her Marysburg's go-to person when a felony was committed.

"You need to call the police. Right now. I'll be there as soon as I can."

Hank put his hand on Darcy's shoulder as she disconnected from the call. "Hold on, young lady. What do you think you're doing?"

"Don't worry. I'm just going to go over there to give the Hobbit some moral support. Let him lean on me some. I don't know if he has the support system I had when I found Eddie. He shouldn't have to go through that alone."

Hank looked at her for a moment. Then he gave Darcy a hug.

"You have grown so much. I'm proud of you." He released his hug, but still held her at arm's length. "Remember to stay in your lane, okay?"

She let out a laugh. Normally, Charlotte was the one reminding Darcy she needed to stay in her lane. Regardless of who was making the admonishment, it was good advice.

"I promise. Scout's honor. Cross my heart and hope to die. Does that cover it?"

"Only if you actually, you know, stay in your lane."

With Hank's words echoing in her mind, Darcy made her return trip to the Magic Box. This time it was behind the wheel of Rusty. The aged jeep took forever to warm up, but it was still better than another walk in the frigid elements.

By the time she pulled into a parking spot across the street from the store, a Marysburg Police Department squad car had already arrived. It was stationed in front of the Magic Box's entrance; the red and blue lights atop it were still flashing.

"Here we go again, girl. Appreciate all the help you can send my way." Darcy tapped the photo of her hero, Go-Go's drummer Gina Schock, that was taped to the dashboard. Somehow, Gina always came through when Darcy needed help.

A uniformed officer the size of a small house blocked her way in. His name badge said "Dickinson." "Sorry, ma'am. This is a crime scene."

She bit back a snarky response to the insulting greeting. She was in her mid-thirties. At least two decades from ma'am territory. Getting into a verbal bout with a cop wasn't going to help the Hobbit. Instead, she gave the officer a big smile.

That she hoped didn't look like a grimace.

"I understand, Officer Dickinson. Mr. O'Sullivan called me. He asked that I be here for moral support. My name's Darcy Gaughan. You can confirm this with him."

The cop gave her a long look, then mumbled something into his radio. Despite the fact that her toes were getting cold, it was a pleasant change to have a member of the Marysburg PD fail to recognize her. Goodness knew, back in her drinking days, she was practically on a first-name basis with the entire force.

After an unintelligible response on the cop's radio, the man stepped aside. She found the Hobbit seated on a stool behind the store's cash register. A flood of memories almost overwhelmed Darcy. Only months ago, she'd been in the same predicament as the Hobbit. She put her hand on a display fixture to steady herself.

"Okay, there Gaughan? No offense, but I didn't exactly call you with the idea that you'd show up and faint."

"Sorry, Sean." She took a deep breath. "Seeing you at the cash register, it was like déjà vu all over again."

"Right, yeah." He scratched his bushy beard. "Sorry about that. I just got done showing the detective where the…you know is. Guess I'm still on edge from that."

"Not a problem. You got me here. How can I help?"

He gestured for her to come up close to him. "I overheard the detective talking to one of the uniforms. They think Angelica was strangled. Her trophy was smashed, too. I mean, not like she dropped it, and it broke. I mean, like someone took it and threw it down on the ground and busted it into a million pieces."

"Interesting." She turned the information over in her mind, looking at it from a handful of different perspectives as if it were a Rubik's Cube. "Sounds like someone was angry. Did you notice anything else at the scene?"

"If we did, it would be inappropriate for us to share it with the public." Detective Paul Gerard walked toward them, leaving wet boot prints in his wake. "Darcy, I understand Mr. O'Sullivan asked for you to be here."

"That's right. Congratulations on the new gig, by the way." Paul had recently been promoted to fill the open detective position that was created when Kaitlin Rosengarten left to work for the Fort Wayne Police Department.

"Thank you. Gotta be honest, I wish it had been longer than a month before I caught my first murder case."

"You think she *was* murdered, then?" The question was out before Darcy had time to reel it back in. The investigator in her was already coming to the forefront, like a lead singer taking the microphone strutting downstage with a microphone in her hand.

Apparently, she was, in fact, getting involved in a murder investigation. Again.

Paul scratched a spot between his nose and lip in a futile attempt to hide a grimace. Darcy withheld comment about the rookie mistake. A murder investigation was a pressure cooker under the best possible circumstances. This situation involved the death of a young woman at a high-profile event.

The pressure had taken no time to go all the way to eleven.

After a moment, he gave a quick nod. "We'll have to wait for a report from the coroner, but it looks that way. Mr. O'Sullivan, can you account for your whereabouts from six o'clock until the time you called nine-one-one?"

"Yeah. Once the awards ceremony ended, people cleared out. When everyone was gone, I closed the store and started cleaning up. It took a while. There was a lot of trash."

"Okay, then." Paul jotted something down in a notebook he'd taken from a jacket pocket. "Is there a place we can talk? I'd like for you to take me through the whole evening, step by step."

"My office." The Hobbit came around from behind the register, then stopped. "Wait a minute. I'm not a suspect, am I? I mean, why would I hurt the person who just won my tournament?"

"That's a great question." Paul gestured for the Hobbit to continue toward the meeting place. "And one I'd love for you to answer. Darcy, thanks for coming by. The Marysburg Police Department can take it from here. I'll make sure Mr. O'Sullivan is treated with the utmost respect."

The abrupt dismissal caused Darcy to take a step back. In the past, Paul Gerard had been an ally. He'd even shown appreciation for her sleuthing efforts. Then again, the man needed to establish his authority over the case. He was the one on the hot seat. She needed to remember that.

"Guess I'll see myself out, then." Darcy scanned the store. A uniformed officer was busy placing numbered yellow triangles wherever she found something that might be evidence. The cop at the door was tapping away at his phone.

In the past, Darcy would have been more than happy to slip out without so much as a wave of goodbye. She'd solved two murders, though. Getting dismissed like someone who'd been dismissed at an *American Idol* audition stung.

She'd just have to get over it.

When Darcy got home, Ringo was sitting next to his empty food bowl. He gave her a long, unblinking stare. Then, he let out an abrupt *mrow*. The cat's disapproval at her late arrival and delayed dinner radiated throughout the room.

"Sorry, dude. Had some extra drama at work." She tossed a few kitty treats into his bowl to make sure he didn't die of malnutrition while she opened a can of fancy, wet food. "My apologies. Have at it."

Darcy brewed a cup of herbal tea while her feline companion attacked his dinner. She massaged the muscles at the back of her neck. The day had started off good enough. And then been turned upside down thanks to that awful, six-letter word.

Murder.

Despite drinking two cups of chamomile tea and watching a nature documentary featuring a narrator who spoke in quiet, soothing tones, sleep evaded Darcy. When she let out a frustrated growl, Ringo glared at her for a few moments before settling back down on her lap.

"Sorry to disturb you, your Lordship." She scratched the cat's head. "I can't stop thinking about that poor girl."

Ringo reached up and placed a paw on Darcy's cheek. He didn't make the gesture often. Only when he sensed she was on the verge of tears. The old tomcat was perpetually hungry and openly hostile to her suggestions that he could use his tail to help get rid of dust bunnies.

When she was at her lowest, though, he was always there for her, offering a comforting paw.

"Since you asked, I can't believe someone murdered her. Right there in the parking lot. And nobody was around to stop it. Or even witness it. I mean, Rafe had his squad at the tournament. And the person who won the card game division had friends there, too. Where were Angelica's buds?"

Ringo blew a blast of air through his nostrils, as if he was as frustrated with the situation as Darcy.

"I know, right?" She ran her fingers up and down his spine. "The whole thing feels weird. Like Gladys Knight doing 'Midnight Train to Georgia' without the Pips singing back up."

The cat yawned, then ran a paw over his gnarled ear. Evidently, her reference to the Empress of Soul was lost on him. She made a mental note to play more classic soul when she was home.

"The question now is, what am I gonna do?" Darcy scratched under Ringo's chin. He responded by purring loud enough to rival the electric snow blower her parents had given to her for Christmas.

She needed to do something. The Hobbit had asked for her help. Hanging out at the Magic Box for a while didn't seem like much of an answer. It seemed like she was leaving him high and dry.

That wasn't cool. Especially after he specifically asked her to find Angelica's murderer.

O'Sullivan was in an awful spot. One she wouldn't want to see anyone put in. Assuming he wasn't the murderer, that is.

Which suddenly made her path forward a clear one.

"The cops should be finished by morning, bud. I think I'll pay the Hobbit another visit. This time, I'll do a lot more than stand around. Not with a killer on the loose."

With her decision made, Darcy fell into a deep slumber with Ringo at her side. Angelica's murderer wasn't going to get away with it. Not if she had anything to say about it.

Chapter Four

Darcy was slicing bell peppers when there were three rapid knocks on the back door. With the knife still in her hand, she opened the door.

"Whoa." Liam put his hands up. "I surrender and will confess to whatever crime I've been accused of committing. Please don't make us stand out here any longer."

She stepped aside as he bolted through the opening. "Spare me. I was only making breakfast."

He hung his jacket on the back of a chair at the kitchen table, then went to the stove to hold his hands over one of the burners. "Didn't think it was going to get so cold overnight. Got any coffee?"

"Why the heck didn't you wear your heavy coat? I mean, there's this thing called the weather app right there on your phone. You could have checked it." She handed him a coffee mug emblazoned with the logo of the goth punk band The Cramps.

"I'm doing this thing with some of the guys at work." He wrapped his fingers around the mug as Darcy filled it with an aromatic Ethiopian blend that was his favorite. "One of the techs is this big outdoorsman. Camps all year round, spends his vacations hiking the Appalachian trail, riding the rapids down the Snake River. Stuff like that. Anyway, he was telling us about this blog post he read with a bunch of tips to help you expand your comfort zone."

Darcy poured some eggs she'd mixed up in a glass bowl into a frying pan. "Why do I not like the sound of this?"

"Because it appeals to people who like spending time outdoors. Taking nothing but pictures and leaving nothing but footprints."

"Sounds like the first year on the road with Pixie Dust." She stirred the eggs, then added the chopped-up peppers to the mix. "Been there, done that."

"Thank you for that editorial, but this is about me, not you." He added shredded cheese to the eggs and peppers. "The point is that we should try to increase our level of comfort in conditions outside of what we're used to. For example, wearing a lighter jacket and turning down the thermostat during the winter so I get a little more acclimated to the cold."

When the moment was right, Darcy slid a spatula under the eggs and flipped one half on top of the other. After adding some diced tomato chunks, she slid the omelet onto a plate and handed it to Liam.

"Your breakfast. You can tell me why you would want to do such a thing while I fix my eggs."

He took the toast that popped up from the toaster and sat at the table. "I want to challenge myself. Do something different, I guess. I'm afraid I'm getting too predictable. I don't want that."

Darcy preferred her eggs scrambled. She pondered Liam's answer while she stirred in her portion of the peppers. At the moment, predictability sounded better than a John Coltrane saxophone solo. Unless she was completely misreading the situation, Liam was unaware of the previous night's horrific developments.

"Predictability isn't so bad." She poured hot water from a kettle into her tea mug. "Especially after last night."

"Why? What happened?" Liam spread margarine over his toast. "Did you catch someone trying to shoplift again?"

She let out a sigh as she took the seat across from him. "If only. You'll hear about it soon enough. A young woman was murdered outside The Magic Box last night."

The piece of toast Liam was holding came to a stop inches from his mouth. He put it down. "You're joking, right?"

"Afraid not." Darcy sat back and stared out the window. The morning light struggled to reach them through a layer of slate-gray clouds. "Her name's

Angelica Stipe. She won the tournament. I was there to hand out a prize package to one of the other winners. Ninety minutes later, I got a call from the Hobbit that she was dead."

Liam took a sip of his coffee. When he put the mug down, his eyes were watery.

"Wow. I know her dad from work. The family must be devastated. Any idea what happened?"

"Not really. O'Sullivan said he found her in the parking lot behind his store when he was taking out the trash." She chewed on a forkful of her scrambled eggs. "That's when he called me."

"Why'd he call you?"

She told him about the phone call and her unexpected second trip to The Magic Box. "I discussed it with Ringo last night. I'm going to go see the Hobbit on the way to work. See if there's anything new he can tell me."

Liam put down his fork. "Do you think that's a good idea? I mean, do you really want to risk putting yourself in danger again?"

"Oh, come on. That's a little dramatic, don't you think?" She took a sip of her tea. The spicy aroma of the chai steadied her as the tension in the room ticked up a notch. "I haven't committed to anything."

He stabbed his fork at his omelet with enough force to knock a chunk of bell pepper off his plate.

"Sorry, but the fact that you're even talking to the Hobbit this morning means it's too late to turn back."

"And what's wrong with that?"

"Because it could be dangerous. Look, you've obviously got a knack for the detective thing. And that's great. It's just that you don't have the things to protect you like the cops do. You know, things like a bulletproof vest and a radio to call for help." He took her hand in his. "I don't want you to get hurt. That's all."

She took Liam's hand in hers. His callouses were rough, but reassuring. He was a solid man. A reliable and trustworthy friend. And a decent boyfriend, too. He wanted what was best for her. Even when he told her things she didn't really want to hear.

"How about we take things one step at a time and not jump straight to the part when I get stabbed in the back or have a gargoyle dropped on me or get shot by a poison dart." She scooped more of her eggs into her mouth.

"Fair enough." He laughed. "As long as you'll let me help you steer clear of any gargoyles when the time comes. Deal?"

They clinked mugs and spent the rest of breakfast chatting about the weather. The forecast was calling for a warming trend. After months of darkness and bone-chilling cold, Darcy and Liam were both ready for the promised uptick in the thermometer.

If only there wasn't a murder hanging over the town's head like a dark winter snowstorm.

A little while later, Darcy entered The Magic Box. She'd texted the Hobbit to let him know she wanted to check in on him. He'd accepted her offer faster than it took to get to the end of a Ramones song.

"You look like you've been on a three-day bender. And I know from experience what that looks like. No offense." Darcy handed the Hobbit a black coffee she picked up for him during her drive over.

The man's bushy hair and beard looked like they were overdue for an appointment with a comb. The circles under his eyes were so dark they could have been made by the same makeup kit the members of Kiss used. To complete the pathetic picture, he was wearing the same clothes that he'd been wearing the previous day.

"Didn't get much sleep last night. Or any, to be honest." He took a long slurp from his coffee cup.

Darcy patted the Hobbit on the shoulder as she guided him to his stool behind the cash register. She could empathize with the guy. Finding a dead body shocked the system. It could be tough to function until the body and mind recover from the horrifying discovery.

"I feel for you, man. From the second I found Eddie, sleep was hard to come by until his murderer was behind bars."

He raised his eyebrows. "Does that mean you're going to look for Angelica's killer?"

She took a deep breath. Like Liam said, there was no going back. She'd

27

been in O'Sullivan's shoes, though. That mattered. "I'll do what I can. Take me through yesterday."

"But I told the cops everything last night." His shoulders sagged. If the writers of the Merriam-Webster Dictionary ever needed a human personification of the word "defeated," the Sean O'Sullivan seated before Darcy was it.

"Tell it to me. Maybe there's something you forgot that you'll remember now." She opened the note-taking app on her phone. "Start from when people arrived Friday."

After some grumbling and chewing on a chocolate Clif Bar he'd stashed behind the sales counter, the Hobbit took her through the moments when competitors began arriving Friday evening through the time he called Darcy. The report painted a grim portrait of the tournament champion.

She'd been condescending to her fellow competitors. She ignored the players from other divisions during breaks in play. While not directly hostile toward O'Sullivan, the young woman had been overheard insulting the store, the staff, the tournament format, the food provided to the players, and even the prizes.

"Good golly, Miss Molly. If she hated everything, why was she even here?"

He shook his head. "You got me. She played last year. She was a lot nicer then. Maybe it had something to do with her boyfriend."

The mention of a boyfriend caught Darcy's attention. The murder, a strangling, had happened in the spur of the moment. Of that, she was certain. She didn't know why; she just did. Maybe it was the experience gained from the other murders she'd investigated.

"Tell me about this dude."

"You're not gonna believe this." He actually chuckled, though his eyes were still sad. "His name is Xander Fleming-Winchester. With an X at the start of his first name."

Darcy grimaced. "Sounds like some Ivy League rich dude who can trace his roots back to the Mayflower. Anyway, tell me about him."

O'Sullivan shrugged. "Yeah, his family's loaded, I guess. Typical spoiled, rich kid. He was here for the last couple of hours of the tournament. He left right after I announced she was the overall winner."

"That's weird." Darcy made a note to see what info she could unearth about Mr. Fleming-Winchester. To leave at his girlfriend's big moment was weird. "Just to make sure, you saw him leave?"

"Yeah. He didn't even stick around for pictures. It wasn't like he was trying to sneak out without being noticed, either. Almost as if he couldn't stand the idea of his girlfriend showing him up."

"What's he look like?"

"Six foot-ish. Short, brown hair, parted on the side. Looks like he stepped out of a J. Crew ad."

She made another note. Why did he leave? Was he angry about something? Jealous of the attention Angelica was getting?

"Did his leaving have any effect on Angelica?"

"Not that I noticed. She was all smiles. She'd just won a bunch of swag and five hundred in cash. Wouldn't you be all kittens and rainbows in the moment?"

"I see your point."

To be honest, if Liam walked out of an event while she was receiving an award, she'd be hurt. Maybe even angry. Then again, it was possible that Angelica felt the same, but had masked her feelings.

It was too bad Darcy couldn't ask her about it. Well, that made for another reason to start her investigation with Xander at the top of the list.

The boyfriend was far from the only suspect, though. Rafe's temper tantrum was still fresh in Darcy's mind.

"Rafe Majors was seriously honked off when Angelica was announced as the winner."

The Hobbit took another drink of his coffee. "I love Rafe like a brother. God knows he's spent enough money next door at The Comic Castle to deserve a lifetime achievement award. But that man is the worst loser on Earth."

"Any idea what made him so mad?" While Rafe had matured a lot in the ten months since his stepdad had been murdered, he still acted like a petulant five-year-old way more often than a man in his late thirties should.

"He won his division last year and has been shooting his mouth off that he was going to win the whole thing this time. I overheard him say he was so confident he'd already spent the grand prize money."

Darcy fiddled with a dangly earring. Liam had given her a pair for Christmas. She was still getting used to them. Adjusting the piece of jewelry gave her a chance to think, though. Something wasn't adding up.

"Let me get this straight. This year was the first time you gave away the big grand prize. And the winner was determined by a secret formula you used. Seems to me, if Rafe had a beef, he should have taken it up with you instead of storming out."

"You'd have to talk to him about that. I can show you how we determined the overall winner. Todd Meadows helped me put it together." He opened a laptop that was on a shelf below the cash register. A spreadsheet with a complicated-looking equation was on the screen. "It was all above board. See? Rafe was the only one who got mad."

"But you didn't show your formula to anyone beforehand, right?"

"No. We decided it was best to keep it under wraps so nobody would have a chance to figure out a way to game it." He closed the computer with a heavy sigh. "If I had to do it all over again, I would have. Maybe then Rafe wouldn't have gotten so honked off. On top of that, whoever killed Angelica smashed her trophy to bits. Who would have been mad enough to do that?"

"That's a good question." And one that Darcy couldn't help noticing directed the spotlight onto someone specific. Which seemed convenient.

Even though the Hobbit had called her, she wouldn't rule him out. Not yet.

"I have to ask, so don't get mad. Can anyone verify your story that when you found her, she was already dead?"

"Come on. Seriously?" He balled his hands into fists. "If I killed her, why would I call you?"

"If you're the murderer, and I'm not saying you are, to cover up the crime. To throw suspicion onto someone else. Like Rafe." She locked gazes with him. "If you want my help, you have to be a hundred percent honest with me. I'm not going to stick my neck out only to have it get chopped off."

Seconds ticked by until he looked at the floor and relaxed his fists.

"I guess I can see where you're coming from. I don't have to like it, though."

"No, you don't. You better get used to it, though. Paul Gerard is smart. This might be his first murder case, but he'll work it a lot harder than Rosengarten ever did."

"Great. I don't know if that's a blessing or a curse."

"Since you're innocent, consider it a blessing. He'll get to the bottom of this."

The Hobbit rose as he broke into a smile. "You believe me, then? Really?"

"Yes, I do. I need to prove it, though. Can anyone verify your story?"

"No. It had been a long couple of days. As soon as everyone was gone and the place was in decent shape, I sent my guys home. You can ask them."

"I will." She placed her fingers on her phone's keyboard. "Why don't you give me their deets now."

Despite his grumblings, Darcy didn't relent until he gave her phone numbers, email addresses, and physical addresses for all six of his employees who worked Friday and Saturday. She'd learned many things running the record store. One of them was how important it was to get complete information the first time around. There was nothing worse than fulfilling a special order and then not being able to reach the customer because phone number digits were transposed or an email address was misspelled.

With a murderer on the loose, getting right the first time was critical.

"Okay. Is there anything else you can remember from the scene? Did she still have her purse? Were her car keys somewhere on the ground?"

"The purse was there. I don't know about the keys. Why?"

"I'm trying to get a picture of the scene in my head." While that was true, it wasn't a complete answer.

If Angelica's purse was at the crime scene, the likelihood that robbery was the motive decreased. If her keys weren't at hand, then that seemed to indicate that she was accosted on her way to her car. Surely, she had been taught to have her keys in hand so she could use them in self-defense, if needed.

Between the prize package and the trophy, her hands would have been full.

31

Maybe she figured she was safe in Marysburg to leave them in her purse until she made it to the car.

If that was the case, then she wouldn't have been on her guard. Who could blame her? She was probably busy enjoying a well-earned state of euphoria as the event's grand champion.

Following that thread would seem to indicate that Angelica was surprised by her attacker. As if someone had been lying in wait for the poor young woman.

Or she knew her murderer.

O'Sullivan scratched at a spot on his forearm. It was redder than the rest of his arm. A symptom of nerves, no doubt. Darcy couldn't help wondering if it was because he was upset over the horrific developments of the last twelve hours or if it was something else.

Like, whether he was hiding something. Something deadly.

Chapter Five

After a quick look around the remnants of the crime scene, Darcy made her way to the comforting environs of Marysburg Music. Sure, the memory of finding Eddie stabbed to death in the store's office would haunt her for the rest of her days. That vision paled in comparison to the good memories Eddie and Darcy had created from the day they first opened the store.

The structure of brick and mortar, with its brushed concrete floor, acoustical ceiling tiles, and memorabilia-covered walls, was her sanctuary. It was where she did some of her best thinking.

Which she was going to need, given the heart-wrenching developments of the last day.

Hank hadn't arrived yet, so once Darcy finished prepping the store for opening, she retreated to her office. It was time for another session with the Suspect Board, the dry-erase board that was normally used to post about upcoming releases.

She was staring at the board's blank surface when there was a knock at the door.

"Morning, Darcy. How's it going?" Hank handed her a steaming cup of herbal tea.

"You're the best. You know that?" She brought the cup to her nose and inhaled until her lungs were full. The floral aroma of chamomile slowed her racing thoughts.

He shrugged. "I try. Your board looks awfully empty. I hope you haven't been staring at it very long."

"Nope. Still getting my thoughts in order. It's early days, as the saying goes." She uncapped a red marker and wrote "Rafe Majors" and "Sean O'Sullivan" on the board. "Better?"

Hank put his hand over his heart. "Yikes. I hate to see any name go up there. But a member of our record store family? That hurts."

Rafe had worked part-time at Marysburg Music over the holiday season. His knowledge of house music had turned out to be quite an asset. He'd also been reliable. Despite her initial trepidation at bringing him on board, not once did she regret the decision.

What a change from her relationship with him only months before.

Now, she had his name up on her suspect board. Yes, it did hurt. It was necessary, though.

"Gotta start somewhere. Just because those names are up there doesn't mean I'm convinced either of them is the murderer."

"The fact that you have them up there isn't exactly encouraging."

Hank was correct. Still, this was one of those times when he was close to entering Drama-land, a locale that was discouraged at Marysburg Music.

"The Hobbit doesn't have anyone who can verify his alibi at the time of the murder. When he wasn't announced as the overall winner, Rafe got angry and left. That's all. Like I said, early days."

"If you insist." He put his arm around her and gave her a gentle squeeze. "Let me know when I can help. I'll be out front."

Darcy returned the hug. He was a good, steadying force at the store. Darcy couldn't keep it going without him. With a kind word, a pat on the back, or a hot cup of tea, the man was truly a father figure in all the best ways.

Once she was on her own again, she created her *Motive, Means, Opportunity* matrix on the board. For Rafe, she noted in the *Motive* column that he was angry about losing to Angelica. For the Hobbit, she jotted down the claim that the deceased had insulted him and the tournament time and time again throughout the event.

"Not exactly chart-topping motives." She drummed her fingers on her thigh as she stared at the board, willing it to offer some answers. After a few moments, one came to her.

"Let's get to know Ms. Angelica Stipe. The Internet's forever, after all."

She was scrolling through Angelica's Instagram feed when the office door burst open.

"Darcy, you gotta help me." Rafe Majors dropped into a chair and grabbed hold of the desk. "The cops think I killed Stipe."

Hank filled the open doorway. His chest was heaving as he scowled at Rafe. "Sorry, Darcy. I tried to stop him, but he's stronger than me."

She put up her hands to get them to stop. At times like this, returning to the footloose and fancy-free lifestyle she led while pounding the skins for Pixie Dust was tempting.

"Hold on, people." Darcy pointed a finger at Rafe. "Stay still and be quiet while I talk to Hank."

Once they were out of earshot of their visitor, Darcy let out a small laugh. "I appreciate the effort. Actually, this saves me time. I was gonna have to talk to Rafe at some point. This saves me the headache of tracking him down."

"Are you sure?" He glanced toward the office. "I mean, if the police think he's involved...."

"I'll be fine. If he tries anything stupid, I'll whack him over the head with the bent cymbal hanging on the wall."

They both laughed at Darcy's mention of the damaged musical instrument. It had played an unexpected role in literally taking a murderer to their knees. In honor of that, she'd put it on display in her office.

Right behind her. Where it was within easy reach.

"Say no more. I can hold down the fort until Izzy gets here."

The second the office door clicked shut, Rafe jumped to his feet. "You need to take my name off that board. Right now. I didn't kill anyone."

Darcy held her tongue as she counted to ten. On one hand, she wanted to knock some sense into him with a bass drum pedal. The nerve of the man to barge into her office and start bossing her around. On the other hand, he was scared. She could identify with that.

"Chill, dude." She put her hand on his shoulder to ease him back into his seat. "That's my *suspect* board, not *murderer* board. Just because your name's on it doesn't mean I think you did it."

"But—"

"No, buts. You want my help? You can start by telling me why the cops think you might have information about Angelica's death." Her word choice was intentional. She needed Rafe calm, so he could think clearly while he answered her questions.

"They said since I got mad about her winning the big prize, I have motive."

"Okay, let's start at the beginning. By 'they,' you mean the police, right? When did they talk to you."

"They came banging on my door at eight this morning. Got me out of bed." He rubbed his forehead. "I might have had one too many last night, so I wasn't happy about being harassed like that."

Conducting a witness interview the morning after a murder wasn't exactly harassment in Darcy's book. Then again, as a white woman, she'd never been profiled, either. She'd let Rafe's grumbling pass. For now.

After all, it wasn't like they kicked down Rafe's door and hauled him away in cuffs at three A.M. If they had done that, Darcy would have been way more sympathetic.

"I'll be honest, lots of people saw the way you took off. You looked pretty mad."

"Sure, I was. Not at her, though. I got robbed by the Hobbit's b.s. secret scoring system."

"Okay, that's good to know. Did the police say *why* exactly they wanted to talk to you?"

He rubbed the three-day stubble on his chin. His eyes were clear and there were no dark circles under them, unlike the Hobbit. At least he'd gotten a good night's rest before everything came crashing down.

"They said I made threats against her. That she didn't deserve the grand champion swag she got."

It wasn't exactly what Darcy was looking for, but it was a start.

"Be honest. Do you remember saying anything like that? I'm not here to judge. I need facts."

"I don't remember exactly, but I might have said a few things." His shoulders sagged. "I was mad. I thought for sure I won the overall. And,

Stipe, she was a piece of work. I'm not saying she deserved to get bumped off, but she didn't make any friends during the tourney."

Interesting. Rafe and the Hobbit shared the same sentiment about Angelica's attitude. She made a note on a sheet of paper to talk to more people about that issue.

"Good. Now, this is important. Did the cops talk to you about the crime scene." She wasn't trying to trip Rafe up. She needed to know what he knew, though. That would help give her an idea of what Paul Gerard and his buddies in blue were thinking about Rafe.

He rubbed his hands together, as if he was trying to figure out a way to respond without incriminating himself. After a while, he nodded.

"At one point, they said the trophy was smashed all to bits. Like, way worse than if someone had dropped it and it broke."

Again, that information aligned with what O'Sullivan's said.

"The detective, Gerard, he also said her prize money was missing. Wanted to know if I knew anything about that. I told him no."

"Is that the truth?"

Rafe had a well-earned reputation around Marysburg for being a poor money manager. He was getting better, with Darcy's guidance. Given his history of spending money faster than he earned it, it wasn't surprising Paul asked him about the cash.

"Yeah, it's one hundred percent the truth." The fury that dripped from every word made a convincing case for Rafe.

Besides, Darcy knew something most people didn't. Thanks to the monthly meetings the two of them had to stay on top of Rafe's finances, he wasn't perpetually broke anymore. He didn't need the money.

Whether he thought he deserved the money as the rightful winner of the tournament was another matter.

"What else did they ask?"

"If I had gloves with me last night." He threw up his hands. "What a stupid question. It was like, twenty degrees out. I might not be a rocket scientist, but I'm not stupid. I got a nice pair of leather gloves from my mom for Christmas."

"Do you know why Paul asked you that?"

"No. By that time, I was tired of answering all his questions. I told him I was done. If he wanted to talk to me again, he could call my lawyer."

Darcy raised her eyebrows. She had helped Rafe find an attorney to help him with estate planning after he inherited Eddie's house and several other valuable assets. She could only hope he didn't think an estate planning lawyer would be sufficient to represent him in a potential criminal matter. Well, it was better to get things out in the open now, rather than later.

"I didn't know you had one."

He laughed. "I don't. But Gerard don't know that."

Playing games with the police didn't seem like a good idea to Darcy. Rafe was an adult, though. If he wanted to play with fire, he was the one who was going to get burned.

"Anything else you can think of?"

"He asked if he could have a look around the house. I told him not without a warrant. I wasn't going to give him a chance to plant evidence. Like I said, I'm not stupid."

Darcy leaned back and blew out a breath while she ran her fingers through her long, brown hair. The conversation had been going so well. And then Rafe managed to step in a proverbial pile of dog poo.

"Okay, Rafe. Here's what I see. You stopped answering Paul's questions. You refused to let him have a look around. You told him to talk to your lawyer. You know what kind of person does those kinds of things from the cops' view?"

He sat up straighter in his chair. "Yeah. A smart one."

"Maybe." She tapped her finger on the desktop. "Or someone with something to hide. Like someone who committed murder."

"Oh." He slumped back into his chair.

"Yeah." Darcy got to her feet. "Rafe, I already promised the Hobbit I'll look into things. I think you better get that fancy new phone of yours out and find a good criminal defense lawyer. Paul Gerard will pay you another visit. You can count on it. When he does, you'll want that lawyer on speed dial."

A dejected Rafe left the store. Darcy's heart went out to the man. She'd scared him to death. That was okay, though. Because she wasn't playing games.

The police wouldn't be, either.

Chapter Six

The following morning, Darcy stopped at her friend Jenna Washburn's diner for breakfast. It wasn't unusual for her to enjoy a bagel or scone with a hot cup of tea before reporting to Marysburg Music. What was unusual was the request she made to Jenna while she spread blueberry cream cheese on her multigrain bagel.

"I need to go to the Chamber of Commerce monthly meeting today. Will you go with me?"

Jenna's mouth hung open for a few moments before she answered.

"But you hate those meetings."

"I do." Darcy took a sip of her herbal tea. "After what happened at The Magic Box over the weekend, I'm betting there will be some fireworks. I don't want to miss them."

"Okay." Jenna shrugged. "Wait a minute. You're not investigating that young woman's murder, are you? I thought you learned your lesson last time about how dangerous that can be."

Darcy grimaced. Her friend on the other side of the counter wasn't wrong. In the past year, she'd been shot at and accosted while on her skateboard. While she escaped both episodes with little more than scrapes and bruises, it was undeniable that neither of those harrowing events would have happened if she hadn't turned to amateur sleuthing.

On the other hand, if she hadn't chosen to channel her inner Veronica Mars and take her lumps in the process, she wouldn't have brought two murderers to justice.

"I did." She took a sip of her tea. "I guess I still have some of the punk rock rebel from my Pixie Dust days in me."

Jenna raised an eyebrow. "I thought punk rock was all about sticking it to the man, not catching killers. I mean, that's what Jack Black said in *School of Rock*. Are you saying he's a liar?"

Darcy's smile morphed into a full belly laugh. *School of Rock* was her all-time favorite movie. She stopped counting the number of times she watched it after her thirtieth viewing. She even spent the summer between her sophomore and junior years in high school learning bagpipes so her first band could perform AC/DC's "It's a Long Way to the Top (If You Wanna Rock 'n' Roll."

"First off, it's Dewey Finn, not Jack Black. If you're going to bring up the greatest movie of all time, get the character names right." She waited for Jenna to deliver an order to a customer and return before continuing. "Second off, and more importantly, I told the Hobbit I'd help him. All of us business owners need to stick together, right?"

"I am so, so proud of you, my friend." Jenna's eyes got misty as she patted Darcy's hand. "If you promise you'll stay safe, I'll make our reservation for the meeting."

"I'll do everything I can to stay out of harm's way. See you at noon."

Charlotte gave Darcy a big hug the moment the store's manager arrived at the store. She didn't even take time to remove her puffy, purple coat, which Peter said made her look like a giant grape.

"I'm so sorry about that girl, Darc. What is happening to our community? Why are people so awful to each other?"

Darcy helped Charlotte out of the coat. Normally, Char was calm and collected. It was a trait Darcy admired the woman for. Having the tables reversed gave Darcy a feeling of accomplishment. To be in a position to comfort someone else was new. To be able to do the actual comforting was better than finishing the last song on an album.

Pride. Accomplishment. A belief that good things were ahead.

She could solve Angelica's murder. She would solve Angelica's murder. And in doing so, she'd be doing her part to make Marysburg, Indiana, the wonderful place she knew it was.

"It'll be okay, Char. The police are on it. Paul Gerard's investigating. I trust him. He'll do a good job. I'm going to do what I can, too."

Char went to the cash register to prepare it for opening. "Hank and I talked last night. How can I help?"

While they put out new stock, Darcy brought her up to speed. The report was shorter than she would have liked.

"Hopefully, I'll learn something helpful at the Chamber of Commerce meeting. So far, I don't have much to go on."

"Do you seriously think that either the Hobbit or Rafe is the murderer?" Char slotted a half dozen new copies of Olivia Rodrigo's latest album into a display near the front of the store called "Hot Young Artists."

"Do I think they did it? No." Darcy drummed her fingers on a stack of compact discs she was holding. "I don't want to rule anything, or anybody, out right now, though. The fact is, the Hobbit admits he doesn't have someone to verify his story and Rafe is acting shifty. I need to look into Angelica's boyfriend, too."

Char raised her index finger. "What's his name? I'll see what I can find out about him online."

"That's a bold move, staking claim to the kids' job." Peter and Izzy were light years more proficient at navigating social media than Darcy would ever hope to be. They'd used that knowledge to unearth invaluable information during Darcy's most recent investigation.

"I can hold my own." Char pulled her phone from her back pocket. "Besides, they have enough to worry about with their auditions coming up."

"Good point. His name's Xander Fleming-Winchester. He's a student at Ball State. A pretty boy, I guess. That's all I know."

"No worries." After a few moments ticking away on her phone, Charlotte smiled. "And here we are. He sure loves his Instagram."

A customer entered the store. Darcy went to greet the man. Despite the Hobbit's request, her investigative efforts would have to play supporting act to her headlining job of running the Marysburg Music.

Darcy was ringing up a sale when Jenna arrived. While she completed the sale, Charlotte and Jenna exchanged greetings and hugs.

"Assistant Inspector Washburn, reporting for duty," Jenna said when the customer left. "Ready to get some dirt?"

"It's not dirt we're after, my dear. It's information. Clues. Actionable Intelligence." Darcy shrugged into her coat. She'd been on the wrong end of gossip too many times in the past to count. Many of the unkind stories and the nasty looks that went with them were deserved. Not all, though. Even today, the false rumors from those days hurt. More than she was willing to let on.

Jenna huffed and crossed her arms. "You're no fun. And I see you've been watching *Chuck* again."

"Someone has to be the grownup." Darcy held out her palm to exchange a high-five with Charlotte. "And Zachary Levi is the total package, right Char?"

"Um, no. Do not try to drag me into one of your disagreements." Char shuddered. "I still have scars from the Mama Mia Misfire of 2021."

"Sorry about that." With her bag over her shoulder, Darcy pointed toward the door. "We gotta run. Before Jenna gets riled up about Pierce Brosnan's singing abilities again."

"Or lack thereof, you mean." Jenna slipped her arm through Darcy's. "He's a wonderful actor, but you have to concede that his singing left a lot to be desired."

"Have a good time, kids." Charlotte raised her voice to drown out any further discussion on the topic. Once they were gone, she put the Mama Mia soundtrack on the stereo. With the intent of reveling in its bright, bouncy songs without having to put up with any commentary from Jenna or Darcy.

"Do we go for the usual spot," Darcy asked upon their arrival at the meeting. She preferred to sit near the back of the room. The old preference was to have one's back to the wall so they could keep an eye on everyone.

"Works for me." Jenna led the way toward an unoccupied table for six. "Anyone in particular you want me to keep an eye on?"

With the meeting only a minute or two from beginning, people were getting seated. Darcy scanned the crowd.

Sean O'Sullivan was sitting at a table in the middle of the room. He was enjoying a laugh with his tablemates. Even from a distance, it was clear the man had slept much better than the night before.

Once they got settled, Darcy covered her mouth with her napkin. "Keep an eye on the Hobbit. He's in a way better mood than when I talked to him yesterday."

Jenna leaned in close to Darcy. "What did you say? And why are you covering your mouth like that?"

Darcy repeated her earlier instruction. "I'm covering my mouth so nobody can read my lips. I don't want to tip anyone off to what we're doing."

"Roger that, Double-Oh-Seven." Jenna poured some Italian dressing on her salad. "Surveillance commencing."

While they enjoyed their meals, Darcy filled Jenna in on what she knew about Angelica's murder.

"Not a lot to go on, Darc." Jenna frowned. "The Hobbit gets on my nerves, but I don't think he's dumb enough to bump someone off in his parking lot right after his own event. I mean, from what I heard, it was a massive success. The tournament, that is. Not the murder."

"Good point." Darcy waited until the server removed their salad plates. "Not exactly hard evidence, though."

"Which is why we need to stop gabbing and get to work observing." Jenna twirled her fork. "And devouring this chicken parm. God, I love it when they serve this. Chicken parm, you taste so good."

Due to her fear of missing something important, Darcy paid little attention to her meal. While she dined, her attention wasn't on the food. Instead, she studied the crowd as the guest speaker discussed the potential benefits of a proposed solar power farm at the edge of town.

Jenna, meanwhile, plowed through her lunch like it was her last meal on Earth.

When the speaker was finished, and the meeting opened for general discussion, Todd Meadows' hand shot up like a rocket.

"Here we go." Darcy took a sip of her water. "Eyes and ears open."

Marysburg's real estate mogul got to his feet. He turned toward the police chief and nodded.

"I'd like to take a moment to thank our public safety heroes for their tireless efforts to keep our community safe. Even during brutal cold conditions, they've been answering the call without hesitation."

The crowd applauded.

"Take this past Saturday evening, for instance. When there was a report of an awful felony committed behind The Magic Box and Comic Castle building, they were on the scene in minutes."

There was more applause. But Todd remained on his feet. Apparently, the blowhard wasn't finished.

"I'd like to invite the police chief to give us an update on their investigation." His smile, which had taken on a predatory menace, grew wider. "I'm sure he understands how important it is to the business community that this horrific event is investigated and the perpetrator apprehended with all due speed."

The police chief exchanged a word with Paul Gerard, who was sitting next to him.

"Looks like the boys in blue came prepared this time," Darcy said under her breath so Jenna was the only one to hear. The last time the Chamber of Commerce had a scheduled meeting shortly after a murder had been committed, Todd had ambushed the chief with questions.

"Good to see they learned their lesson." Jenna took a pen and a piece of paper from her purse. "You keep an eye on Meadows. I'll cover the cops."

The chief cleared his throat as he removed a sheet of paper from his pocket.

"I'd like to thank Mr. Meadows for his thoughtful comments. As with any investigation, I'm at liberty to discuss details, but we've already conducted a number of interviews and are exploring multiple lines of inquiry."

"Really?" Todd crossed his arms. "And what, exactly, does that mean?"

A murmur went through the crowd. The chief had dedicated his life to protecting the citizens of Marysburg. Over the course of those thirty-five years, he'd become the gold standard of reliable public service. When he spoke, people listened. More importantly, when he spoke, the community believed what he said.

The business community did, at least. Marysburg was becoming more diverse. As it did so, more folks, especially young ones, tended to look at law enforcement the way Rafe Majors did. With a healthy dose of skepticism.

That made Todd's challenge all the more astonishing. This was normally friendly territory for the police.

"I'll take that, Chief." Paul rose to stand next to his boss. Dressed in a navy blue suit with a Kelly green tie, the detective radiated a sense of calm control. He wasn't going to let Todd Meadows, or anyone else, mess with his investigation.

"For those of you who don't know me, I'm Detective Paul Gerard. I can confirm we've spoken to Mr. Sean O'Sullivan. He owns the store where the victim had been participating in a gaming tournament and is also the one who found her. He's giving us his full cooperation."

In response, the Hobbit's head bobbed up and down. It was as if he was hoping he could prove his innocence by giving his full agreement to whatever the detective was saying.

"We've spoken with Mr. O'Sullivan's staff, along with a number of other witnesses. I can assure you all that we're working this case as hard as possible."

"Is her boyfriend among these other witnesses?" Todd's smile was gone, replaced with a hard stare. "There's been a rumor that he disappeared Saturday night and hasn't been seen or heard from since."

"I don't deal in rumors, Mr. Meadows." Paul took a sip of water. "I deal in facts. Normally, I wouldn't comment in this amount of detail, but in order to quell this rumor, I've spoken with Mr. Fleming-Winchester myself."

"Does he have an alibi," Jasmine Longoria, who was sitting next to Todd, asked.

"We located him at his fraternity house yesterday afternoon. He was questioned but claims to have no memory of the events of this past Saturday night."

"What's that mean?" This time, the question came from Jenna. "Is he trying to say someone roofied him?"

Laughter rippled through the room, cutting the tension that had been rising faster than a new Taylor Swift release shot to the top of the charts.

While the Chief joined in with the laughter, Paul shot a death glare at Jenna.

"Hmm, wonder if you hit a nerve." Darcy offered her friend a fist bump under the table with one hand while she made a case note in her phone with the other. She'd learned from her dealings with Paul's predecessor that an odd or unexpected reaction from the investigator meant something.

Something important.

"I appreciate that these are stressful times for everyone here, Ms. Washburn. I'd rather not make light of something as serious as a murder investigation, though."

Jenna was a decent enough person that her cheeks turned pink at the admonishment. Darcy managed to contain a laugh when it occurred to her that Paul's retort wouldn't have bothered her in the least.

It also reinforced her resolve that she needed to have her own chat with the elusive Mr. Fleming-Winchester.

Chapter Seven

On the way back to Marysburg Music after the meeting, Darcy and Jenna hashed over what they'd learned. The main thing they agreed on was that Paul had done a masterful job of keeping information under wraps.

"What's the deal with Todd?" Darcy came to a stop at a cross street. "I get his play when he confronted the police about Derek Tufnell's murder. He got to act like the business leader whose only concern was the welfare of the community's image."

"That, and he got to take a swipe at you in the process." Jenna bumped her shoulder against Darcy's.

"Truth." Once a silver SUV cleared the intersection, they began crossing it. "He seemed a lot more heated this time, though. You don't think he was messing around with her, do you?"

Jenna grimaced. "That'd be gross. He's old enough to be her father. It's not that. They worked together. Angelica was interning for him. She was working on a business degree."

"I didn't know that. Guess it helps explain why he was at The Magic Box Saturday night." Darcy recounted Todd's role in presenting the grand prize.

"That tracks. It makes things look even worse for Rafe, though."

Marysburg Music's familiar purple and red marquee came into view. It was time to return Darcy's focus to her first love—music. She couldn't dismiss the implication of Jenna's comment, though.

What if Rafe knew that Angelica was working for Todd? He knew Todd was there to present the grand prize to the overall winner. The scoring system was secret. Who was the beneficiary of the secret system? And who got the five hundred in cash?

Angelica Stipe.

The dots connected themselves. Especially regarding Rafe, who had pulled a fast one on Todd and scuttled a big development the real estate kingpin had been working on.

Darcy groaned. She was going to have to have a hard conversation with Rafe. Well, if anyone in town could pull it off, she was the one. Good times.

"I'll talk to him again." She wrapped up Jenna in a tight hug. Her bestie was a godsend in every sense of the word.

"Given the circumstances, be careful, hon. Let me know if you want me to sit in when you chat. Just to be on the safe side."

They parted ways with Darcy's promise to keep Jenna in the loop. It seemed that one couldn't be too careful in Marysburg, Indiana, anymore.

The store was calm upon Darcy's return. A few customers were wandering up and down the aisles, stopping from time to flip through a selection of albums. A couple with matching cobalt blue hair who appeared to be in their mid-twenties was chatting with Charlotte while they gushed over a Bluetooth-enabled turntable.

The sweet voice of Norah Jones floated on the airwaves, feeling the store with mellow, jazzy pop.

The way the customers were *oohing* and *ahhing* over every new feature Char showed them, a sale was a foregone conclusion. The only question that remained was whether the final purchase would include a copy of Norah's album that was being used in the demonstration.

After checking in with the browsers to make sure they were good, Darcy settled herself behind the cash register. She had a lot to think about, and with Char the only other teammate around until the kids arrived after school, any ruminating would have to take place on the sales floor. The question before her was a simple one.

Had the results of the tournament made Rafe so angry that he turned to murder?

The man had spent so much of his adult life slacking off whenever possible, it was incomprehensible that he would have it within him to literally take someone else's life.

Then, the stories of Rafe arguing with Eddie popped into Darcy's head. Sometimes, the battles got so heated that things ended up being thrown and broken. Still, it was still a big step from throwing a coffee cup at someone to murdering them.

Wasn't it?

Good fortune intervened, as Char closed the sale. Darcy let her ring up the turntable purchase. While that was going on, Darcy called one person who might have insight on that question.

"Darcy, this is a surprise. What can I do for you?" The woman on the other end of the line was Heather Ewing, Rafe's next-door neighbor. She was the one who initially told Darcy about the rows between Eddie and Rafe.

"I need to pick your brain." Darcy signaled to Char and headed to the office so she could speak freely. "It's about Rafe Majors."

"That poor man. I didn't want to pry, but it was impossible to miss how long the police were at his house yesterday. This is about that young woman who was murdered, isn't it?"

"Yeah." Darcy massaged her temples with her free hand. It was a futile attempt to ward off an incoming headache. If only the discomfort was due to something simple, like the need for her to start wearing glasses. There was no such luck.

"Fire away." Heather had played a small but important role in Darcy's investigation into who murdered guitar legend Derek Tufnell. The woman was kind, discrete, and smart, and because of some unfortunate circumstances in her life recently, she wanted to help the Marysburg community any chance she got.

"You told me about the knock-down, drag-out fights Eddie and Rafe got into. Do you think Eddie's life was ever in danger?"

The woman was quiet for a few moments. That was Heather. She never spoke without thinking.

"I can't deny there were a few times I heard Rafe say some harsh words to Eddie. I never heard or saw anything that made me think I needed to rush over there to stop them."

"Never felt the need to call the cops?"

"No. Claude wanted to, but I always managed to talk him out of it."

"Why was that?"

"Sure, the fights were unsettling, but the next time I'd see Eddie, he'd be smiling and insisting there was nothing to worry about. He said they were just a couple of passionate people who didn't believe in bottling up their emotions."

Heather's description of Eddie was spot on. The man was a big believer in forgiving and forgetting. Darcy debated her next question. She hated to ask it. There was no getting around the issue, though.

"Do you think Rafe's capable of murder?"

"Well," Heather drew out the word, like she was playing a 45 record and slowed it down to 33 speed. "He's never seemed to be the brightest...."

"Yes, he's no mastermind. I want, I need, your honest opinion. We all get angry. Do you think Rafe Majors is capable of getting so angry that it could lead to murder?"

"By accident, maybe."

The clouds parted as the words registered in Darcy's brain. Of course. That made a ton of sense/

A scene formed in Darcy's mind. Rafe was angry about how the tournament had finished. After he stormed out, he went for a walk or something to cool off. He must have returned about the same time that Angelica came outside. He confronted her.

Angelica didn't seem the empathetic type, so they got into an argument. In the heat of the moment, Rafe grabbed her around the neck. Before he knew it, he'd strangled her until she lost consciousness. Rafe being Rafe, he most likely took off without bothering to confirm whether she was still breathing.

"Darcy? Are you still there?"

"Yeah." She shook her head. "I am. Thanks for your time, Heather. You've been a huge help. Come by the store soon. I've got some new jazz artists to introduce you to."

"I'm glad I could help. Should I keep an eye on Rafe? Let someone know if it looks like he's getting ready to leave town?"

Good golly, what have I done? What if he's the murderer? I can't ask Heather to put herself in harm's way. The thoughts flashed across Darcy's mind in the blink of an eye. It was time for prudence to take the lead.

"Go about your day like normal. You don't want him to think you're watching him. If you notice something weird, call the cops ASAP. Not me. Them. And above all, keep your distance. At least for now."

"So, you think he did it." The statement carried an unmistakable note of sadness to it.

"I don't know. Rafe's come a long way since Eddie died, so I hope he didn't. Until I can rule him out, though…"

Heather confirmed she understood the implication. Given the weight of the topic, they ended the call with little more than a promise to keep in touch.

Darcy tossed her phone on the desktop. then rubbed her eyes. Good golly, could it really be that simple? Could Heather Ewing, who lived alone, be residing next door to a murderer?

Her thoughts were interrupted by a knock on the door, followed by three more rapid knocks. It was Peter. He'd assigned all Marysburg Music employees their own unique knock so Darcy would know who wanted to see her.

At first, she thought it was silly. Undeterred, Peter convinced his co-workers of the brilliance of his scheme. When he invoked "Can't You Hear Me Knocking" by the Rolling Stones, he won everyone over.

In the end, it had turned out to be a decent idea.

"Come on in, Peter."

"What up, Boss?" The young man extended his fist for a knuckle bump, then sat down. His brow was furrowed. "I know I'm supposed to be out on the floor, but this'll be quick. Char said it was okay."

Normally, Peter was a reliable source of light and silliness at Marysburg Music. His serious demeanor meant something significant was on his mind.

"There was non-stop chatter at school about Angelica Stipe. Thought you'd want to know about it." He pointed at the whiteboard behind Darcy.

"Shouldn't you be more focused on your audition than on rumors?"

While Darcy appreciated Peter's willingness to help with the investigation, she wanted him to be thinking about his own future. And that future included his impending live audition for a spot at the Jacobs School of Music at Indiana University.

The prestigious program was super tough to get into, accepting only fifty incoming freshmen from within the State of Indiana. The last thing Darcy wanted was for Peter to lose focus with his audition mere days away.

"I am. I've been rehearsing before school and when I get home in the evening every day for the last three weeks. Trust me on this, Boss."

Darcy drummed her fingers on the desktop for a moment. At this point, any information was welcome. She could decide later on whether the intel was worth pursuing.

"Lay it on me."

"Yesi." He opened an app on his phone. "I wrote stuff down so I didn't forget it. Angelica went to high school here. A lot of people didn't like her. She was a bully. Always wanted to have her way with everything."

A picture of the young woman was becoming clearer in Darcy's mind. It would be a mistake to assume that image was correct, though.

"Was she popular? Like a cheerleader or class president? You know, those kinds of things."

Peter glanced at his phone. "She was in charge of the business club all four years. She ran for student council president her senior year but lost."

"What was she like personally? Did she have any enemies?"

"It was like she thought she was better than everyone. That the first chance she got, she was going to head off to New York for some big time career in international finance. As for enemies, Angelica and Bethan McDougal, her next-door neighbor, hated each other. One time, Angelica ran over Bethan's cat."

Darcy hugged herself. The thought of someone trying to hurt Ringo made her blood run cold.

"Do you know if this Bethan is still in town?"

"Yep. And there's more." He recounted another handful of anecdotes involving Angelica and Bethan. None of them were pleasant. And in each one of them, Angelica was the aggressor.

"Good golly, Miss Molly. Our victim was a piece of work, wasn't she?" Darcy put her hands up in surrender fashion. "Not that makes it okay for her life to be taken."

"I hear you, Boss. It's a sad world we live in." As the young man shook his head, his dreadlocks swung from side to side, as if to emphasize his statement.

"Which is why the world needs musicians and other creatives like you. Now more than ever. Thanks for the info." Darcy rose to her feet to signal the meeting had concluded.

Peter headed for the door. "I'll send Izzy in. She's got some stuff to tell you, too."

"Sorry about this, Darcy." Izzy closed the door but remained standing. "I know I'm supposed to be on the floor, too, but this is important."

"That's okay, Iz. What's on your mind?"

The young woman ran her fingers through her long pink hair. A Christmas gift had paid for the color. "While Peter was talking to people at school, I was talking to friends on campus at B.S.U. There are stories Angelica was up to some shady stuff over there."

"Can you be more specific?"

"Yes. Angelica was on the Dean's List. Some people think she got her good grades by cheating."

Darcy thought about it for a moment. Obtaining answers to a test was as bad as a band lip-synching at a concert. The circumstances might be different, but the outcome was the same. The perpetrator got credit for something they didn't deserve.

Did that provide motive for murder, though?

"Was she doing this on her own, or were other people involved?"

Izzy raised her eyebrows. "That's exactly what I asked. Supposedly, her boyfriend was involved. I don't know how, though. Sorry about that."

"No, this is really helpful. Getting caught and then kicked out of school or going to jail would give someone motive for murder."

Izzy frowned.

"I know that look, and I agree," Darcy said. "It does seem like a huge leap. Between your information and Peter's, I've got a lot to go on. Thank you."

"No problem." Izzy's smile returned. "My work here is done."

As the young woman returned to the sales floor, Darcy turned around. There was no doubt about it now. She uncapped her dry-erase marker.

It was time to add Bethan McDougal and Xander Fleming-Winchester to her suspect list.

Chapter Eight

Tuesdays were Darcy's day off from Marysburg Music. She adored her job of providing countless kinds of tunes, from classical to gospel to show tunes to the latest chart toppers to the community. She wouldn't trade it for anything in the world, either. Not even for a chance to return to her life as a touring musician.

She also loved the one day of the week she didn't have to go to work.

Darcy Gaughan was a practical woman. Her days off were filled with the mundane tasks of everyday life. After breakfast in her pajamas with Ringo on her lap, she'd prepare a to-do list. Normally, the list included things like doing laundry, getting groceries, and working in the yard.

On this Tuesday, she added a few new items to the list. Once her regular chores were finished, she was going to check in on Rafe. Then, she was going to pay a visit to Bethan McDougal. Xander would have to wait for the time being.

"Good times today, buddy." She scratched Ringo under his chin. "At least it's warming up. In a few days, all this snow will be gone."

The cat stared at her, then climbed down to the floor. It was as if he was telling her she'd better get a move on.

Such was her life as a former punk rock star.

She wouldn't have it any other way.

Later, she pulled to a stop in front of Rafe's house. It was weird for her to think of it that way. For years, it has been Eddie's house, a dwelling filled with music, good times, and love.

What kind of dwelling was it now? Was it really the refuge of a murderer?

There were no police cars parked nearby, so she took that as a positive sign for Rafe.

Darcy patted the photo of Gina Schock taped to the jeep's dash. The picture served as a great focal point when Darcy wanted to think out loud.

"I know things look grim for Rafe right now, Gina. Maybe it's because he was Eddie's stepson, but I don't see him doing it. Pouting in a corner? Yes. Complaining on social media? Totally. But resorting to violence? No way."

The picture looked back at her. It didn't offer any advice. That was probably for the best. Darcy would have gotten worried if an image of her hero actually started speaking to her.

She navigated the snow-covered walkway to the house with a sense of dejection. Eddie had made it a point to shovel and salt his driveway, front and back walkways, and the sidewalk with care. Rafe, obviously, hadn't bothered maintaining his stepfather's practice.

After knocking on the front door, she sent Rafe a text letting him know she was there. During the best of times, the man wasn't great at responding when someone showed up. In his current situation, he was probably ignoring any visitors.

After waiting long enough that the winter chill began to penetrate her Doc Martens, her phone buzzed. It was a text from Rafe instructing her to come to the back door.

With a grumble, she trudged through the snow to the other side of the house. He waved her in and even held the door open for her.

Her appreciation for the kind gesture dissipated when he told her reporters had been staking out the house, and he didn't want to let them know he was home.

"Dude, nobody is watching your place. I learned how to keep an eye out for stalkers back in my Pixie Dust days. You're safe."

Rafe's shoulders sagged. His disappointment with no longer being monitored, if he ever had been, would have been laughable if the stakes weren't so high.

She strode into the living room. Empty pizza boxes were strewn among crushed beer cans and sports drink bottles. It looked like a 1970s rock band had spent the night there. Biting back a growl, she pushed a pile of laundry aside and sat on the edge of the couch.

"How are you?" She looked him in the eye. "Be honest."

"Trying not to freak out." He dropped into his favorite chair, a leather recliner, like a sack of potatoes. "The cops want me to come in for an interview. My lawyer's working on that. Meanwhile, the library gave me the week off. To focus on my mental wellbeing, whatever that means."

It's a nice way to say you're a distraction right now, and they don't want you around. Darcy kept that thought to herself.

"It means you still have a job. And the sooner the murderer's arrested, the sooner you can go back to work."

Rafe stared at her for a moment, with the look of a hopeful puppy in his eyes.

"You believe me. You think I'm innocent."

She wanted to believe him. If for no other reason than she didn't want Eddie's legacy tarnished by having his stepson convicted of murder.

It was more than that, though. Darcy didn't believe Rafe Majors was capable of murder. She wanted to prove to herself and others that her intuition was spot on.

"It's not me you need to convince. It's the cops. One way to do that is to give them a full accounting of your whereabouts the night of the murder."

Rafe balled his hands into fists. "I told them already. I went for a walk to cool off. After everything that went down, I wanted to be by myself. How was I supposed to know someone was going to kill her while I was getting some steps in?"

His story hadn't changed since the last time they talked. That was encouraging. If he was lying, he'd eventually trip himself up.

Or, it was a demonstration of how good of a liar Rafe was. Well, a little more digging would help clear up that question.

"Do you remember where you went on your walk?" If she could establish the route of Rafe's stroll, she could check to see if he passed within the vision of any security cams. Not all businesses had them, but she only needed one or two to help confirm his story.

He shook his head. "I took a right when I went outside. That's all I remember."

Not helpful. And this guy wants me to save his bacon. She stifled the negative thought. Despite his request for assistance, Rafe got hostile when someone asked him tough questions. He'd been that way for as long as Darcy had known him.

"That's okay. Did you cross paths with anyone? Jenna takes her dog out for a walk every evening. Maybe someone like that?"

"Don't think so. I wasn't exactly in the mood for sightseeing." He unwrapped a piece of gum and popped it into his mouth. "Besides, I thought the whole reason the Hobbit called you is because the cops think he did it."

The change in direction gave Darcy pause. It wasn't an unreasonable question, though.

"That's true. I've already talked to him twice. I thought since it's been a couple of days, it couldn't hurt to check back in with you."

He clasped his hands together as he chomped down on the gum. His head started bobbing up and down in time with his jaw movements, like he was keeping up with a song going through his head.

Was it a matter of him thinking before speaking? Or was it something more sinister, like plotting before speaking? Darcy could only hope it was the former because, at that moment, she couldn't get a read on him.

An unreadable Rafe was problematic Rafe.

He glanced at his wrist when it beeped. "I got a call with my lawyer in a few. I need to get ready. Thanks for coming by."

"Do you want me to sit in on it with you? I'm happy to."

"Nah, I'm good."

"Oh." Since the visit was apparently over, she stood. "You can trust me, Rafe. I'm not gonna screw you over. I'll see you later."

On her way back to Rusty, Darcy slowed her pace and scanned the area. It was a subtle move, one she hadn't used in years. It all came back to her, though. Muscle memory in action. At the jeep, she even took a look at the house next door. Heather Ewing was nowhere to be seen.

"Sorry, Rafe. No 'Hollywood Insider' action for you today."

Darcy keyed the engine. It was time for a visit with a much more friendly face.

"Lunch delivery for Liam Hewson." Darcy gave Charlie, the young man at the service counter, a smile. "And a super-size soda with all the caffeine and calories for you."

"Sweet." He inserted a straw into the drink. "The Boss is working on a tire alignment. I'll let him know you're here."

Over the past year or so, Darcy had gotten to know the team at the auto service station. They liked Liam. He was a good boss, approachable and clear with his instructions and expectations. That made it a welcoming environment when Darcy visited. Nobody minded if she made her own way to Liam's office. Small-town life at its best.

She'd just finished laying out their lunch spread, submarine sandwiches, and chicken noodle soup from the local sandwich shop when Liam arrived.

"Looks amazing. To what do I owe the honor?" He took a big bite out of his sandwich.

"Can't a girl just want to treat her guy to lunch?"

"Totally." He took another bite. The sandwich was disappearing faster than a crooked concert promoter with a night's cash box. "But you're no ordinary girl. And these not ordinary times."

She blew on a spoonful of her steaming soup. "Fine. Since I'm busted, what can you tell me about Bethan McDougal? I hear she and Angelica had issues."

Liam slurped a big serving of his soup, then another. The man had a fireproof palate. "From the stories her dad told me, the McDougal and Stipe parents got along fine, but the girls hated each other. He placed the blame on Angelica. Said that practically from day one, Angelica bullied Bethan."

"How so?"

He recited a litany of abhorrent behavior that ranged from face-to-face name-calling to online harassment to the attempted murder of Bethan's cat. Darcy had been quiet, alternating between note-taking and munching on her lunch.

"This is the second time I've heard about the cat."

Liam shrugged. "Depends on who you ask. According to Mr. McDougal, the cat was sunning itself on the Stipe's driveway while Bethan was weeding in the front yard. Angelica came home and seemed to aim for the cat when she turned into the driveway. The cat escaped, but the young ladies had a serious throwdown."

Darcy chewed on a bit of a sandwich while she pondered the story. She had to admit that if someone tried to hurt Ringo, she'd be out for blood. Figuratively, not literally. But that was her.

It might be different for Ms. McDougal.

They chatted about the other subjects while they worked through their lunch. Darcy was picking crumbs off the paper her sandwich had come in when there was a knock at the door.

Liam wiped his mouth. "Gotta get back to it. Thanks for lunch."

"Appreciate the intel." Darcy gave him a hug. She cared for the man with all her heart but wasn't ready to move to the kissing in public stage in their relationship. "I think I'll swing by the McDougal place. See if Bethan's up for a chat."

"Make sure you take some personal protection. She's got a short fuse." Liam laughed. "Just kidding."

The problem for Darcy was that she wasn't sure whether she should take the joke seriously or not. One could never be too sure when conducting a murder investigation.

Chapter Nine

Before Darcy could go see Bethan, she had an appointment she couldn't miss under any circumstances. It was with her next-door neighbor and cat sitter, Hallie Birch. At age thirteen, the middle-schooler had started to show an interest in music outside of her band classes at school.

That interest had manifested itself most prominently in the area of percussion. And in drumming, specifically. Whether Darcy's status as a former touring drummer had anything to do with Hallie's interest was unknown. What was known was that the girl had a true interest in learning how to play the instrument, not simply wanting someone to oversee her while she banged away on the drums and cymbals.

After chatting with Darcy, Hallie's parents had gotten the girl a drum kit for Christmas. In addition, they arranged for Darcy to give her lessons on Tuesday afternoons.

At 4:15 on the dot, Hallie knocked on Darcy's back door and let herself in. Since she looked after Ringo occasionally, she already had a key. That way, Darcy didn't have to be on the alert for her arrival.

"What up, Teach?" The girl exchanged a high-five with Darcy as she dropped her backpack on a chair in the kitchen.

"Sticking it to the Man by showing a lack of respect for your instructor. Very punk rock of you." Darcy poured each of them a glass of ice water while Hallie shrugged out of her winter garb.

"I knew you'd understand." Hallie pulled a pair of drumsticks out of her backpack. "If I tried that at school, it would be Detention City."

Darcy laughed out loud. Hallie was the stereotypical good kid. She got above average grades, helped with the community's annual Riverwalk Clean Up Day, and stayed out of trouble. To think of her figuring out how to avoid detention made the rebel inside Darcy do a fist pump.

"No detention here. Instead, I'll put you on litter box duty." Darcy led the way into the spare bedroom. Her drum kit, was located to the left of center of the room. A smaller kit sat next to it.

The smaller setup was identical to the one Hallie had in the basement of her home. It was the arrangement Darcy started out with back in the day.

The hour spent with the girl was like a ray of sunshine on a cloudy day. For those sixty minutes, Darcy forgot all about Angelica Stipe, Rafe Majors, the Hobbit, and the whole murder investigation. Instead, that precious block of time was spent discussing music theory, practicing fundamentals, and then playing a song.

At that moment, it was exactly what the doctor ordered.

When the drum riff from Phil Collins' "In the Air Tonight" blasted from Darcy's phone, teacher and student sat back and exchanged a fist bump. Another lesson had concluded, and both of them were a little sweaty from the session. They were both smiling, too.

And Darcy's elbow didn't hurt, either.

"Great work, kiddo. Keep practicing your fundamentals, and before you know it, you'll be ready for your own drum battle with Nandi Bushell."

"Sick. I'd totally be down for that." Hallie had admitted that meeting Nandi one day was one of her life goals.

With a wide grin, Hallie skipped down the hall toward the kitchen, drumming on her thighs along the way. The only time she put down the sticks was to put her coat and boots on. As she headed out the door, she had them back in her hands.

"See ya next week, Teach." The girl saluted Darcy with one of her sticks.

"Same Bat time. Same Bat-channel." Darcy leaned out of the doorway so she could shout one more instruction to Hallie. "And keep stickin' it to the man. Just not your folks or in school."

As a former punk rocker, it was a lame order. There was no denying it, though. Darcy was a businesswoman, a homeowner, and cat mom.

My, how things had changed.

A little while later, Darcy brought Rusty to a stop in front of a split-level ranch. The white exterior featured a blue door and shutters. A flag on a post in the middle of the front yard fluttered in the breeze. It featured a blue field with crossing, diagonal white bars.

Darcy smiled at the flag of Scotland. Pixie Dust had played both Glasgow and Edinburgh during a twelve-stop tour of the U.K. and Ireland. The Scottish crowds had been boisterous beyond belief, which made for ideal conditions for a punk rock show.

After a moment, reveling in the memories, Darcy shook her head. She was there on a serious matter, not for a stroll down memory lane. She gave the Gina Schock photo a quick pat for good luck; she made her way to the front door.

A tall, young woman with reddish-brown hair and freckles answered Darcy's knock. Dressed in a plain yellow T-shirt and blue shorts, she had wary gray eyes and an athletic build that showed off muscles with some serious definition.

It was Bethan McDougal. She was a soul not to be trifled with.

Darcy introduced herself and asked if she could have a moment of Bethan's time.

"What's this about, then?" She didn't move from her position, filling the doorway.

"I was wondering if I could talk to you about your neighbor, former neighbor, Angelica Stipe." Darcy nodded in the direction of the Stipe home. "She was murdered the other day."

"And you think I had something to do with it, do ya?" She crossed her arms. The sleeves of her shirt strained against her biceps.

This woman radiated more toughness than Darcy's favorite leather jacket. That piece of clothing had somehow survived the Pixie Dust days without so much as a scratch on it. Underneath the jacket's durable surface was a lining that was soft to the touch, too. If Darcy was patient, maybe she could find a part of Bethan that was as dependable as the jacket.

"A friend asked me to look into the matter." She shrugged. "I've had some success helping the police catch a couple of recent murderers."

"Have you, now?" Bethan raised an eyebrow, then pointed her finger at Darcy. "Now I know who you are. You own the music store. You caught that fella who knocked off your boss, yeah?"

The question caught Darcy off guard. She had to close her eyes for a few moments to prevent a stream of tears from escaping. It had been almost a year, but the mention of Eddie's death often took her right back to the awful Monday morning when she found him.

She took a deep breath and opened her eyes. "Yeah, that's me. I'm trying to do the same thing for Angelica that I did for Eddie Maxwell, my boss. I trying to figure out who murdered her."

"All right, then." Bethan led Darcy through a tidy living room and into the kitchen. An island with a gray granite surface commanded the center of the room. Four barstools lined one side of the island.

While Darcy got settled at on a barstool, Bethan took two mugs from a cabinet. "I'm having some tea. Care to join me?"

"Sure." Since it was late in the afternoon, Darcy only wanted herbal tea or at least something decaffeinated. Given the challenge, it had been simply to get in the door, being picky about the woman's choice of tea might be counterproductive.

Bethan filled both mugs with a dark brown tea that had a floral aroma to it. She slid a small cup and saucer in Darcy's direction. A dainty serving spoon lay on the saucer.

"Some sugar if you want it." She took a sip. "I think it's best straight, but some folks find Scottish Blend a bit strong if they haven't had it before."

Darcy took a sip. And almost choked. "Wow. That's strong. Really good, though."

Bethan smiled and raised her mug. "Slàinte."

The moment their mugs clacked together, the tension in the room dropped by half. To ingratiate herself with her host further, Darcy took another sip. A small one.

"Please don't take this the wrong way. If I drink too much of this, I'll be up all night."

"That's why I drink it. I often work into the wee hours of the morning." The younger woman settled onto a stool that left one between them.

Keeping a barrier between us. Interesting. "What do you do?"

"Medical coding. It's not a bad gig. I get to set my own hours and work from home."

Darcy became all too familiar with medical billing and coding when she was going through rehab. To her, the people who did that work were unsung heroes of the American medical field.

Bethan's career choice didn't mean she wasn't a murderer, though.

They were at the point in the visit where Darcy wished she was better at small talk. If she had Eddie's gift of gab, she could have had the younger woman at ease in no time. Well, some people appreciated her directness. Maybe Bethan would.

"Have you liked next door to the Stipes a long time?"

"Aye. Ever since we moved here. My mam took a job at Ball Memorial Hospital. That's been ten years now." She let out a little huff. "Ten long years."

"What makes you say that?"

"The reason you're here." Bethan barked out a laugh. "Angelica Stipe. That harpy had it in for me from the day we first laid eyes on each other."

"Seriously? Right from the start?" Darcy was familiar with the concept of long-running feuds between neighbors. But it always seemed that some sort of inciting incident started the feud. She'd never heard of a decade-long bullying campaign simply because someone moved next door."

"Oh, aye. She was nice enough in the beginning. All neighborly-like when her parents dragged her over to welcome us to the neighborhood. The next day, though, I was going out for a walk. You know, to explore the surroundings. When I waved at her, she flipped me the bird, then turned her back on me. It got worse from there."

Bethan recounted story after story of appalling behavior on Angelica's part. They made Darcy's blood boil. She made constant fun of Bethan's ginger hair. When school started, she belittled Bethan's Scottish brogue, often not bothering to wait until they were out of earshot of each other.

"That's horrible. Didn't anyone help you?" Images came to Darcy's mind of her middle school years when kids tried to make fun of her passion for drumming and punk music. She used those hateful words to motivate her so much that sometimes she'd finish a practice session and find her fingers were bleeding.

"My mam and da did what they could. Which most of the time involved preaching to me about the McDougal clan's historical toughness. A lot of good that did for a girl in a new country who didn't have any friends."

"The middle school years are the worst. I take it things didn't get any better when you got to high school."

"They changed." Bethan took a drink of her tea and stared out a window. It was like she was looking into her past. "We didn't see as much of each other. She was into the cheer squad thing, while I played for the girls' football and rugby teams. She got more subtle with her bullying. Less often but more hateful."

"Like the incident with your cat." The words were out before Darcy could do anything to bring them back. Well, she was going to have to broach the subject at some point. It might as well have been then.

"Yeah." She drank the rest of her tea. "Not my finest moment."

At Darcy's prompting, Bethan related the story in detail. The blow-by-blow account sent shivers down Darcy's spine. What first started as an exchange of harsh words quickly escalated into a shouting match. First, there was pushing and shoving. When Bethan tried to call the police, Angelica slapped her phone to the concrete surface, breaking the device in the process.

The situation got even worse when Angelica used her own phone to livestream the encounter. The video caught Bethan threatening Angelica with what a police report later described as "grievous bodily harm."

"Let me make sure I have this straight. Did you make a specific threat, or was it more something like, 'I'm gonna get you.'"

"Wait a minute. You're not trying to say I had anything to do with her murder, are you?"

Darcy put up her hands. "No. Not at all. Your name's come up during my investigation, though. I'm just trying to gather as many facts as I can. Figures the best way to get your take was to ask you."

Bethan, who had started to get up, sat back down. She tilted her head to one side. "I guess that's fair."

"Do you remember what you said during the faceoff? My guess is it won't be long before the police pay you a visit. If it helps, think of this as practice for talking to them."

"You really think they want to talk to me? That fight was a long time ago."

"I know the investigator. He's super thorough. He'll be in touch. You can count on it."

"Lucky me." Bethan balled up a paper napkin, then flattened it back out. "I might as well tell you what I said, then."

Darcy held her tongue. Trying to force it out of her or trying to speed things up would backfire. She could wait.

The second hand on the wall clock made a complete sixty-tick rotation before Bethan moved. First, she let out a long sigh. Then, she blinked a few times, as if to get rid of tears that were threatening to form. Finally, she made eye contact with Darcy.

"I told her one day she'd pay for what she did to my cat and to all the things she'd done to me. And the payment wouldn't be in money. It'd be in blood."

Darcy let the words tumble around in her mind for a few moments. Were they harsh? No doubt about it. Were they a real threat to Angelica's well-being? That was tougher to say. Especially since they were uttered in the heat of the moment. Shoot, she could recall threatening each of her bandmates with violence a half-dozen times. None of those outbursts ended up on the Internet, though.

"Thank you for being straight with me. I can't imagine how tough it was living next door to someone like that."

Bethan gave her a quick nod. "I'm not going to lie. Angelica Stipe was a malignant tumor in this town. Eventually, you have to remove the tumor, or the body dies. Marysburg's better off now. I'm not sorry she's dead. I didn't murder her, though."

"Any thoughts about who did?"

"No." Bethan got to her feet. Apparently, the visit was evidently over. "But I wouldn't mind shaking their hand."

A chill came over Darcy as she stood. The woman standing mere feet from her carried a lot of bottled-up anger. An angry person was a dangerous person. She started toward the door, then stopped and turned, just like Detective Columbo.

"Just one more question, then I'll get out of your hair. Where were you Saturday night?"

Bethan stared at Darcy, her jaw clenched so hard it looked like it might crack. She gestured toward the door.

"It's none of your business where I was Saturday night. Goodbye."

Chapter Ten

By the time she got home from her chat with Bethan, Darcy was ready to forget about the real world for a while. She made some chicken stir fry in the wok her parents had given her for Christmas. The sizzling oil commingled with aromatic spices and tended chicken strips to re-create a scene from her favorite Asian restaurant. The concentration required to prepare the meal helped make the stress from the day's activities fade away, like the steam from the wok.

After giving Ringo his portion, she settled into her recliner with dinner on her lap and All *Creatures Great and Small* on the TV and made a mental note to use cooking therapy more often.

The next morning, she was awake before her alarm went off.

"Sorry, buddy." She had to move Ringo so she could get out of bed. "Lots to do and not enough time to do it."

The cat glared at her for a moment, then yawned so wide his face disappeared. After licking a paw, he descended the set of stairs at the end of the bed and strolled out of the room. Any other time of the day, he would have gone back to sleep after giving her his death stare.

It was breakfast time, though. The most important meal of the day for a cat. At least until the second breakfast.

After taking care of Ringo's dietary needs, she got cleaned up and headed out the door.

"Later, skater." She tossed a few kitty treats into his food bowl. "Got people to talk to and records to sell."

She stepped outside and stopped on a dime. The sun was rising in a cloudless sky. What caught her interest wasn't above her head, though. It was under her feet.

The snow was melting. Patches of grass could be seen in the yard among the remaining accumulation.

According to an app on her phone, the current temperature was forty degrees, with a forecasted high near fifty. Darcy did a little happy dance. If the warmer temperatures held for a while, the snow would be fully melted by the weekend.

With the snowmelt a hint that Spring couldn't be that far off, Darcy gave the Gina Schock photo a good luck tap as she rolled down the gravel driveway.

A few minutes later, she eased into a parking space near Jenna's diner. The spot was next to one occupied by a nondescript silver sedan. The vehicle had a law enforcement plate. It was the one assigned to Paul Gerard.

"Detective, good morning. What a surprise running into you here at my bestie's diner." Darcy took a seat in a chair across from the man.

"Or not." He glanced at his wristwatch. "Since I have breakfast here most Wednesdays."

"Guilty as charged." Darcy chuckled as she pointed a finger at him. "The benefits of paying attention and learning the habits of people around me. Your predecessor taught me that."

He sipped his coffee, then placed the cup back on the tabletop and crossed his arms, remaining silent the entire time.

"Another thing I learned from her is that when you're talking to someone, a great way to get them to start talking is to be quiet. People can't stand the silence." She dipped a bag of herbal tea into a mug the server placed in front of her. "Have you heard from her recently?"

"She texted me when she heard about the Stipe murder." He smoothed his tie with his fingers. "Offered to help any way she could."

"Speaking of which, how's it going? The case, I mean."

"We're pursuing a number of avenues of inquiry." He sat back to let the server place Jenna's Full Hoosier Breakfast in front of him. The meal consisted of two eggs, two pieces of bacon, biscuits & gravy, and toast.

"Good golly, Miss Molly. Are you going to eat all that?" Darcy shook her head. Paul could be a poster boy for a fitness program. There were an awful lot of calories for a single meal on his plate.

He unfolded a napkin. "Have a lot to do. A cop cannot live on coffee alone."

"Good on ya, then." Darcy slathered a bagel she ordered with cream cheese. "Since it's gonna take you longer to power through all that than it'll take me to eat this, mind if I tell you what I've learned the past few days?"

At his nod, she gave him a report on the results of her sleuthing. "I'll admit, right now, I'm thin on hard evidence. Rafe's not your guy, though."

"Why do you say that? It sounds like he still doesn't have an alibi."

Darcy took a bite. While she chewed, she considered Paul's question. It got to the root of the matter with Rafe. She didn't have a good answer to it. That wasn't going to stop her, though.

"Come on, man. Think about it. We both know Rafe. God love him, the guy isn't smart enough to commit something as serious as murder without getting caught."

"You sure about that?" Paul gave Darcy a half smile as he picked up a piece of bacon.

The hair on the back of Darcy's neck stood on end. Paul seemed to know something she didn't. Not surprising, since he was investigating the case with a variety of tools at his disposal, and she...wasn't.

She knew Rafe, though. At least, she thought she did.

"I've known the guy as long as anyone in this town. When he realized he needed help managing his money after Eddie died, who'd he turn to? Me."

Paul stared at her, almost through her, as he chewed a piece of gravy-laden biscuit. He took a drink of his coffee, then wiped his mouth. All the while, it was impossible to get a read on his thoughts.

He pointed a finger at her. "All true. And kudos to you for taking him under your wing. One thing I know is how much a pain in the backside he can be in the best of times. There are a couple of other things I know, too."

"Are you going to share them with me?" Despite her best effort, Darcy couldn't keep the annoyance she was fighting out of her tone. Though, to be fair, she was the one who interrupted his breakfast.

"Sure. Since they aren't related to the case." He chuckled. "One, Rafe may not be Einstein, but he is crafty. I believe you have your current location for the record store, thanks to said craftiness. Two, Rafe's got a pronounced narcissistic streak, and his pride was wounded. He thought he was going to win that tournament. That's why his group of friends was there. Not winning embarrassed him. With his personality, that's a troublesome combination."

The man was right. Darcy took another bite of her bagel. Being a wily, self-absorbed man-child wasn't a good combination. It didn't make Rafe a killer, though.

Did it?

Darcy wasn't ready to give up on her mission. "The way you sound, I'm surprised you haven't arrested him."

"I'm not going to arrest someone just because they fit a certain profile. Or to make certain people happy, if that's what you mean."

Darcy let out a breath in relief. Rafe wasn't even the person who'd gotten her involved, and here she was, acting like his defense attorney. It was time to go back on offense.

"I do. And speaking of personality profiles, have you verified the Hobbit's alibi?" She held up her hand. "Since he asked me to help him, I think that's something you should be able to share."

Paul shook his head. "Or lack thereof, you mean? He's admitted his staff was already gone. Now, that could mean he was being a nice boss. Or..."

It took Darcy a few seconds to catch up. She didn't like the result when she did.

"Or, he sent everybody home so nobody would be around in case he happened to run into Angelica when he was taking out the trash."

Paul tapped the side of his nose with his index finger.

"But that assumes the Hobbit knew Angelica would still be around when he took the trash out. Or, maybe he wasn't planning anything and just snapped when he saw her. I mean, it sounds like they had taken the snark and turned it up to eleven during the tournament."

"It's a possibility." Paul's noncommittal response wasn't a denial. At least there was that.

"What a minute. What about the marks on her neck? Like fingerprints, or maybe scratch marks or bruising?"

"The murderer wore gloves. We're waiting on additional information from the coroner."

"So, he's still a suspect." When Paul shrugged again, Darcy changed her approach. "I talked to Bethan McDougal yesterday. She's an interesting one."

Paul put down his utensils and even leaned forward. So much for his poker face. "Why do you say that?"

Darcy shrugged. "Oh, I don't know. Maybe because she didn't hesitate to admit she's not sad Angelica's dead. I'd be out for blood if someone tried to hurt Ringo."

"Understandable, but a lack of mourning does not a murder suspect make."

"That's what I thought." Darcy drank her tea, savoring the flavor as much as the suspense she was creating. "Until I asked her what she was doing Saturday night."

Paul chuckled as he shook his head. He wiped his hands with a napkin. "I see what you're doing. Are you going to keep me in suspense?"

"She told me it was none of my business. Then said it was time for me to leave."

"That's interesting. I'll give you that. But—"

"But, what? Come on, Paul. Angelica bullied Bethan for years. Have you seen this woman? She's almost as big as Thea. Someone with that size and strength could easily have strangled Angelica."

"Look, Darcy. Everyone at Marysburg PD knows about the long history between the Stipes and the McDougals. The police reports take up a whole drawer of one of the filing cabinets at the office."

"Wait a minute? You keep paper records?"

"It's an expression. The point is, the dispute goes back a decade, and while there's been plenty of name-calling, nothing's ever risen to the level of threats of bodily harm."

"That's not what Bethan told me when her cat almost got run over."

Paul scratched his forehead. "Those were words spoken in the heat of the moment of an emotional situation. Eventually, cooler heads prevailed."

Darcy drummed her fingers on the tabletop. "So, that's it? Nothing more to be said about Bethan McDougal?"

"I didn't say that. Since she didn't want to share her whereabouts for Saturday night, I'll pay her a visit. Satisfied?"

She smiled. "I will be if you tell me where she was. After all, I'm the one who tipped you off to her lack of an alibi."

"Don't push your luck. I'm still not officially talking to you about the case, remember?"

They finished breakfast on good terms, chatting about the warm-up that had arrived, then went their separate ways. On the short drive to Marysburg Music, Darcy dictated her thoughts about the case into an app on her phone. She was still speaking into the device when she entered the store.

"What up?" Charlotte waved at her with a feather duster from a corner of the store. She had a hand-held vacuum in the other hand. "Saw a cobweb by the ceiling, so I'm getting a head start on spring cleaning."

"I love you more than life itself, Char." She scanned the store. Everything was in order. "Do you mind if I spend some time in the office? I'd like to update the suspect board."

"No prob. Just a reminder that I have to leave at eleven to look at a record collection. It's supposed to have a lot of classic and prog rock."

One of the ways Marysburg Music maintained its inventory of used records was by purchasing personal collections. Someone from the store would visit the seller, give the collection an inspection, and, if the albums were in good shape, make a purchase offer. It was a task Darcy had been responsible for. She'd given the responsibility to Charlotte the previous October.

Darcy gave her general manager a thumbs up and made for the office. Normally, she started her Wednesday mornings catching up on email and other important things from her day off. On this day, she gave her inbox a quick scan to make sure there were no fires that needed to be extinguished, then removed the Ziggy Marley blanket from the suspect board.

First, she added Bethan's name to the suspect list. As imposing as the woman was, there was no doubt she had the strength to commit the murder. Her motive, revenge for all the abuse she suffered at Angelica's hands, wasn't a smoking gun, but wasn't without merit, either. It wasn't any weaker than

Rafe and the Hobbit's motives.

Opportunity was the thing. Until Bethan shared where she was and what she'd been doing the previous Saturday night, Darcy was going to assume the worst. What if Bethan got word that Angelica won the tournament and snapped? She could have waited for her nemesis, remaining hidden behind a vehicle or trash container, until it was time to strike. Then she choked the life out of the smaller woman.

An image of Bethan committing the crime flashed before Darcy's eyes. A chill went down her spine. It was a terrifying scene, indeed. And one that required further investigation.

A while later, Darcy was at her desk, making a list of items to order for Record Store Day. The annual event held every April celebrated the world of music and independent record stores. The store phone rang. With Charlotte out front, Darcy ignored it.

There was a knock on the door moments later. Char came in with the sales floor's cordless phone in her hand. Her complexion was pasty white, as if all the blood had drained from it.

"Are you okay?" Darcy leapt from the desk to guide Charlotte into a chair.

"Yeah. It's a call for you." She held the phone close to her chest, as if to keep it from her boss's prying hands.

Darcy knew evasive behavior as well as anyone. She'd practiced it for too many years. There was something Char really didn't want to tell her.

"Come on. Hand it over." Darcy kept her tone friendly as she gestured toward the suspect board. "It can't be as bad as a murder, right?"

"I'll let you be the judge of that." She held the phone out. "It's the manager from Pixie Dust. He wants to talk to you about playing a gig with the band."

Chapter Eleven

The office door closed with a click behind her. It had been a conversation like no other in Darcy's life. She made her way toward the cash register with an unsteady gait. It was as if she was walking on a carpet made of marshmallows. It wasn't an unpleasant sensation, but there was a tinge of danger with each step. If she wasn't careful, she'd trip and plummet through the softness under her feet and into an abyss, never to be found again.

"Darcy, darling?" Hank, who had arrived while she was in the office, guided her by the elbow to the stool behind the cash register. "You don't look like yourself. Do we need to call someone?"

"No. I'm okay." She chuckled as she shook her head. "At least I think I'm okay."

"What did the snake want?" Charlotte's words dripped the venom from the most dangerous pit viper on Earth. Like everyone who worked at Marysburg Music, Char knew the tragic downfall of Darcy's career as a touring drummer. And how Pixie Dust's manager had been the one who put the final nail in the coffin.

"To make, actually." She laughed again. "Dust is out on tour. They're playing Indianapolis on Friday, March third. Something happened at the following night's venue, so they had to cancel that gig. They booked a replacement one at Emens Auditorium. He wanted to know if the band could do a meet and greet and play a reunion set here at the store that afternoon before they play the show."

Silence hung over the trio like a heavy raincloud moments before bursting.

Hank and Charlotte exchanged glances as Darcy kept shaking her head. There was no denying that Darcy's alcohol abuse was the main reason for her getting kicked out of Pixie Dust. It also couldn't be refuted that her elbow injury made it impossible for her to play for more than thirty minutes at a time. That kind of limitation wasn't going to work for a band that had spent the last decade playing between one hundred and two hundred gigs per year.

Still, Pixie Dust was Darcy's band. She started the group. She was the one who found the perfect bandmates. To be fired from the thing she created still hurt worse than the most massive multi-day hangover she'd ever suffered through.

And now, the man who had delivered the devastating message that she was no longer part of the band, the one that sent her into full freefall, wanted to visit her store.

As if she didn't have enough going on at the moment.

"What did you tell him," Char asked.

"I told him, sure. Why not? Time heals all wounds, right? This is the ultimate chance to be the person Eddie always wanted me to be." As she got to her feet, she handed a piece of paper to Charlotte. "Here are some of the deets. If you could order some Dust music and merch, that would be great."

While the store's general manager studied the page, Hank stepped forward. "How can I help?"

She responded by hugging him. His decision not to analyze anything or talk her out of agreeing to the appearance meant more than she could put into words.

Darcy might be the heart of Marysburg Music. Char was the brains of Marysburg Music. Hank was, without a doubt, the soul of Marysburg Music.

"Work with Char on a To-Do list. Let's schedule everything so it leads up to open mic night, with Dust doing the closing set. There's not much time, but if we're gonna do this, we're gonna do it right. Sound like a plan? For now, at least?"

Hank gave her two thumbs up. "Sounds like an excellent plan. Leave it to us."

"Good. I could use some fresh air, so I'm going for a walk."

Darcy didn't have a destination in mind as she set out. With her earbuds in so she could listen to *Questlove Supreme*, her favorite podcast, she was content to wander at a casual pace. The sun was a beacon of warmth in a cloudless sky and helped make the stroll truly stress-reducing.

When she found herself passing The Magic Box and Comic Castle, she laughed. Apparently, her subconscious did have a destination in mind. It was the stream of water flowing into a drain that made things click into place.

"The snow that was on the ground Saturday night. What if it's gone?" She snapped her fingers as she picked up her pace. What if there was a clue to be found now?

Upon rounding the corner of the building, she did a little happy dance. The parking lot was clear of all snow. More importantly, the mounds that had been built along the edges of the parking lot had decreased in size by half or more.

Another thing was in her favor. The area where Angelica had been discovered was unoccupied. There were no vehicles to impede a search.

Police crime scene tape had been removed, which made things even easier. She wouldn't get in trouble for crossing into somewhere she wasn't supposed to be.

Not that some yellow tape would have stopped her, anyway.

The lot's damp asphalt surface shimmered in the bright sunlight as the ring of snow drip, drip, dripped away. It was almost as if someone had removed a giant mirror from a wall and placed it on the ground.

Her first move was to turn off the podcast. She wanted one hundred percent focus. A few feet away from the crime scene, she stopped to take a few photos with her phone. While nothing currently suggested there were clues to be found, she could study enlarged shots on her computer later.

Despite her challenges with former Detective-Sergeant Rosengarten, Darcy had learned a number of handy investigatory tricks, like enlarging photos, from the woman.

"Thank you, Detective."

She also snapped a few shots of the surrounding area. If the murderer had lain in wait for Angelica, where could they have hidden if not behind a vehicle? There was the dumpster, of course. O'Sullivan claimed he'd been taking out the trash when he came upon Angelica's body.

She lifted the dumpster's lid. It was half-full of plastic garbage bags, flattened cardboard boxes, and the usual detritus to be found after an event. The amount of trash seemed to verify the Hobbit's reason for being in the parking lot at the time of the murder.

The police would have confirmed the same thing already, but one could never be too sure. Paul Gerard was meticulous in his investigations. Those working under him might not have the same attention to detail.

With no surprises in the dumpster, Darcy turned her attention back to the crime scene. An alley ran alongside the edge of the parking lot farthest from the building. Another lot of similar size was on the other side of the alley. That lot ran up to the backside of a row of two-story commercial structures, not unlike the Hobbit's building.

There were no nearby trees, shrubbery, or man-made structures that could serve as a hiding place for a potential murderer. Two aluminum light poles straddled the alley.

"Someone might have been able to hide behind one of these if they were skinny." She took photos of the poles, then gave them an up-close inspection. They wouldn't have provided complete cover, but on a dark night, someone could have remained partially concealed. If the victim had other things on her mind, she would have even known someone was lying in wait for her.

It wasn't out of the question that the murderer used the element of surprise. If that was what happened, then Rafe and Bethan needed to be moved up on her suspect list. They were angry with Angelica and couldn't, or wouldn't, account for their whereabouts on the night in question.

While she mulled that scenario, Darcy began walking the parking lot's perimeter. One thing she didn't see was a makeshift memorial. There were no flowers, stuffed toys, or photos near the scene of the crime. It appeared that if folks wanted to memorialize Angelica, they chose someplace else to do it.

Or nobody cared enough to create a memorial. Not even Xander.

Was there anything to be made of that? Darcy shook her head. It was clear that Angelica wasn't universally loved. So what? With the exception of Dolly Parton, who was a true gift to all of humanity, pretty much everyone in the world had their detractors.

Deservedly so, for a fair number of them.

Darcy's musings came to an abrupt halt. Her gaze landed on something in the remaining snow a few feet from where Angelica's body had been found. It was a small black object, circular in shape. She took a photo, then got down on one knee for a closer look.

It was a button, about an inch across, with four holes in the center. Too big for a shirt button, it belonged on another piece of clothing. A piece of outerwear, in fact.

"A coat button. Well, what do you know." With a gloved hand, she picked up the button to get a close-up look. Her heart started beating faster when her thumb ran across a thread that was still attached.

The button could be a critical piece of evidence.

She called Paul Gerard. "I'm in the parking lot behind The Magic Box. I found something you should see."

Instead of asking why she was poking around the crime scene, Paul promised to be there in a few minutes. Apparently, he agreed that the button held some significance.

Darcy hadn't moved from the spot when Paul arrived. She dispensed with exchanging pleasantries. Instead, she held the button out to him.

"I found it right there." She pointed to a snow mound that was almost melted away. "I wonder if Angelica tried to fight off her attacker, and it came off the murderer's coat in the struggle."

Paul raised an eyebrow. After a few seconds, he removed a paper evidence bag from his coat, which had a zipper.

"It's possible." He kept his gaze locked on Darcy as she dropped her find into the bag. "I appreciate you calling me about this. I have to ask, though. Why are you here?"

"What's that supposed to mean? I found a piece of evidence in your murder case. And you ask why I'm here? Isn't it kind of obvious?"

A ghost of a smile crossed his face. Then it was gone. If he was enjoying his little game, the feeling wasn't mutual.

"You know how it goes, Darcy. It's a mistake to make assumptions. So, why don't you tell me what brought you here? Then we can move along to more interesting topics."

"You can be really infuriating, you know that? Like having your opening act not show up for a show kind of infuriating."

"So, I've been told. Especially when I'm putting people in a holding cell after charging them with breaking and entering." He tapped his toe on the asphalt surface. "Though they usually use more colorful language than you."

She wanted to argue the point but needed to get back to the store. "Fine. I got some news when I was at work. I took a walk to decompress and ended up here. It wasn't intentional. I figured while I was here, I might as well take advantage of the snow melting and have a look around."

"Are you okay?"

"Yeah, I'm fine." Darcy waved the question away. "It was a call from Pixie Dust's manager. It was totally out of the blue, so…"

"I get it. And I'm glad things are okay." He gave the evidence bag a shake. "As for this, it might be a critical piece of evidence. The coroner found a piece of thread caught in one of Angelica's fingernails. The color appears to be the same, but we need to do some testing to see if they're a match. But you didn't hear that from me."

"Because police protocol says no sharing of information with the public." Darcy shoved her hands into her pockets. Despite the sun, the temperature was still hovering around forty. Hardly weather to be hanging around outside for too long.

"Exactly." Taking a cue from Darcy, he zipped up his coat.

"Well, I better get back to the store before Hank starts worrying that I slipped on some ice and bonked my head." She nodded at the evidence bag. "Looks like you have some work to do, too."

"That is a fact." He chuckled at his own joke. "You're not going to ask me if we have an idea who this button belongs to?"

"Nah. I figure you can't share it with me, so I'll figure it out on my own." She tipped an imaginary hat to him. "See you around. Got a few leads to track down."

Chapter Twelve

That evening, Darcy was going through the inventory of the record collection Charlotte had checked out. It was an impressive lot, covering multiple genres and artists from four decades, but the seller wanted more than Char was comfortable agreeing to on the spot. Since the store belonged to Darcy, the decision to either buy, pass, or make a counteroffer was hers.

"The records are all in good to excellent condition, right?" Darcy tapped her finger on the report.

"Yeah. According to the owner, her son left the collection when he moved out. It's been sitting in a closet for twenty years."

"Three thousand dollars is a lot of cash."

"Yes, but for that we get 450 albums and a receiver and turntable that are both in working order. I got her down from thirty-give hundred by offering her cash. We could use the inventory for Record Store Day."

"All righty, then. Make it so." Darcy handed the tablet back to Char. The woman had done a thorough job logging the records and providing sound reasoning for making the purchase. It was great to see. "I'll leave it to you to work out the details. Now, I need to check on the kids."

Peter and Izzy were placing their instruments in a corner of the store's stage. "You two ready for tonight?"

"Oh, yesi." Peter grinned and rubbed his hands together. "It'll be good to perform our audition pieces in front of a crowd."

Izzy bounced up and down on her toes. "Yeah. Will totally help with the nerves when it's time to perform them for our admissions people. We've got a new piece to play tonight, too. It's called 'Mayhem.'"

"You two are amazing. Can't wait."

They discussed the line-up for the evening's open mic performances. The program continued to gain in popularity, with ten musicians scheduled to perform. Before that, though, Darcy needed a different kind of information from her high schoolers. She put her arms around them to prevent them from being overheard by the handful of shoppers in the store.

"Any luck on the button quest?" She had asked the young ones to identify what kinds of coats her suspects wore.

"I texted Rafe, like you asked," Izzy said. "He said he has a red, green, and black zip-up parka he was wearing that night. It doesn't have any buttons. He has a few Instagram posts where he's wearing a coat that matches the description."

"And I called the Hobbit. He said he was wearing a hoodie when he found Angelica. Pictures from the awards ceremony show him wearing a gray hoodie with the store's logo on it." Peter beamed, clearly proud of his thorough report.

"Excellent." Darcy had initially worried about asking the young ones to contact Rafe and O'Sullivan on her behalf. They'd been eager to contribute more to the investigation, though. To their credit, they had obtained the information she needed from the safe environs of Marysburg Music.

"But, wait. There's more." Peter raised his eyebrows. "The boyfriend, Xander. In some posts, he's wearing a navy peacoat. He's not in any of the pics from the tournament, though."

"We hit a roadblock with McDougal." Izzy tugged at the sleeve of her shirt. "She doesn't have much of an online presence. Almost all of it is reposting anti-bullying messages."

"With everything she's been through at Angelica's hands, that's not surprising. You both did great work. Now, have fun tonight."

For the first time since open mic night had started, a spoken word artist took the stage. She shared a powerful story, and her rhythmic presentation had folks in the room comparing her favorably to Amanda Gorman. The crowd was as outstanding as the performers. The aisles were full, but the huge throng was respectful of each performer, remaining quiet during performances, then giving them warm rounds of applause when they finished.

On top of opening their hearts to the performers, the crowd opened their wallets to Marysburg Music. Even though the store normally closed at eight, Darcy was ringing sales until almost nine. It was a night of unabashed creativity and generosity. The kind of community Eddie and Darcy had dreamed about when they opened the store.

It also meant Ringo was displeased with Darcy's late arrival home. It took two offers of kitty treats, in addition to his regular dinner, before he would even look at her. By the time she hit the sack, though, he was curled up in his usual spot at the foot of the bed.

He was no dummy. It was going to be a cold night, after all, and Darcy was a reliable source of warmth.

The next day, she was awakened by the feline pawing at her face. "Come on, dude. I apologized last night."

Undeterred, the cat wouldn't stop bugging his human until she got him breakfast. To make sure he was satisfied, she added some shredded chicken to his dry food.

Once Ringo was taken care of, Darcy's mind shifted to the mysterious button. While her herbal tea steeped, she reviewed the information obtained the previous day.

If the button really did come from the murderer's coat, then Rafe seemed to be in the clear. That was good. Darcy didn't want to think of the man as a capital felon. The jury was still out on Sean O'Sullivan, though. Just because he told Peter he was wearing a hoodie didn't make it true. As for Bethan? Darcy would have to figure out what kind of coat the woman wore.

It was also time to finally pay Xander a visit, too. She didn't want to jump to conclusions. If he was the only suspect to own a winter coat with buttons, though, that would vault him to the top of the list.

When it was time for lunch, Darcy ordered carryout from Selena's for Hank and Char.

"To what do we owe this act of kindness?" Hank rubbed his belly and licked his lips.

"The weather's nice again. It gives me an excuse to go for another walk." She rocked back and forth on her heels. "And y'all deserve it. Putting up with me the way you do. Just a little way to say thanks."

"You're welcome." Charlotte wiped her hands on a rag. She'd been in the office, making room for the collection she'd hauled into the store earlier in the day. "Don't let us delay you. I'm famished."

After a quick salute, Darcy made her exit. Charlotte was a kind soul, but everyone in the store knew all too well how cranky she could be when she got hangry. That wasn't going to happen this day. Not after all of her hard work to obtain the new collection.

On her way to pick up the order, Darcy made a detour.

"What up, Gaughan?" The Hobbit was sitting on his perch behind the cash register when she entered. "Any news for me?"

"The search continues. I'm making progress, though." She leaned against the counter. "Be honest. Were you being straight with Peter when he called yesterday?"

He put his hands out to the side. "Totally. I mean, look at me. I've got plenty of insulation. Besides, you saw the coat I wear when it's super nasty outside when I picked up the gift cards. No buttons."

Darcy stared at him, but he didn't look away. That was good enough for her. For now.

"I believe you. Any chance you remember what Angelica's boyfriend was wearing when he was here?"

"Not really. What's this about?"

"I found a button in the parking lot yesterday. It wasn't far from where you discovered Angelica. The police have it now."

O'Sullivan leaned back and smiled. "I see where you're going. Whoever murdered her lost a button in the process."

"Yep. Now, I'm eliminating people who don't have a coat with buttons. It's not a smoking gun, but it helps."

Her phone buzzed, notifying her the lunch order was ready. "Gotta rock n roll. One more question. Was Angelica taller than you?"

"Yeah. She was about your height. Why?"

"I couldn't remember. Later." An idea was coming together in her head. Was there a way to prove whether the murderer was taller or shorter than Angelica based on neck bruising? If so, that would help eliminate suspects.

On her way to Selena's, Darcy passed by, among other businesses, Jasmine Longoria's gallery. While she thought the art dealer was a snob, she loved the pieces the gallery carried. In recent months, she'd made it a habit to slow down while passing the gallery so she could enjoy the art.

While a new watercolor painting of the St. Mary's River caught her attention, what made her come to a stop was an animated discussion going on inside the gallery. Jasmine was poking Todd Meadows in the chest with her index finger. Between that and voices that were loud enough for Darcy to hear, it wasn't a pleasant conversation.

"Well, well. Sounds like trouble in paradise. I can spare one minute."

She headed straight for the watercolor upon entering the business. While she kept her gaze on the artwork, her attention was really on the arguing couple.

"...I don't care what your excuses are. I had to wait forty-five minutes until you got there. It was unforgivable. I've had enough—" Jasmine stopped.

"Well, I'm sorry if I can't be at your beck and call twenty-four hours a day, your Majesty. If you'll excuse me, I have an appointment." Todd spat out the words barely above a whisper, like the hiss of a snake.

Trouble in paradise, indeed. Darcy coughed to cover her smile as the clicks of Jasmine's stilettos grew louder with the woman's approach.

"Welcome back to the gallery, Darcy." Jasmine gave her a smile that made Darcy think of the barracuda from the animated film *Finding Nemo*. "It's always a pleasure to have you visit."

The statement couldn't have been further from the truth. Jasmine despised Darcy. While it was in large part due to Darcy suspecting her in a previous murder investigation, there was a deeper reason for her antipathy toward Marysburg Music's owner.

Darcy was privy to some of Jasmine's most closely guarded secrets.

Even worse, though, was the fact that Darcy had the money to purchase any item in the gallery without a second thought. The art dealer had taken great pleasure in looking down her surgically-perfect nose at the rough-and-tumble former punk rocker. That was until Darcy dropped her Black Card in front of Jasmine to purchase an oil painting.

Jasmine adored money more than she loathed Darcy, though. Thus, the warm welcome.

"I like this watercolor. I'll take it." She handed over the credit card. "I'm in the missile of some errands, though. Could you arrange to have it delivered to the record store?"

"Of course." The woman's waist-length ebony hair swished from side to side as she made a ballerina-like spin before gliding to the sales kiosk.

Darcy waited until she was in the middle of recording the sale before she spoke. Women needed to be there for each other, even if they didn't care for each other. Especially if a man was being a jerk. "I'm sorry if I interrupted your conversation with Todd. Are you two all right?"

"Couldn't be better." Jasmine forced an unconvincing smile. "All couples have disagreements from time to time. Obviously, not everyone saw eye to eye one hundred percent in your band. Am I right?"

The verbal punch was a low blow. Though not totally surprising since Darcy, in general, and Marysburg Music had been a thorn in Jasmine's side for a half-decade now. So much for sisterly support.

"Touché."

She completed the transaction and made a graceful exit. Darcy was happy and healthy. She wasn't going to let another woman's anger at her bring her down. She had better things to do with her time.

Like solve Angelica Stipe's murder.

At Selena's, Thea had Darcy's order waiting for her. "What up, girl? How about this weather?"

"Not quite ready to break out the skateboard yet, but I hope this means the worst of Winter's over."

"Cheers to that." Thea lifted her glass of ice water to Darcy. "How goes the sleuthing?"

"Making progress. Just had a weird experience at Jasmine's, though." She recounted the brief but eyebrow-raising moment at the gallery.

"Probably just a lover's quarrel. Two total type-A personalities butting heads, it's bound to happen."

"Good point. For a second, I couldn't help wondering if Todd's up to something besides his usual habit of checking out any woman under the age of twenty-five. Must be the investigation making me paranoid."

"You're not paranoid, honey. I see those two in here a lot and I wonder if they'll ever be happy. It seems like they're always so busy plotting their next big score. I wonder if they ever take the time to appreciate what they have. Know what I mean?"

"That I do, my friend. I'd love to hang, but I have food to deliver. See you soon."

As she exited, an image popped into Darcy's head. Todd and Jasmine had been seated together at Selena's the night of the murder. If her memory was accurate, they hadn't been happy. Todd was all smiles and handshakes during the awards ceremony, though.

And then there was the tidbit from the Chamber of Commerce lunch that Angelica had been working for Todd. Had the man's involvement with the college student become a source of friction between him and Jasmine?

It was a crazy scenario. Todd was old enough to be Angelica's father. The man had left his second wife, who was already fifteen years his junior, for Jasmine. And he'd claimed the art dealer was his soul mate.

Darcy pocketed the idea. Lovers Triangles were too much of a cliché for her to take the scenario seriously. She had other, more promising, leads to follow.

Like tracking down Xander. She had serious questions for that young man.

Chapter Thirteen

Darcy was setting out new BLACKPINK and Pitbull albums when her phone buzzed. It was a call from Rafe. He never called; he only texted. This couldn't be good.

"Darcy, the cops are here. They want to take me in for questioning. What do I do?"

She closed her eyes. Why was the man calling her when he had a lawyer?

"Why are they there, Rafe?"

"That Gerard dude said, since I don't have an alibi, I must be hiding something. What do I do?"

"Tell them the truth. Where were you?"

The line went silent for way too long. Then he let out a long sigh. "I told you before. I was out walking. Nothing more, nothing less."

"Okay, man. If that's the truth, stick to your guns. And call your lawyer." She ended the call.

Rafe Majors was an adult. He had to learn to stand on his own two feet. That included being honest and cooperating with the police. Paul was a good man, a trustworthy one. If Rafe was guilty of murder, so be it. On the other hand, if he wasn't, Paul wouldn't sell him down the river just to close the case.

From Darcy's perspective, the situation was still too cloudy for any judgments to be made. Too many moving parts. Which meant Darcy would maintain course. With a slight change of direction.

Fridays were busy days at the record store. There was always work to be done to make sure the sales floor was fully stocked, and the fixtures were dust-free. The customers and community of Marysburg Music had to come first.

Which meant Darcy wasn't able to turn her attention back to the case until her lunch break. As she munched on a chicken Cesar wrap, she stared at the suspect board with a new approach.

Instead of focusing on who had an axe to grind with Angelica, she decided to step back and take a metaphorical look around the crime scene. Give thought to what evidence had been recovered and what seemed to be missing.

Darcy didn't want to put blinders on herself. She recalled reading a mystery featuring one of her favorite amateur sleuths, a spunky woman named Allie Cobb, who often talked about needing to follow the evidence. Narrative couldn't take priority over facts. The facts and the evidence had to inform the story.

With a new thought process in place, she turned her attention to the right-hand side of the whiteboard. Earlier in the investigation, she'd made a list of Angelica's possessions that had been found at the scene. There were the remains of the obliterated trophy. The purse, keys, and wallet were accounted for. The swag she'd won had been found in the back seat of her car. What did those various puzzle pieces reveal?

"A trophy doesn't break into a thousand pieces if all you do is drop it."

Darcy glanced at an Independent Music Award sitting atop a set of shelves. A corner of the base was chipped away from the time she'd lost her grip while polishing it. That had been an accident. Whoever murdered Angelica had destroyed her trophy in an act of all-out rage.

Most people didn't get furious with someone they didn't know. That likely meant the murderer knew Angelica well enough to be angry with her. Over what, exactly, was another question begging for an answer.

"Okay. What wasn't found at the scene?"

The list was shorter. The five hundred in cash was missing. Her phone was missing, too. So, what did those two things mean?

The disappearance of the cash could be explained in any number of ways. The murderer may have been after the money and killed Angelica in the struggle. Or the murderer might have simply decided to take the money after strangling her. After all, what was a little theft compared to taking someone's life?

Darcy chuckled at the grim thought. Sometimes gallows humor was a good coping mechanism for her, though.

There was a more pertinent question to be answered, though. Was the money the motivation behind the attack? If so, how did the killer know about it? These days, most people carry little, if any, cash on them. To take Angelica's cash winnings while leaving her purse and any cash or credit cards it contained indicated the mugger wanted that money. That would mean the murderer was someone who knew what she'd been awarded as tournament grand champion.

The phone, though. That was a different tune altogether. The cash could be long gone by now. A cell phone might take longer to get rid of. There was little doubt Paul and his team were searching for it. If it was a high-end model, the murderer might have turned it off and removed the SIM card to sell it. From what Darcy had learned about Angelica, the young woman wasn't the type to use a budget model.

If the case was a matter of robbery gone wrong, why was her wallet left behind? Any credit cards it might have contained could have been used the night of the murder, then tossed in the trash.

Would a thief take the energy and time to destroy the award, though? It seemed unlikely.

If it wasn't a robbery gone wrong, what was it? A lover's quarrel that got out of hand? Once again, that would elevate Xander to the main suspect. But why did he take the money and the phone?

Darcy drummed her fingers on her thigh as she stared at the board, letting the rhythm help her focus. After a few moments, the answer popped into her head, like the perfect lyric to a song.

What if there was information on Angelica's phone the murderer wanted? Or, perhaps, information the murderer wanted to make sure nobody else obtained. The police would be able to get text messages and call logs, though. There might have been something else on the phone.

Something incriminating. Like pictures.

Darcy wasn't oblivious to the fact that some people liked to send racy photos to their partners. She'd always thought it was a bad idea, especially as news-grabbing revenge porn cases popped up in the media. If there were pictures or other incriminating bits of data on the phone, they didn't have to be sexually explicit, though.

The information could simply be embarrassing to someone. Or it could be some type of intelligence Angelica had obtained that someone wanted back.

With a black marker, Darcy drew a line connecting the phone to the trophy. What if the murderer found out Angelica had something incriminating on her phone and was angry about it? The murderer might have confronted Angelica. They argued. The trophy got smashed as the conflict elevated. Then, the assailant strangled her. When the murderer realized what they'd done, they made off with the phone and took the cash.

It seemed like a plausible scenario.

The next question stepped to the metaphorical microphone. Who would be so desperate to get information from Angelica's phone that they were willing to kill for it?

"Can't put it off any longer, girl. Time to talk to Xander."

She had to wait until after work, but Darcy was able to track down the young man at a hole-in-the-wall pub close to the Ball State campus. He was alone, seated at a table in a shadowy corner, nursing a dark beer from a pint glass.

"Xander Fleming-Winchester?" Darcy extended her hand to shake as she introduced herself. "I was hoping to have a chat. Do you mind?"

She eased into the seat across from him without waiting for a response.

"I've heard of you." He kept his gaze on his drink. "I'd like to be alone, thank you very much."

Darcy put her elbows on the table's wooden surface and propped her chin in her hands. "Yeah, I get that. Your girlfriend's been murdered. Your whole life's been turned upside down. On top of that, the cops think you might have done it. Tough times."

"I don't know what you're talking about." He took a long pull of his beer, draining a third of the glass.

"Come on, dude. You say you've heard of me. If that's true, you know why I'm here. Talk to me. I'm two for two when it comes to catching killers. With your help, I can make it three for three."

He finally looked her in the eye. "Why should I believe you? You're nothing but a has-been rocker running a two-bit shop catering to sad souls clinging to some sense of lost nostalgia."

Darcy let out a laugh, loud and long enough that a server approached. "Is everything okay here?"

"We're fine. How about another round for my friend here, and I'll have an ice water."

"I insult you, and then you buy me a drink?" A smile curled up at one end of Xander's mouth. "You must be desperate. Or you want to get me in the sack later."

She sat back and smiled as she shook her head. Over the years, Darcy had seen too many petulant, self-absorbed people who weren't anywhere near as smart as they thought they were to count. Most of those encounters were during her Pixie Dust days. Even during the hazy days of her addiction, she could spot Xander's personality type.

And knew how to deal with it.

"For the record, neither. I thought you'd want to help bring Angelica's murderer to justice." She waited a beat while the server dropped off their drinks, then got to her feet. "But, whatever. No skin off my nose. I've got resources the cops don't have. I'll figure it out. With or without your help."

She'd taken two steps when Xander asked her to wait.

"How did you find me?"

Darcy returned to her seat. She kept her expression neutral but was grinning on the inside. She called him on his tough guy bluff with indifference, and now he'd caved. Now, she was going to get to see if he was innocent or not.

"Seriously, dude? Your Insta feed's a virtual road map. If you don't want people to know where you are, don't post pics of the beers you're drinking to drown your sorrows. Oh, and turn the location feature off, too."

"Oh, right." The dim light couldn't hide the fact that his cheeks got red. At least he had enough self-awareness to be embarrassed. Darcy wasn't going to tell him that Izzy had done the locating for her. The two women considered that a trade secret.

"Ang's funeral was today. Did you know that?" He took a big swig from his beer. "They called it a private service. I wasn't invited even though we were together for two years."

Darcy sat back. She'd been so focused on other things that she'd never even thought about a funeral for the young woman. It was a timely reminder that a real person had died. Angelica Stipe had been a member of a family. People were grieving her loss. The man across from her was among them.

"I didn't know that. I'm sorry. You must be hurting right now."

He ran a finger around the rim of his mug once, then a second time. When he looked from the drink to Darcy, his eyes were watery.

"You're the first person who's said that to me. 'I'm sorry.' My parents haven't even said it. They didn't like Ang, so there you go, I guess." He scratched his chin. "What do you want to know?"

"Angelica's phone's missing. Did you know that?" When he nodded, she took a drink of water.

"Yeah, the cops told me that when they talked to me."

"I take it to mean you don't know what happened to it." When he shook his head, Darcy made a mental note that he was much less talkative and much less arrogant when he was under the gun. That was good to know.

"I understand you two were together for a while. Do you have a key to her place?"

"Yeah, why?"

"I'm kind of surprised the cops didn't make you give it to them."

He finished his beer and immediately took a drink from the one Darcy ordered for him. "That's because I told them I don't have one."

She raised an eyebrow. The man across from her was either playing a game of 3-D chess with the authorities or was stupid beyond belief. Her money was on the latter, but that wasn't the key issue. At least, not for her.

"Gutsy move, lying to the Man. They could charge you with interfering with an investigation."

"Yeah, well, I did it for Ang. She didn't want her parents to know I had a key, so we kept it on the lowdown."

"When did you use it?"

"Between classes and the internship, she was always on the go. A couple of times a week, I'd stop by and make her dinner. While I was there, I'd water the plants and pick up around the place. You know, so she didn't have to."

"A real one-person domestic service team." Darcy didn't buy his story for a second. The real story was probably closer to something along the lines of him using the key to come by late at night for some fun and lock up after leaving in the morning if she was already gone.

Whatever the reason, he had access to her place. That was what mattered.

He shrugged, completely missing Darcy's note of sarcasm. "I did what I could. People liked to say Ang was hard to get along with, that she was mean. They didn't know her."

"And you did, I take it?"

"You bet I did. That's what happens when you're together as long as we were. Because of that, I know her mom and dad put a ton of pressure on her. And not to just do well. More like, have a four-point-oh on her GPA. Get the best internship out there. Leave school with a job paying her six figures. You know that saying, 'Failure is not an option?' Well, for Ang, even being second best wasn't an option."

It was an impressive speech. Almost as if he'd rehearsed it, should the need ever arise. It painted a lovely picture of the good-hearted, supportive boyfriend. Unsure if he was being honest, Darcy didn't press the issue. It would be easy enough to find out if he was lying.

He'd made a mistake, though.

"Sounds rough. Situations like that can lead people to take desperate measures." She tilted her head to one side. "Like cheating on exams, for instance."

His glass stopped halfway between the table and his mouth. It hovered, motionless for a moment or two. Then he took a drink, followed by another one.

"That's a bold accusation. Especially against someone who can't defend herself. Be careful. If Ang's parents find out you're saying things like that, they'll slap you with a lawsuit."

Darcy smiled as she put her hands out to the side. Xander had walked right into her trap. He'd confirmed the rumor Izzy reported was, in fact, going around. Rumors were cheap, though, like second-hand cassette tapes. Some were reliable; some weren't. Relying on them usually didn't end well, though.

"I don't believe I mentioned her or anyone else in association with any cheating." With him no doubt about to get defensive since she'd caught him out, she pounced. "Anyway, you want to help her? Play your part in making sure justice is served. Let's go take a look around her apartment."

Even in the semi-darkness, it was impossible to miss the color draining from his face. He gulped down the rest of his beer, rattling the table as he brought the glass down with too much force.

"We can't go there. It's a crime scene. Isn't it? What if the cops are there?"

"No, it's not a crime scene. The parking lot where she was strangled to death is a crime scene." She rose, never breaking eye contact with him. "Let's go. For Angelica. It's time to avenge her."

His shoulders slumped, and he let out a loud groan as he stood. Darcy made a show of looking at her phone while he shrugged into a jacket that had been hanging over his chair. The garment had a clean sheen to it that brought a question to her lips.

"Nice coat. Is it new?"

"No. I've had it for a while. Ang gave it to me."

"Looks nice." She ran her hand down one of the sleeves. "I like it."

She especially liked the fact that it was different from the Navy peacoat he'd been wearing when he'd posted on social media recently. Which begged the question.

Why wasn't he wearing that coat? Was it because it was missing a button?

Chapter Fourteen

"Do you really think you'll find something the cops missed?" Xander smirked as he inserted his key into the lock to Angelica's apartment.

"You never know." She gestured to him to open the door. On the drive from the pub, Darcy tried to engage him in conversation with no luck. He'd responded to question after question about the case with the same shrug or a mumbled, "Dunno."

For someone who claimed to be innocent, he was proving to be surprisingly uncooperative. Darcy had hoped that some of her questions would give her a sense of who Xander thought the murderer was. She'd given him a perfect opportunity to lay blame at the feet of someone else.

He refused to take the bait, though. Cagey, this one was proving to be. Not unlike Pixie Dust's first international tour manager, a British woman named Glynnis. Darcy never got a read on her. To be fair, Darcy had spent more time those days with a bottle than getting to know Glyn.

She wasn't going to make the same mistake twice.

The door opened into an airy living room, featuring a gray loveseat and two matching recliners. To the right, a half-wall provided separation from the kitchen. A quick look around confirmed a short hallway led to two bedrooms, a bathroom, and a utility room. A sliding door opened onto a concrete patio.

"Sweet digs." Darcy ran her finger along the frame of a sixty-inch flat screen mounted on the wall. "A lot more posh than my place."

Xander dropped into one of the chairs. "Her parents wanted nothing but the best for Ang."

"Mind if I look around?"

"That's why we're here, right?" He waved his hand as if he was flicking away a fly.

Darcy turned on her heel and wandered through the kitchen, then down the hallway. Her gaze passed over everything without focusing on any particular item. When she saw what she was looking for, she'd know it.

Paul Gerard and his team were competent and thorough. Compared to Darcy, though, they were amateurs when it came to hide and seek. Her years of alcohol abuse turned her into a master at keeping things from prying eyes.

Evidently, the majority of folks in Marysburg thought Angelica was a hardworking young lady. Not the nicest, by any means, but a decent young woman, in general. Nobody would have any reason to suspect she was literally hiding something.

The most likely places for Angelica to hide something important would be either the bedroom or bathroom. Since Darcy arrived at the bathroom first, she checked it out first.

An initial scan revealed nothing beyond a typical utilitarian bathroom. The diamond pattern shower curtain matched the toothbrush holder and tissue box cover. The teal and gold colors coordinated with the towels and area rugs.

"Nice setup, Angelica. I sure never had anything this nice when I was your age. Nice and neat, too."

Darcy removed the liner from the trash can. There was nothing underneath. She let out a chuckle as she was flooded with memories of her senior year of college. She lived with three roommates in a two-story clapboard structure built before World War II. Her dad had dubbed it the "Scary House" since it looked like a strong wind would knock it down.

She loved it, though. There might not have been modern conveniences like a dishwasher or a fridge with an ice maker, but there was rehearsal space for Pixie Dust and plenty of room in the fridge for cold beverages.

Back in the present, Darcy put the liner back. She removed the lid from the toilet tank. Nothing out of the ordinary was to be seen. To be sure, she gave it a flush. As the water drained, she was able to confirm no items wrapped in plastic were fastened to one of the tank's sides. That was a trick she'd learned that allowed her to grab a swig of booze while on tour without Glynnis finding out.

For a while, at least.

The last place she checked was the air vent. After Glyn found a bottle stashed in a tank during an overnight stay in Hamburg, Darcy resorted to even more desperate measures. That included hiding bottles in the ductwork. All it took was a screwdriver and an attention to detail sharp enough to make sure the vent was replaced in the same position it had been in prior to removal.

The heads of the two vent screws in the bathroom were in pristine condition. Other than being probably dusted from time to time, this particular vent probably hadn't been touched since the last time the room was painted.

To make sure, she popped the cover off the light fixture in the ceiling. Other than an LED bulb, there was nothing to be found.

"The bedroom it is, then."

She checked on Xander. He was staring at his phone. If the young man had intended to do something nefarious while they were here, he'd either done it already or was waiting to make his move.

Or, possibly, he wasn't the murderer and was only killing time while Darcy looked around.

"Everything okay out here?" His only response was a half-hearted wave. "I'm finished in the bathroom. Gonna check out her bedroom now."

When he didn't respond, she headed back down the hallway. Her report was a subtle attempt to prompt him into action. If he was going to do anything, he'd have to do it now. It was a long shot, but one couldn't be too careful when a murderer was on the loose.

Angelica's bedroom was just like the rest of the apartment. Decorated in tasteful shades of seafoam green and beige. The only thing that seemed out of place was a half-full laundry basket in one corner by the closet. Romance author Nan Reinhardt's latest novel lay on the nightstand next to a round device about the size of a bagel. It was one of those devices that could do everything from play music to tell Angelica the weather to serve as an alarm clock.

A peek in the closet didn't reveal any home safes or hidden panels. She'd once resorted to hiding airplane bottles of whiskey behind can light fixtures. The overhead lighting for this room came from an LED fixture integrated into the ceiling fan.

"Gotta hand it to you, Angelica. You were doing a nice job in the energy-efficiency department."

She opened the dresser drawers but didn't go through the contents. Instead, she ran her hands along the undersides of each one. Her fingers came across a piece of masking tape underneath the bottom drawer. It wasn't attached to anything.

Had it been used to fasten something to the wooden surface sometime in the past, though? Something important? There was no way to know for certain.

One thing was certain, though. The air duct next to the dresser was askew. It was barely discernable. A thin stripe of off-white paint had been exposed when the vent cover was moved.

"Find anything yet?" Xander appeared in the doorway.

"Nope." Darcy gave the room another scan. "Thanks for letting me do this. It was worth a shot."

He looked at his phone when a notification went off. Then, he started tapping away at the keyboard and wandered back down the hall.

Darcy wasn't going to let a golden opportunity go to waste. She needed to finish soon, though, so she didn't have to risk Xander's reappearance due to boredom or impatience.

She'd have to come back. By herself so there would be no prying eyes. And with a screwdriver in her pocket. Angelica had hidden something in the vent.

Darcy was going to find out what it was. And follow the clue straight to Angelica's murderer. That was for later, though.

There were two windows in the room. She released the locking mechanism on both. As she made her way to the living room, a plan was forming in her head.

"Welp, I didn't find anything." She massaged the back of her neck. "Thanks for your help. Let me get you back to the pub."

With a shrug, he followed Darcy out of the apartment. He remained silent until they were in the jeep.

"What's up with the picture?" He pointed to the Gina Schock photo.

"She's my hero. Wouldn't have become a drummer if not for her." Darcy tapped it with her index finger. "I keep it here for good luck. And for someone to talk to when I need to think out loud."

"Does she ever answer?" Xander cracked a half smile. His green eyes sparkled in the illumination when they passed under a streetlight. His teeth were as white as snow and straight as train tracks.

When he wasn't pulling the brooding bad-boy act, he was a handsome young man. It wasn't hard to figure out why Angelica had been attracted to him.

What was harder to figure out was whether that attraction proved to be fatal. After all, what motive did he have? Well, no time better than the present to find out.

"I heard you were at the tournament but left before the awards ceremony."

He stared out the passenger window. "That's what everyone says. Like I told the cops, I don't remember."

"I get it. Back before I got sober, there were a lot of times I'd wake up in the morning with no idea what I did the night before." It was true. And if a little empathy coaxed information out of Xander, it was all good. "Wasn't the best feeling in the world. That was for sure."

"Yeah, well. Thanks, but it wasn't on account of too much to drink. I don't know what happened. That's the God-honest truth."

The pub was only a couple of blocks away. If Darcy was going to get an answer from him, it needed to be now. Given the circumstances, in a few days he might not be willing to talk to her ever again.

Or be able to. A trip to prison might make him tough to track down.

"Okay, how about this? Witnesses have confirmed you left when the games ended. You must have known Angelica was going to win something. What would make you take off instead of sticking around to celebrate with her?"

He rubbed his chin. At least he was giving her the appearance of mulling over the question. Then again, with the pub's sign coming into view, he may have been stalling.

"I know leaving early makes me look like a jerk. Since everyone says I did, I must have had a good reason to. I don't know. Maybe there was someone there I didn't want to see."

That was promising. She took advantage of the time provided by a four-way stop to ask a final question. "If you don't mind me asking, who do you not like enough that you'd rather leave than stick around? Especially at your girlfriend's moment of triumph?"

"That's easy." He put his hand on the door handle as Rusty rolled to a stop in front of the pub. "Todd Meadows. That dude was totally taking advantage of her internship status. If he was there, I would have punched him the first chance I got."

Chapter Fifteen

With the echoes of Xander's bombshell still banging around inside her head, Darcy piloted Rusty toward Marysburg Music. It was only a ten-minute drive, but she needed to think. She slid *The Very Best of Enya* into the CD player. The New Age music calmed her as she drove, the mellow tunes smoothing out her frayed thoughts.

Xander didn't like Todd Meadows. That much was as obvious as Peter's status as the number one fan of reggae music in Marysburg. Did his antipathy for the realtor have any connection to Angelica's murder, though? After all, the line to get into the I Despise Todd Meadows Club, if there really was one, would stretch for blocks.

Darcy slowed as she approached a roundabout. The bends in the road reminded her of the investigation. Just when she thought she was getting somewhere, a curve popped up, making her ease off and rethink the situation.

If the young man was being honest about Angelica's internship situation, why would that be motivation for him to murder her? It made no sense. It was way more logical that, in a testosterone-fueled and misguided attempt to stand up for his girlfriend, he'd try to tangle with Todd.

Unless he tried to talk sense into Angelica. Or, at least, what he thought of as sense.

What if she didn't agree with his assessment of the situation? What if she was finding the internship more valuable than her relationship with Xander? What if that led to an argument?

An argument that got out of control and ended in murder?

As Darcy passed a sign welcoming her to Marysburg's Business District, she gave the photo of Gina a soft fist bump.

"How about this? Xander gave her an ultimatum to quit the internship. She said no. Then he upped the ante by saying she needed to choose. The job or him. When she chose the job, he smashed the trophy and stomped on it. Then he strangled her. But it was an accident. In his remorse, his brain blocked out all memories from the night. It was possible."

Gina didn't respond. Neither did Enya, who was singing ethereal tunes about trains and winter rains. That was okay. Probably for the best, actually. The two artists had somehow combined forces to help Darcy come up with motive, means, and opportunity for Xander to murder Angelica.

All Darcy needed was evidence connecting him to the scene of the crime. Like the navy peacoat he'd stopped wearing. As she rolled to a stop in her parking spot behind the record store, she was bursting at the seams with excitement. Finally, she had something tangible. Something she could hash out with her team.

Any attempt to do just that had to be put on hold when Darcy entered the store. Rafe was waiting for her. It was time for their Friday evening check-in.

At first, the sight of Eddie's uncooperative stepson deflated her. Then she noticed he was wearing a new pair of hi-top athletic shoes. The iridescent black patent leather made them impossible to miss.

She might be hot on Xander's trail, but all of a sudden, Rafe had some serious explaining to do.

Lucky for Darcy, she used an agenda for these meetings. The goal was to make sure Rafe was managing his money properly so he could eventually do it on his own. A notorious spendthrift, the man never needed to worry about mundane things like keeping the lights on while Eddie was alive.

As much as Darcy adored her mentor, she couldn't deny her frustration at her dearly departed friend's inability to get Rafe to stand on his own two feet. Whatever reasons Eddie may have had didn't matter now, though. The task had fallen to Darcy. It was one she was going to see through.

It gave her a perfect opportunity to ask about the shoes when they got to the topic of Rafe's expenses.

"The utilities, Wi-Fi, all that stuff. You've got them all on autopay, right?" Darcy had been after him to put his monthly bills on an automatic payment system for months. That way, there was a smaller chance of something getting turned off.

"Yeah, yeah." He leaned his head back and stared at the ceiling. "Going without an Internet connection for a week was torture. Won't let that happen again."

She covered her mouth with her hand to hide a smile as visions of the man unable to participate in his beloved online gaming flashed before her eyes. Sometimes, the consequences of one's actions were enough punishment.

"I know I keep harping about this, but you need to keep an eye on your discretionary spending. I totally get treating yourself from time to time and having fun with your buddies—"

"But. What is it this time?"

"Those are some nice kicks you're wearing. Are they new?"

"Yeah." He propped his feet on the corner of her desk. "What do you think? Sick, right? Even got them on sale."

"Nice." The last name of the footwear's Italian designer was spelled out in a garish font on the red soles. She resisted the urge to push Rafe's feet to the floor as dollar signs that went into four figures started blinking in her head. She didn't want him on the defensive too quickly, though. "How much? Be honest. I recognize the designer. His shoes don't go on sale."

"Okay, fine. They were a grand. My accountant said I'll be getting a refund on my taxes this year, so I treated myself."

Darcy rose to her feet. "Seriously, dude? A thousand dollars? Did you learn nothing from your little trip to the police station this morning? You've got a receipt for those, right? Because if Paul Gerard finds out about them, he's gonna want to know how and when you paid for them. Am I making myself clear?"

"Loud and clear. That trip to the station was b.s. My lawyer had me out of there just like that. "Rafe stood and snapped his fingers. "They've got nothing on me and never will. We're done here."

He opened the office door, then turned to her.

"You know, one night, after one too many old fashioneds, the old man let slip that you've got some big stash of cash in the bank. Why not treat yourself from time to time? After all, you can't take it with you. Or did *you* learn nothing from his murder?"

Rafe's words hit her like a slap in the face, followed by a punch to the gut. She dropped back into her chair as the door closed behind him with a bang. It was the lowest of low blows.

And he knew it.

Darcy took the pain and let it course through her, like the water flowing down the St. Mary's River. Rafe was crafty. As much as the words may have rung true, there was still a possibility he'd uttered them in fake outrage.

"Methinks he doth protest too much." Things were beginning to come into focus. But, like the first time she listened to Miles Davis's groundbreaking jazz album *Bitches Brew*, Darcy didn't quite understand the picture.

She grabbed her cell phone. If anyone could help her think things through, it was Jenna.

"You free tonight? I need to pick your brain."

A few hours later, Darcy found Jenna perched on her favorite stool at Selena's bar. "What up, girlfriend? I figured last time you wanted to talk about...you know, the stuff you said you wanted to talk about; we met right here at these stools. Thought they might have good karma."

Darcy waved at Thea, who was pouring two glasses of wine, as she eased onto the stool next to her best friend. At first, she had wanted to talk in private, but Jenna told her she needed an evening away from her family. Hanging out with Ringo at Darcy's house wasn't appealing to her.

When in doubt, Selena's was always the way to go.

"Living the dream." Darcy leaned closer to Jenna. "Things okay on the home front? You sounded awfully eager to get out of the house."

Jenna waved Darcy's concern away. "We're fine. Hubs and the kids are all into watching the NBA All-Star Game Friday Night events. Boring."

"What are we having tonight, ladies?" Thea placed a glass of ice water in front of each of them. "The special's fish tacos."

"Works for me," Darcy said. "And an iced tea. Could use the caffeine boost."

Jenna asked for shrimp fajitas and a mojito. When Thea stepped away to put their orders in, she placed her palms against the bar top, as if to steady herself for the upcoming conversation.

"Let me have it. What's on your mind?"

Darcy took a sip of her water. What, exactly, was on her mind? Further, how could she share her thoughts in a coherent manner when they had her head spinning?

"This case is driving me crazy. Every time I think the clues are coming together, something pops up and sends me in another direction." As she filled Jenna in on recent developments, the words rushed out, almost as if she was trying to keep up with the pace of R.E.M.'s "It's The End of the World as We Know It (And I Feel Fine)."

Jenna chewed on a tortilla chip for a moment when Darcy had finished. Then, she took a drink of her mojito.

"Let me recap to make sure I've got things right. You've got four suspects. One, Bethan McDougal because Angelica bullied her, and when you asked her where she was last Saturday night, she told you to get lost. Two, the Hobbit because he doesn't have anyone to verify his alibi, and Angelica spent the whole tournament dissing the store and the event. Three, Rafe because he doesn't have an alibi, doesn't want to cooperate with the cops, and now shows up with some uber-expensive shoes. Four, the Xander kid because he's wearing a new coat with a zipper instead of one that buttons up and claims he can't remember that night."

"Incoming hot plates, friends." Thea served them with her trademark wide grin, topped off their waters, and left them to their conversation. The bar was hopping, and Thea was dashing from customer to customer right along with it.

While they ate, Jenna dissected each of the suspects, along with Darcy's reasoning for including them on her suspect board. Then, they discussed the apartment trip while Thea removed their plates. After dinner, Jenna steepled her fingers in front of her.

Darcy kept quiet. She'd seen the gesture when Jenna's kids were fighting about something and wanted their mom to be referee. It wasn't a good idea to interrupt the woman at moments like this.

"The only thing I can think Angelica would have hidden is something that ties her to the cheating rumors. Assuming they're true, that is. And you haven't told Paul about the vent thing?"

"No." Darcy's cheeks got warm. "After dropping Xander off, I was thinking about the case. Then, I had to meet with Rafe. Then, after I called you, I needed to close the store. It kept slipping my mind."

"Which would mean there's no reason the cops would be there tonight. Hmm." Jenna's eyes began to sparkle in the way they always did when she came up with a far-out idea.

"What are you thinking?" At times like this, Jenna's ideas usually focused on unusual bakery concoctions or impromptu trips to Indianapolis or Fort Wayne to see a movie or stage play.

"I'm thinking we take a look inside that vent. I mean, you went to the trouble of unlocking the windows, right? And the apartment's on the first floor, right? And there could be a clue there that might crack the case right open, right?"

"Sure." Darcy's spine began to tingle. "But, that's like breaking and entering. What if we get caught? We could go to jail."

Jenna took Darcy's hand in hers. "If we call Paul right now, he'll have to get a search warrant, and who knows how long that'll take. That's time that Xander or someone else could sneak in and get their hands on whatever stashed there. Or, we could go right now and make sure the evidence ends up in the right hands."

Darcy sat for a moment, watching the tiny droplets of water trickle down the sides of her glass. After a while, she nodded. Jenna was right. Marysburg was a small town. Word about a warrant would get out. And tip off the murderer that something worth looking for was in the apartment. The chances of that happening were low, but not zero. The two of them could prevent the murderer from finding out there was potential evidence in the apartment.

It was a stretch in logic, but Darcy had used a thought process like that too many times to count. When she did, things had turned out okay. Usually.

"You convinced me, Jenna. In the immortal words of Pixie Dust, let's ride. I'll drive."

At the apartment complex, they found an out-of-the-way place to park only after they were convinced the apartment was empty. Next, they made a quick dash to a bedroom window under the cover of darkness. With a screwdriver taken from a small toolbox in Rusty's storage compartment, Darcy removed the screen. She was going to enter the abode while Jenna served as lookout.

"Here goes." She pushed the window up. "My phone's on vibrate. If you see anyone, text me. Now give me a boost."

Once Darcy was perched safely on the windowsill, Jenna saluted, then strolled around the corner of the building so she could keep an eye out for approaching vehicles or pedestrians.

Reaching the opening had been as easy as mounting a step ladder. Getting through it without making a racket was tougher. It took some adjusting, but eventually, Darcy settled herself on the sill like she was riding a horse, with one leg indoors and one outdoors. She shifted her weight indoors and let gravity do the work until her toe contacted the bedroom carpet.

After that, it was easy. She put her full weight on the inside leg, turned her torso toward the inside of the room, and put her hands out to catch her fall.

"Just like old times." Darcy allowed herself a grin as she got to her feet. She hadn't snuck in through a window since her Pixie Dust days. It had been like riding a bike. Seven years or so since her last attempt, and she hadn't forgotten a thing.

In a flash, she was on one knee in front of the vent. The screws came out with such ease it was like they'd been lubricated. Within a minute, Darcy had the screen off and was feeling around inside the vent with her hand.

After a few seconds, her fingers came across something smooth to the touch. The sensation was different from the slightly textured feel of the aluminum duct. Whatever the mystery item was, it was affixed to a portion of the vent that someone making a cursory look would miss.

She found an edge to the object and pulled. It came loose with the familiar ripping sound made when Velcro was separated.

"Using a command strip to attach a plastic bag to the top of the vent. Clever thinking, Angelica."

Despite her desire to check out the contents of the bag, Darcy set it aside. The longer she lingered, the odds of getting caught increased. She replaced the vent cover, then wiped it and the screws to remove any fingerprints. Before making her exit, she locked the second window. The devil was always in the details.

Then she sent Jenna a text, asking if the coast was clear. The response was immediate. A thumbs-up emoji. With a surge of adrenaline, she closed and locked the window she entered through, sprinted through the apartment, and slipped outside.

They didn't speak until they had the screen back in place and were inside Rusty.

"Any luck?" Jenna's eyes were wide. The adventure had apparently energized her.

"We'll know soon enough." Darcy showed the bag to Jenna. It was clear plastic and contained 8 ½ by 11 pages that had been folded in half.

"Holy Secret Message, Batman, what do you think's in there?" Jenna was giving off a vibe closer to someone who just got their hands on Beyonce's latest album, not someone who'd participated in a burglary. Though, in her defense, it had been conducted with the best of intentions in mind.

"Here's what we're not going to do. We're not going to open this right now. We're going to my place, and then we'll figure out what's next." Jenna's enthusiasm was appreciated, but Darcy wanted to bring her back to Earth. The papers, whatever they contained, were presumably related to Angelica's undoing.

It didn't get more serious than that.

At the cabin, Darcy switched out her leather gloves for surgical ones while Jenna fed Ringo. Despite the importance of the find, the old tomcat wouldn't let his mom get anything done until his belly was full. That was life in the Ringo Gaughan household.

Darcy tossed a pair of surgical-type gloves to Jenna, then gestured to the kitchen table.

"I want you to take pictures of whatever is on these pages. Then we're going to put them back and call Paul."

With a frown, Jenna accepted Darcy's phone. "What if there's something important there? Like, I don't know, the key to break the whole case wide open?"

Suppressing a chuckle, Darcy patted her friend's hand. Jenna had watched one too many episodes of the glorious mystery show *Psych*. In Darcy's real-world experience, it was way harder to find the key piece of evidence than Shawn Spencer and his pal Gus made it appear.

"Hope springs eternal, my friend." Darcy removed the pages from the bag. It wasn't a voluminous collection. There were four pages in total. What the papers lacked in number, they made up for in content.

"Holy spreadsheet, Batman." Jenna clicked away with gusto as soon as Darcy placed each sheet on the table. "These are ledger entries."

Darcy studied the information for a full five minutes before speaking. "Looks like it's mostly receipts. Nothing to show where the money came from, though."

"Agreed." Jenna had come around the table to study the documents from over Darcy's shoulder. "Look at the date column. The numbers there must be some kind of code. I don't know of any dates that end in forty-eight."

"I hear you. We can figure that out later. Look at the size of some of these numbers in the credits column." She pointed to a number near the bottom of the first page. "Five hundred here, and I saw a thousand-dollar entry on the last page. There must be between fifty and a hundred grand here."

"Seventy-three, unless my math is off." When Darcy looked at her slack-jawed, Jenna shrugged. "What can I say? I look at numbers every day."

"And that is the latest example of why it's good I pursued music and not business. We need to get this to Paul ASAP."

"Do you think that's necessary?" Jenna ran her gloved fingers over the pages, as if she was mentally checking her math.

"Yeah. I'm not sure what exactly was going on, but I know one thing. Angelica had a seriously lucrative side hustle. What if this is income from people paying for her help cheating on tests? Paul will freak if he finds out I kept it from him. Maybe arrest me for tampering with evidence or something."

At the mention of the detective, Jenna swept the pages together and slipped them back into the plastic bag. The woman had played her part in the little caper, but reality seemed to be setting in on her.

"Here you go, then." Her gaze darted from side to side, as if she was trying to spot criminals who might be hiding in the shadows. "You're going to leave me out of this, right?"

"Totally." Darcy wrapped her arms around Jenna. Her bestie was an honest soul who was at her best, making amazing delicacies and offering sage advice. While she was a woman of action, putting herself in peril while serving as an amateur sleuth's sidekick was not the kind of action she was accustomed to.

Nor should it be.

"You've been amazing and now your work is done. I'm going to take you home right now. We can cook up a cover story on the way, but I think the best one is the simplest. I wanted to have a look around Angelica's apartment, but you convinced me not to. Instead, we went for a drive and had some nice girl time."

"You think that'll work?"

Darcy grabbed her keys. "Sure. And when I give this to Paul, your name will never enter the conversation. This is one time that my checkered past will come back to help instead of haunt me."

"What are you going to tell him?"

"It's best you don't know." Darcy gave Jenna a big smile. "Plausible deniability is a powerful tool to employ."

Chapter Sixteen

"I told you already. I don't know where it came from." Darcy massaged her temples. Her attempt to turn her find over to Paul wasn't going as expected. "I was on my way to work—"

"On your skateboard. In February, really?" The detective leaned back in his chair and stared at the interview room's acoustical ceiling tiles.

"Yes, really. It's supposed to be in the upper fifties today. And it's how I get my exercise." She crossed her arms. The defensive posture wasn't the most helpful one to take. Paul would pick up on it. His lack of gratitude was to blame for that.

"Okay, fine." He put his hands up in surrender as he looked at the pages that were spread across the table between them. "You found this package by the side of the trail. What made you stop?"

"Because I care about my community. I can't stand litterbugs. Is that so wrong?"

"Of course not. Did you pick anything else up on your clean-up commute?" A slight smile betrayed his stern tone. He apparently wasn't buying her story.

"Check the trash can outside the entrance. You'll find a plastic grocery bag with trash in it. Today's haul. It's not full because once I found the plastic bag, I came straight here."

He looked Darcy in the eye. The second hand on the clock hanging on the wall behind him made a full rotation before he turned his focus back to his notes. His shoulders sagged. They'd spent fifteen minutes going round and round about the package's origin. All attempts to pierce a hole in Darcy's story had failed.

After taking Jenna home the night before, she'd spent two hours coming up with the story. By the time her head had hit the pillow, she was satisfied it was bulletproof. Pleased with her preparation, she suppressed a smile. It was a small victory. The thing that mattered was that now he'd turn his attention to the information in the documents.

"Why'd you look inside the bag instead of dropping it into your little collection sack with the rest of the trash?" The man was relentless. He'd asked the same question, using different words, twice before already.

"It seemed out of place. Ninety-nine percent of the trash on the trail are things like plastic bottles, candy wrappers, beer cans. Things like that. I thought maybe someone dropped it by accident. I mean, come on, who puts a bunch of pages of ledger entries into a plastic bag and then loses them?"

"You're certain these are from a ledger? You know who it belongs to, then." Paul kept his expression neutral. It didn't work. It was an obvious attempt to get her to admit something. The man's predecessor had tried the same trick on Darcy on a handful of occasions.

With the same result.

"I'm not a hundred percent certain. I run a business, though, and those pages look like someone was tracking income and expenses. In my experience, that's what a ledger's for. As for who it belongs to, I have no idea."

"Humor me, then. Take a guess." Paul sat back and put his hands behind his head. In the glare of the fluorescent lighting, the dark circles under his eyes stood out like stage makeup. That, and the two cups of coffee in front of him were a giveaway. It had been a week since Angelica's murder. The Marysburg Police were no closer to solving the case than Darcy was.

"Someone doing something illegal. I'd bet my drum kit that these transactions were made in cash. The obvious guess is a drug dealer." Darcy had arrived at the make-or-break moment of the conversation. She drummed her fingers on the surface of the table while she watched the clock.

After thirty seconds passed, she raised her index finger. "What if it's related to the stories going around about Angelica Stipe cheating on exams?"

Paul stopped in the middle of having a drink of his coffee. He put the cup back down. "What do you mean?"

"I talked to Xander yesterday. The exam cheating thing came up. He denied knowing anything about it." Darcy leaned forward. "What if he was lying? Or what if Angelica was running the scheme? What if these are payments for exam info?"

Paul tilted his head to the side. He scratched his chin with one hand while he tapped on the tabletop with the second finger of his other hand. Apparently, he thought there was merit to Darcy's supposition.

"For argument's sake, let's say these documents did belong to Angelica. If that's the case, and I'm not saying it is, why did they end up by the trail?"

Darcy spread her hands out wide. It was better for her story to play dumb. "Beats me. Maybe she lost it. Maybe her murderer lost it or tried to throw it away."

"Sure, but just tossing it away instead of destroying it? Why not burn the pages or tear them up? This seems sloppy to me."

"Maybe it was a panic move. I can take you to the spot where I found the bag. It's not far from The Magic Box. What if Angelica had it on her, and the murderer took it when they killed her?"

"It's a possibility. I'll give you that. Assuming that these pages are actually connected to Angelica Stipe. So far, I don't see any evidence of that."

Darcy's phone buzzed. It was her daily reminder to leave home for the record store. She needed to go. It had been time well spent, though.

"I gotta get to work." She stood. "My gut tells me there *is* a connection. And I've had some good luck following my gut recently. If you know what I mean."

"I do." He let out a laugh as he gathered the pages together. "Thanks for this. We'll look into it."

Paul escorted her out of the building. When she asked him if it was an excuse to check the trash can, he went over to it. With a shake of his head, he pulled out the plastic grocery bag.

"You'd think people who use the trail would be more inclined to take care of it." He peeked inside. "There's a lot of trash in this town."

"That's why we all need to do our part to clean it up. If you know what I mean."

"Go to work, Gaughan. If I need to talk to you, I know where to find you."

As was typically the case on a Saturday, Marysburg Music was filled with customers and friends from the moment Charlotte unlocked the front door. With business brisk, Darcy had little time to think about the case. She had other things on her mind.

Like Peter's music school audition, which was happening as they spoke.

"Any news," Darcy asked Izzy as she placed a purchase the young woman rang up into a paper shopping bag.

After thanking the customer, Izzy checked her phone. "No. You?"

"Nothing. He promised to let you know when he was finished, right?"

"Yeah." Izzy turned her attention to a woman and her tween daughter who had placed two P!nk albums on the counter. While she rang up the sale, she told the girl how much she loved the artist and complimented her on her fabulous musical taste.

The mother gave Izzy a big smile and thanked her for the kind words.

"You're going to make an amazing music teacher." Darcy draped her arm over Izzy's shoulder.

"Thanks. I just wish Peter would text me. I'm sure he killed it, but..." Izzy couldn't hide the worry in her eyes. Her concern for her friend was heartwarming. It was also unnecessary.

"He's been rehearsing for weeks. His performance was flawless the other night. He's probably checking out the campus with his folks. Enjoying his moment now that the audition's over."

"You're probably right. It's weird. I'm not worried about my audition at all, but I've been worried about Peter's for weeks."

"That's because you're a good friend. You know in your head you've both done everything you can to prepare. You have control over your audition but not over his. I remember the early days of Pixie Dust. My mom and dad were worried sick those first shows would be disasters. That something would go wrong and kill the band before it had a chance to build a following. I knew different."

"Did their worrying make you mad? I mean, I know you haven't always had the best relationship with them." Izzy's cheeks turned pink. "Sorry."

"No apology needed. My mom and dad were worried about me because they cared about me. I appreciated the sentiment. I still do. Things went south between us when alcohol took over my life. The choices they made in our relationship were made with the best of intentions. The decisions they made had one goal in mind. Help me get treatment and kick my addiction once and for all."

Darcy was more than willing to talk about her alcohol dependency. To anyone at any time. This was the first time she and Izzy had discussed the topic, though. She appreciated Izzy's interest. Hopefully her candidness would help steer her young employee from making the unfortunate choices she made.

"Must have been hard. Not speaking to your parents for such a long time."

"It was. In my heart, I knew they loved me. My sister, too. In my brain, it was different. I had a medical condition in my head that needed treatment. They knew it. I refused to face the facts. It took a long time to regain their trust. I spend every day working to keep it. And not just with them, but with everyone who helped get me to where I am now."

"Pardon me for interrupting, ladies." Ace, one of the store's best customers, joined them. "I kind of overheard your conversation. I just want to tell you, Darcy, that you've earned this town's trust. Between this space and the murder cases you've solved, we owe you. Big time."

Darcy's cheeks got warm. She tried to speak, but a lump formed in her throat. To top it all off, her vision got watery.

"That's, uh." Darcy coughed as she dried her eyes with a tissue Izzy gave her. "Thank you, man. That means more than you can imagine."

He leaned toward her. "How are things going on your new case? A buddy of mine started a pool. He's taking bets on how long it will take you to solve it. All the money that's collected is going to the performing arts center."

"Wow. No pressure there." Darcy let out a shaky laugh. "I'm making progress. Better not say any more than that right now."

Ace looked around. Nobody was approaching the sales counter. "Can I talk to you for a minute? Someplace private?"

"Go ahead, Boss." Izzy nodded toward the office. "I'm good here."

When they were seated, with the door closed, Darcy opened her note-taking app.

"What's on your mind?"

"It's about Angelica. Stipe. I've heard rumors floating around town that she had dirt on someone."

"What kind of dirt?"

"Personal. Embarrassing, I guess."

She raised an eyebrow. "Any idea who?"

Ace shook his head. "Not specifically. Just that it was someone important in town."

"That could be a lot of people." Darcy put her hands up. "Don't get me wrong. I appreciate the info. It gives me something to think about. Have you told the cops this?"

The man ran his palms along the thighs of his sweatpants. "No. I was afraid they wouldn't take it seriously since it's only a rumor. I knew you would."

"Appreciate the confidence, buddy. I think you should contact Detective Gerard. Tell him the same thing you've told me. He won't laugh, I promise."

For a moment, Ace stared at the floor.

"Look. I know the guy. I trust him. We all want the same thing, right? To catch Angelica Stipe's murderer." Darcy waited for him to say something. When he nodded, she barreled on.

"The police have access to resources I don't. Sure, there are things I can do that they can't, but at the end of the day, the police will be making the arrest. They're the ones who'll need to have evidence to make a conviction. Any help you can give them is a good thing."

"But."

"No buts. Angelica Stipe is dead. Someone took her life. She might not have been awful to a lot of people, but that doesn't make it okay for someone to cut off her life like pulling the plug from an amp."

"Okay. I get it." He pulled out his phone. "Give me his number. I'll call him right now."

While Todd spoke with Paul, Darcy had an epiphany. Ever since the moment the Hobbit had asked for her help, she'd thought she agreed to investigate because she wanted to help a fellow business owner. Then, when Rafe contacted her, she pledged her assistance out of a sense of loyalty to Eddie.

Good reasons, certainly. Honest and true reasons, definitely. But the real reason? The one that had her looking for clues so hard she was taking risks of landing herself in jail? No.

Clarity came to Darcy. The day Eddie literally pulled her out of the gutter down the street from Selena's, Darcy had been given a second chance at life. An opportunity to change her ways. To become the woman she was today. Business owner, cat mom, and community musical resource.

Angelica had been robbed of that chance.

The moment the young woman's heart stopped beating, any chance for her to see the error of her ways was taken from her. There would be no mending fences with Bethan. No apologizing to the Hobbit and all the other people in town she'd denigrated. No coming clean with the officials at Ball State over the exam issues.

No becoming the woman Angelica Stipe was meant to be. No graduating from college, no making an impact in the business world, no finding someone to spend the rest of her life with. No future.

Darcy couldn't change the past. She could shape the future, though. She could find Angelica's murderer. Make sure the heartbreaking story wasn't forgotten.

She would not stop until that future included Angelica Stipe's murderer behind bars for the rest of their life.

Chapter Seventeen

Darcy was enjoying a cup of rooibos tea with Ringo on her lap when there was a knock on the back door. She ticked out a text to Liam with instructions to let himself in. She couldn't bring herself to disturb her beloved tomcat.

A few moments later, he strolled into the living room. A paper sack was in one hand. A drink caddy holding two paper cups was in the other. A blue and white scarf that reached his waist was draped around his neck, the colors of his favorite English Football Club, Everton.

"Here I am, bringing you breakfast, and you can't be bothered to greet me at the door." The admonishment was betrayed by his wide smile.

"Don't blame me." She pointed at Ringo, who was giving Liam a one-eyed glare. "I can only do what the Boss Cat allows. Are those donuts from Jenna's? Gimme."

He handed her the sack as he put the drinks on the end table next to Darcy's recliner. While she inspected the aromatic bakery delights, he turned on the flatscreen TV.

"I thought your game didn't start for another hour. Do you really need to turn it on already?"

"It's a match, not a game, my dear. And it's a big one with Liverpool. So, yes, I need to watch the pre-match coverage." He took a big slurp of coffee before plopping down in the loveseat catty-corner from Darcy. The one with a direct view of the television.

Liam cared deeply for Darcy. He *loved* his Premier League Football.

"If you say so. You mind if I pick your brain while you watch? I mean, about the case?"

"Sure." He bit into a cream-filled donut. "Fire away."

She decided to wait for a commercial break to begin the discussion. While he gave his rapt attention to the talking heads on the screen, Darcy munched on the pastry. It was warm, sugary, and practically lighter than air. Just the way she liked her glazed donut. Some extra time on the skateboard was going to be in her future in the coming week to work off the calories.

But, as Prue from *The Great British Baking Show* was known to say, the donuts were worth the calories.

When the TV went dark for a moment, she swallowed and wiped her hands on a paper napkin. The time spent chewing had given her a chance to figure out how to frame her questions. The last thing she wanted to do was drag Liam into her web of investigatory rule-bending.

Which was a much more socially acceptable term for breaking and entering. And possibly burglary.

What he didn't know couldn't hurt him.

"Let me run a scenario by you. What if robbery wasn't the reason for Angelica's murder? The prize money's gone. But her phone's missing, too. What if the murderer wanted something on her phone?"

"Like what?" Liam's short response wasn't due to lack of interest. He had learned it helped Darcy more when he forced Darcy to share her thoughts clearly.

"There are allegations she was involved in cheating on exams at BSU. What if she actually did supply test info? And then, instead of being happy with a single payment, she demanded more money from her customers to keep quiet?"

Liam nodded. "I see where you're going. That'd be a gutsy play on Angelica's part; God rest her soul."

"And a dumb one, too. I know from experience that people, especially desperate ones, don't respond well when they think they're cornered. And people willing to pay for exam info sound desperate to me."

"So, whoever killed her took the phone to destroy any incriminating evidence that might be on it. Do you have anyone in your sights that fits the profile?"

"One and a half, maybe. Her boyfriend, Xander. He seems like a little weasel. I don't like him. And then there's Bethan McDougal. With the way Angelica bullied her for years, it wouldn't surprise me that Angelica had things on her phone that she could use to harass Bethan. Even though she says the bullying tailed off in recent years, it didn't stop. I get the feeling Bethan's wounds are deep."

"Have you talked to Bethan again?" When Darcy shook her head, put his donut down. "You need to. I get it if you sympathize with her because of what she went through at Angelica's hands. You can't let that cloud your judgment, though."

"Don't worry about that." The broadcast came back on. It gave Darcy time to assess the situation with Bethan. Specifically, whether Liam's suggestion about her judgment was on target.

It would be easy to dismiss Bethan as the murderer. There was no evidence tying her to the scene of the crime. Besides, she'd been victimized for years. That made her a sympathetic suspect. While she might have wanted to strike back at Angelica, there was nothing to suggest she ever did.

Unless Darcy could find out what Bethan was doing the evening Angelica died.

"Bethan told me she works from home," Darcy said when a commercial came on. "Do you know if she has another job?"

"I don't. Why?"

"I'm trying to figure out if there was a reason she wouldn't be at home the night of the murder. Like, I don't know, maybe she has a part-time job someplace not far from The Magic Box."

"Seems to me, if she does have a job somewhere and was working that night, she would have told you that." Liam's phone chirped. It was a text message. He started ticking away a response. "Sorry. I need to respond to this. A buddy who's a Liverpool supporter is trying to run some smack. I cannot let that go without a response."

One Darcy wanted to ponder Liam's point further, but the real world got in the way when she glanced at her phone. She needed to get ready for work.

A few hours later, Darcy was helping a customer pick out some contemporary blues music when Peter arrived. He took one step inside Marysburg Music, spread his arms wide, and asked for everyone's attention.

"Behold, you are looking at a future student at the Jacob's School of Music. Feel free to ask me for an autograph now so you can say you knew me before I hit the big time."

Darcy rolled her eyes at the young man's dramatics but joined in the round of applause. The announcement was the first report on his audition. When he hadn't texted by the time Darcy got ready for bed the night before, she had begun to fear the worst.

The rest of the team that was working, Izzy and Hank, hadn't heard from Peter, either. The three of them had reached an unspoken agreement to refrain from talking about the audition for fear of jinxing their friend.

Relief coursed through Darcy as she exchanged a look with Hank. In unison, they each let out a long breath.

Izzy wasn't so reserved. She practically tackled Peter with a hug. She only released him when it looked like they might fall into the "New Releases" display.

"Way to go, dude." Then she punched him in the arm. "That's for keeping all of us in suspense. Don't do that to me ever again. I couldn't sleep worrying about how things went."

Peter covered his cheeks with his palms. "Aww, you do care, Iz. You shouldn't have worried, though. Between my folks, you, and the Boss over there, I was so prepared, I could have nailed it blindfolded."

"And doing well on your audition gives you permission to roll in to work twenty minutes late?" Darcy pointed at the Michael Jackson clock on the wall.

"I am truly sorry about that, yesi." He dashed behind the sales counter. "To celebrate the audition going so well, I spent the afternoon touring campus with the fam. Then, we went to dinner. By the time we got home, I still had to call my relatives in Jamaica. I fell asleep without setting my alarm. Won't happen again, Boss."

Darcy grimaced, then scratched her cheek. "I dunno, Hank. You buying this tall tale?"

Everyone, employees and customers alike, laughed when Marysburg Music's head of Customer Satisfaction gave Peter an exaggerated head-to-toe look. The older gentleman loved to give Peter a hard time. Always in jest, though.

After a while, Hank took hold of Peter's hands and inspected them. "Palms aren't sweaty. Breathing isn't rapid. Pupils aren't dilated. I believe our young musician is telling us the truth."

"In that case, congratulations, dude." Darcy led those in the store in another round of applause. "We all knew you could do it. When do you get official word?"

Peter was grinning from ear to ear. "I should hear something in April. Man, I wish you all could have been there to see me."

"Too bad they didn't have a livestream. I would have totally watched it," Izzy said. "Do you know if anyone recorded it?"

"Nah, sorry." When a customer approached Peter with an LP and Marysburg Music T-shirt, Peter held out his hands. "Want me to autograph this shirt? You never know. It might be worth a million dollars someday."

"More like a million pennies." Izzy bumped Peter's shoulder as she went behind him to place the purchase in a bag.

While the customer laughed along with her teenage employees, an idea came to Darcy. Like a lightning bolt out of a clear blue sky, the revelation sent a surge of electricity through her, almost buckling her knees. She grabbed hold of one of the record bins to steady herself.

Hank was at her side in the blink of an eye. "Are you okay, Darcy? You look like you were about to faint."

"I'm fine." She shook her arms out. "In fact, I'm better than that. I think I just figured out how to ID Angelica's murderer."

Hank led Darcy by the hand into the office. While the store would get busy later, the young ones could handle the existing crowd for a few minutes. He closed the door.

"What are you talking about?"

"Getting a little dramatic, aren't you?" Darcy leaned against her desk.

"One never knows who's listening. For all we know, someone who knows the murderer could be out there right now. I didn't want you to say something that might tip them off."

"Good point." She swallowed. "Didn't even think about that."

Hank gave her a slight nod. "Now. Out with it."

Her apology accepted, Darcy rubbed her hands together. "I can't believe I didn't think of it before. It hit me when Peter and Iz were talking about video of his audition. What if one of the businesses in the area caught the murderer on a security camera?"

"Wouldn't the police have already checked that?"

"Yes. The question is, how far away did they check? And how long is it taking them to check? A quick sprint can get you three or four blocks away from the Magic Box in a couple of minutes. That's a lot of ground to cover, and I'm sure this isn't the only thing the cops are working on. Can't hurt to look into it myself, right?"

"How will you know what you're looking for.? After all, you could be staring at a lot of video of people coming and going who are well within their rights to do so."

"It's like an up-and-coming band that's destined for greatness, my friend." She patted him on the shoulder. "I'll know it when I see it."

After solving two murder mysteries, Darcy had a reputation as Marysburg's version of Dex Parios, the sleuth from the *Stumptown* graphic novels. If she showed up on someone's doorstep in the aftermath of a murder, odds were good she wanted to talk about it.

That reputation made it easier for Darcy to get permission to view surveillance video local businesses had recorded. Despite unanimous cooperation from every fellow business owner, she visited Sunday evening after work and Monday morning, nine in all, she failed to find anything helpful.

By the time she rolled into Selena's after her shift Monday afternoon, she was beginning to think the idea was nothing more than a fool's errand.

"I really thought I'd see something by now." She dipped a tortilla chip into a bowl of chori queso. The spicy chorizo and cheese dip warmed her insides. "Maybe it was a dumb idea."

"I don't know." Thea took a break from placing freshly washed pint glasses on the bar back. "Since Eddie was murdered, a lot of people have put security cams in place. Whether it's out of fear or wanting to cover their backsides or something else, the businesses around here have finally realized a lock on the door and an alarm system might not be enough to deter crime anymore."

"That's a depressing thought." Darcy took a drink of her ice water to cool her tongue. The dip brought more heat than she first thought.

"Maybe so. It is what it is, though. You want to take a look at our video? I know we're a few blocks away from The Magic Box, but it couldn't hurt. And you can do it while you finish your chips and dip."

Darcy didn't need any more convincing. While Thea went to get approval, Darcy studied a map of Marysburg in her mind. All routes between Selena's and the crime scene involved making two turns at intersections. With no straight-line connections, it seemed like any video catching the murderer was unlikely.

Not impossible, though.

Zig-zagging their way through town to avoid being apprehended after murdering Angelica wasn't a bad idea. Given the state of the investigation, if that was the move that had been made, it worked.

Thea skipped up to Darcy, snapping her fingers in rhythm with each step she took. "Green light from the boss. Go on back. He's pulling up the video now."

"Alrighty, then." Darcy took her plate in one hand while she exchanged a high-five with her friend.

Selena's owner, Nathan Echols, and Darcy went back years. His support of Pixie Dust in its fledging months had been invaluable and much appreciated. The Saturday nights the group spent playing in the bar, learning how to perform songs they'd written, how to be more than three young women with a dream to be famous provided the launching pad from which the band lifted off into orbit. The gigs were good for the restaurant, too. By the time Pixie Dust released its first single, the Saturday nights the band appeared were full houses.

Neither Nate nor Darcy had forgotten their partnership. Which was one of the reasons Darcy dined at Selena's so often. Becoming fast friends with Thea had been a huge bonus.

"Nate, my man." Darcy took a seat across from the restauranteur. "I appreciate you letting me do this."

"Hey, if it helps catch a killer, Selena's is ever at your service. Mind if I watch with you? I guess you could say I have a vested interest."

They spent the next thirty minutes chatting and studying video of the restaurant's entrance. Watching people come and go in black-and-white without any audio made her thankful for the fast-forward setting.

When the time stamp on the screen flashed past the ten P.M. mark, she held out the remote to Nate. "Thanks, man. It was worth a shot."

"Anytime. You know that." He furrowed his blond eyebrows. "You're not giving up, are you? We've got more video to watch."

"What do you mean? There's no point looking at the rest. If the murderer had been caught on the video, we'd have seen something by now. I didn't see any of my suspects or anyone acting sketchy." She got to her feet. "Don't get me wrong, I appreciate it, but I've taken enough of your time."

He lifted his index finger. "Aha, the amazing investigator doesn't know about the camera I installed in the back. Have a seat. Time for the second half of the double feature."

"When did you do that?" Despite the heat warming her cheeks, she let out a laugh. "Sorry about that. I mean, I'm sorry you felt you needed to."

"I'd been thinking about it for a while and decided to go for it last fall. It's not exactly something that was worthy of an Instagram post, if you know what I mean." He entered a few commands on his keyboard. "We were having a few problems with vandalism in the alley. Broken bottles, trash being dumped, stuff like that. Once word got out that a kid who tagged the wall got busted because of the video, things improved back there."

"Cheers to that." Darcy sent up a thank you to the spirits above that there had never been problems behind the record store's building. Whatever the reason for her good fortune, she was appreciative.

"And away we go." Nate helped himself to one of Darcy's tortilla chips as the video played.

The view was mind-numbingly dull. Other than a few people strolling into and then out of the camera's view, there was nothing more than a shot of the alley. Until the restaurant's back door opened, and someone exited the building.

"What the…" Nate hit the pause button before Darcy had time to ask him to do the exact same thing.

"Let it play." Darcy noted the timestamp. It read "6:32:49." As the video progressed, the person in question stood in the middle of the alley. After looking one way and then the other, they lit a cigarette, then pulled out their phone. They kept their back to the camera. Whether intentional or not, the move kept their features hidden.

"Whoever it is, they're tall," Darcy said. "One of your employees?"

Nate shook his head. "I don't mind if my people step out back there for a smoke break. Nobody on the schedule that night smokes, though. There's a smoking area out front for customers, so there'd be no reason for one of them to be there."

In tandem, they leaned toward the screen, as if getting closer would reveal the smoker's identity. Their effort was eventually rewarded, as the subject turned and headed out of the camera's field of vision. Before disappearing from view, the individual glanced in the direction of the camera.

"Good golly, Miss Molly, I know her." Darcy shot to her feet. "That's Bethan McDougal. This is a game-changer."

As she shrugged into her coat, she gave Nate an edited version of her conversation with Bethan. She skipped over most of the details. It wasn't appropriate to share too much with him, after all.

She had no hesitation in telling him that Bethan had lied to her about the night in question, though.

"What are you going to do now?" Worry lines creased Nate's forehead. "Go to the police and let them take it from there, right?"

"Not quite." She pointed her phone at the computer screen. The ghostly image of Bethan was still on it, frozen in time. With a push of an icon, a copy of the image showed up on her phone's screen. "I'm going straight to Bethan. She owes me an explanation."

Nate put his hand on her arm. "Isn't that dangerous? I mean, what if she's the murderer? Won't you be putting yourself in harm's way?"

"Maybe. Then again, that woman's never faced me when I'm as mad as I am right now. She's the one who better be on her guard."

Chapter Eighteen

By the time Darcy arrived at the McDougall residence, her anger had subsided. She shut the engine off and took a deep, cleansing breath. After a look at the photo of Gina taped to the dash, she took another breath, counting to ten as she blew out.

"You're right. I need to be calm and focused." She tapped the photo for good luck. "Here goes."

Bethan's father answered Darcy's knock on the door. She barely had time to introduce herself before he ushered her inside.

"Of course, I know who you are." The man offered her a friendly smile; his dark brown eyes sparkled behind a pair of steel-rimmed glasses. "Bethan told her mother and me you came to visit the other day."

"Oh really?" The warm welcome caught Darcy off-guard. She placed her coat into Mr. McDougall's outstretched hands.

"Indeed, she did. Said you were investigating the murder of the Stipe lass." He lowered his head for a moment. "Such a sad thing. She may have been awful to my daughter, but nobody deserves to have their life taken from them."

Darcy followed him into the kitchen. She took a seat on the same barstool she used during her visit with Bethan. He put a kettle on the stove and asked her if she'd like some tea. She nodded, still attempting to regroup from the greeting so different than the one Bethan gave her.

"Be right back." He strode away with a spring in his step, humming a tune. The man was as friendly as his daughter had been surly. Go figure.

A moment later, he returned with Bethan in tow. The young woman's scowl was in direct opposition to her father's grin.

"Hi, Bethan. Great to see you again." Darcy waved as she got to her feet. Being friendly was the play to be made, at least as long as Mr. McDougall was around.

"To what do we owe this unexpected pleasure?" Bethan headed straight for a cabinet, where she withdrew three mugs. She didn't even glance at Darcy.

"Since you were kind enough to talk with me the other day, I wanted to give you an update on my investigation. There have been a few developments. I thought sharing them with you was the right thing to do."

"Bless you, young lady." Mr. McDougall poured steaming water into the three cups, then offered Darcy a variety of teas to choose from. "A few people seem to think Bethan had something to do with that woman's unfortunate end. Can you believe it?"

"If there's one thing I've learned over the years, it's that you never know what people think." Darcy looked Bethan in the eye. "And you have absolutely no control over what they do."

"Aye. Isn't that the truth." He shook his head, but the smile was still there. "Well, you don't need an old man hovering over you. I'll let you have a proper chin wag."

Silence hung over the room. Darcy kept her gaze on her tea. It might be a silly power game, but she would wait for Bethan to speak first. After a few moments, her patience paid off.

"What are you really doing here?" Bethan moved next to Darcy. Her voice was low. Those were the actions of someone who didn't want their conversation overheard.

It was the kind of reaction Darcy had been hoping for.

"Wanted to clear up a few things from our last convo." She took a sip of her herbal tea.

"What makes you think there's anything to clear up?" Bethan pulled her long hair back into a ponytail. Another sign of nerves, perhaps?

"Because you lied to me. When you told me, it was none of my business what you were doing the night Angelica was murdered."

Bethan shook her head. "Nope. It wasn't your business then. It's not your business now. That's the truth."

"Yeah." Darcy spread her palms on the island's cool, granite surface. "You see, here's the thing. I get it that you hated Angelica for what she did to you. Bullying you year after year after year. I don't blame you for feeling relieved that your tormenter can't hurt anymore."

"Wow, thanks. So, you're an amateur psychologist, along with all the other amateur things you do?"

Darcy let out a laugh. "Nice one. Let's just say I know a thing or two about living with an unrelenting antagonist. My point, though. On the night of Angelica's murder, you were observed behind Selena's Mexican Restaurant smoking something. Not only that, the time you were seen was not long before the murder. To top things off, you were walking toward The Magic Box. Those are the kind of things that make me go, huh? Can you see why I might think you lied to me?"

"You're full of it." Bethan's gaze darted left, then right. "Whoever your witness is, they're wrong."

"I don't think so. My witness is a security camera." Darcy slid her phone toward Bethan. "As the saying goes, 'The camera don't lie.'"

The younger woman muttered something under her breath as the color drained from her face. She began chewing on a fingernail. Eventually, she threw her hands in the air.

"Okay, you got me. Work has me stressed out. I met a friend at Selena's. I slipped out the back to take a few hits. I was hoping it would mellow me out. I didn't go anywhere near The Magic Box, though."

"Where'd you go, then?"

"Another friend's house." Her fingers trembled as she took a sip of her tea. "A close friend, if you know what I mean. My friend's folks don't know about us. We need to keep it that way."

Darcy sat back. She did know what Bethan meant. To her, people loved who they loved. End of story. Not everybody agreed with that assessment, however.

"I hear you. It would be helpful if your friend could confirm this for me. Can I get a name?"

"Really? As if her life doesn't have enough challenges already, you want to go bother her?"

"No. But, for all I know, you could be lying to me."

Bethan stirred some sugar into her cup. She let out a sigh. "I hate this. That witch made me miserable for years, and nobody did a thing. I didn't have anything to do with her murder, but I'm getting screwed over again. Even from beyond the grave, she's torturing me."

"You're not wrong. All I can say is that I'm really sorry for all you went through. The sooner you can get your alibi verified, the sooner you can go along with your life. I want to catch the murderer, the real one. Not just somebody to sit in jail to make Marysburg folks feel safe."

"Justice for Angelica, the angel herself." Bethan practically spit out the words.

"And for the innocent people the police have as suspects. Sean O'Sullivan, Rafe Majors, you."

"Fine. You win." Bethan wrote her friend's name and phone number on a piece of notebook paper. "When are you going to call her?"

"The second I set foot outside your front door. Don't worry. I'll be friendly and promise to keep your secret." She finished her tea and got up. "By the way, it wouldn't hurt for you and your friend to make sure you have your stories straight in case the police ask you about your whereabouts. I'll see myself out."

After taking a moment to thank Mr. McDougall for his hospitality, Darcy left. She dialed the number Bethan gave her once she was buckled into Rusty's driver's seat.

It turned out that Bethan's friend knew Darcy from the record store. Once she'd been assured the nature of her relationship with Bethan would be kept confidential, she spoke without hesitation.

In fact, the woman was so chatty, the conversation didn't come to an end until Darcy came to a stop in the driveway at her home. The ten-minute chat included enough detail and specifics as to timing and location, that by the time Darcy ended the call with a hearty amount of thanks, she was confident in her decision to remove Bethan from the suspect list.

After a night of undisturbed sleep, Darcy awoke the next morning ready for action. On any other day of the week, she would have been excited to get in front of the suspect board in her office at work. Since it was Tuesday, her one day of the week off, she decided to analyze her suspects over a bowl of granola and blueberries and a cup of chamomile tea.

The last time she showed up at Marysburg Music on her day off, Hank had bawled her out. He'd been right to do so. She loved the store, but for her own mental well-being, she needed to allow herself time away from it. Her team was full of kind, trustworthy, and smart people. The store was in good hands.

"Help me out here, Ringo." Darcy gave him a soft kitty treat even though she'd given him breakfast less than an hour earlier. "I need to talk my way through my suspects. Let me know what you think."

The cat leapt up onto a seat by Darcy. He faced her and put a paw on the table for a moment. Maybe it was merely a smooth attempt to get more treats. She chose to believe he was really interested in helping.

"Okay, here we go. Assuming her friend didn't lie to me, we can take Bethan off the list. I'll admit, it was a phone call, which isn't nearly as effective as a face-to-face. I got the sense she was being straight with me and appreciated my promise to keep my big mouth shut about their relationship."

Ringo responded with a quick *meh*. It was a vocalization he made when he was okay with a situation. In appreciation for his support, Darcy gave him another morsel.

"Cool. That leaves us with Rafe, the Hobbit, and Xander."

Ringo pinned his ears back when Darcy finished the list of suspects.

"I know. They are not the most likable group around. The Hobbit's not a bad guy, once you get to know him. Kind of like a certain cat I know." When Ringo chose not to respond, she chuckled. "The Hobbit's problem is nobody can verify his alibi. Sending his employees home and cleaning up himself after a super long day is something a good boss would do. I hope I'd be that aware of my teams' long hours if I put on a marathon event like that."

Ringo licked a paw, then let out a *mrrow*.

"Record Store Day's a good point. I do let everyone go home and save as much clean-up as I can for the next day." She gave Ringo another treat. "And therein lies the rub, dude. The Hobbit could have locked up and gone home for a good night's sleep. Instead, he stuck around. Why did he make that decision? I need to check in with him, anyway. I'll ask him."

She texted the Hobbit to let him know she wanted to give him an update on the investigation and would be by early in the afternoon.

"We'll keep the clean-up question between the two of us for now, buddy. Somehow, I need to get Paul to tell me about bruising on Angelica's neck and, if that helps, figure out the height of the murderer. Next up is our frenemy, Rafe Majors."

The cat growled.

"Oh, come on. He's not that bad. Yes, he's a dipstick, but a murderer?" She fixed herself another cup of tea while she debated her own question. "How's this? Rafe may not want to admit it publicly, but he was humiliated by not winning the tournament. Knowing him, he probably already had the prize money spent."

When Ringo remained silent, Darcy continued with her train of thought.

"Yes, he's better with his money. Refusing to admit where he got the cash for those Louboutin high tops makes me wonder. On top of that, he still won't tell anyone where he went when he left the store." Darcy scratched her elbow. "I'm going to have to talk to him again, aren't I?"

The feline blinked.

"That's what I thought." Darcy placed another treat between his front paws. "Don't get any ideas that this is going to become a regular thing. You're enough of a fat cat as it is. Anyway, what's your take on Xander?"

Ringo was too busy licking his chops to respond.

"The sad boyfriend act doesn't work for me. The bit about losing his memory that night? That's totally sketch. I could see him getting mad at Angelica, losing his cool, and killing her. Sure, if he did it, it was probably an accident. Doesn't make it okay, though."

The chat with Ringo raised Darcy's spirits. It also gave her a new game plan to follow. It was time to lean on some folks. Hard. The approach always worked for Deputy Marshall Raylan Givens. Maybe it could work for her, too. First, the Hobbit, then Rafe, with Xander to wrap things up.

The sun was a blinding orb in a bright blue sky when Darcy exited the cabin. Without a cloud to be seen, she was tempted to grab her skateboard. There were too many places to go, though. For this mission, she needed Rusty's trusty, and powerful, four wheels.

She found an unoccupied parking spot behind The Magic Box. Normally the daytime business crowd filled the lot. Darcy chose to look on the opening as a positive sign that she was on the right track.

As she crossed the parking lot, Todd Meadows emerged from the back entrance of The Comic Castle. He had a clear plastic bag in his hand.

"Why, Mr. Meadows, I never figured you for a fan of graphic novels."

"Greetings, Darcy." Todd gave her a quick nod. "I'm not. Jasmine's niece has a birthday coming up. Apparently, she's a fan of *Shadow and Bone*, whatever that is. O'Sullivan took care of me, though, so all's well."

"I've seen the Netflix adaptation. It's good. She'll love it."

He gave her another nod and took a step as if to pass her by. The movement spurred an idea to life in Darcy's brain.

"Hey, while you're here. I wanted to express my condolences. I understand Angelica worked for you and that you thought a lot of her. I'm sorry."

The man looked away for a moment, his lips in a straight line. After a moment, his gaze returned to Darcy. "Thank you. Yes. She was such a promising young woman. It's a great loss."

A shiver went through her. It wasn't due to the breeze. Such a cold statement from Angelica's boss seemed uncaring and cold-hearted.

"Do you know of anyone who had it in for her? Maybe was harassing her?"

He rolled his eyes. "Don't tell me you're doing your Nancy Drew thing again."

"I wouldn't put it that way, but yes, I'm looking into some things. Someone asked me to, and I said I would. I'm a woman of my word. You should know that."

"Indeed, I do." With his free hand, he pulled the zipper of his coat down, then back up to where it was. "I've already given my statement to the police. You remember them? The experts in law and order. I'll tell you this, I the spirit of cooperation. If I was investigating this case, I'd be taking a hard look at that Xander. He was nothing but trouble for Angelica."

"Thank you. I appreciate the suggestion." Despite the fact that she despised Todd every but as much as he hated her, Darcy chose to be cordial. Antagonizing the man wouldn't help. Besides, the investigation wasn't about either of them. It was about justice for Angelica.

It was one of those "The Enemy of My Enemy is My Friend" situations.

"One more question. I understand she put in a lot of hours working with you. In that time, did she ever share her troubles with you or anything like that?"

"No. When I took her on, I made it clear that I was happy to mentor her, but if she was looking for a friend, she was looking in the wrong place. Now, if you'll excuse me, I have a listing appointment I need to get to."

He gave her a curt nod and strode to his vehicle, a low-slung, sleek sports car with a glossy black finish.

"Compensating much?" Darcy kept the comment under her breath but entered the Comic Castle with a spring in her step, thanks to getting in a final jab at the jerk.

She exchanged greetings with one of the store's employees, then wandered around the store while she waited for the Hobbit to finish a phone call. A *Wynonna Earp* comic was in her sights when the Hobbit came alongside her.

"Any news?"

"Hello to you, too." Darcy put the comic back. "Progress is slow but steady."

"Is there any way you can speed things up?" He gestured toward the sales floor. There were no other customers to be seen. "This investigation is killing my bottom line. Receipts are down by half since...you know what. If this keeps up much longer, I could be in trouble."

It didn't surprise Darcy that customers would steer clear of the Magic Box for a day or two. But since the crime scene tape had been taken down, there was no reason for people to stay away.

Unless Sean O'Sullivan was a murderer.

"Situation same for both stores?"

"Yep. Worse over there." He kept looking at the entrance in the vain hope he could entice customers to come inside through the sheer force of his will. "Only half of my regular crowd showed up for Dungeons and Dragons game night last week. I ended up closing early when a group of people showed up with signs and started protesting outside the store, demanding justice for Angelica."

"Seriously?" Darcy was all for freedom of expression, but protesting in front of the police department seemed a more logical place than at the Hobbit's store. "That stinks. I swear to you that I'm doing all I can to get to the bottom of this. I'm sure Detective Gerard is doing the same."

"Be that as it may, if this lingers for too long, I'm going to be looking at a serious cash flow problem."

"How long is too long?" Darcy's mind flashed back to the crushing weight she was operating under during after Eddie's death. Small businesses like Marysburg Music and The Magic Box didn't have a ton of cash reserves. Profit margins were typically fairly thin, too.

A downturn in business, even one as short as a month, could be fatal.

And it made her wonder. Who benefited from the Hobbit's stores shutting down?

One person always came to mind when Marysburg real estate was involved. Someone who loved to speak out about murder. The man himself, Todd Meadows.

Chapter Nineteen

Darcy wrapped up her conversation with the Hobbit and double-timed it to Rusty. Her fast footwork was struggling to keep up with her racing thoughts. Could Meadows really be the murderer? By all accounts he'd thought highly of Angelica. If that was true, what could possibly propel him to take her life? Shoot, he'd been there at the end of the tournament, so he could present Angelica with her grand prize awards.

The facts didn't seem to fit. One thing was inescapable, though. Todd loved to get his hands on real estate to redevelop it. And the block that was home to the Hobbit's businesses was an attractive location to resurrect the mixed-use condo project Darcy and Rafe had scuttled.

"Wait a minute. Slow down." She put her hands on the jeep's hood. The metal was cold. The sensation penetrated her skin and provided a jolt to the system she needed. "Let's not get off track, girl. Don't let your feelings get in the way. You won't find Angelica's murderer running around like your hair's on fire and jumping to conclusions."

She tugged at the cuffs of her coat's sleeves. When she was satisfied with the fit, she climbed into Rusty.

There was still an appointment with another murder suspect number one. She'd be foolish to blow it off. Rafe needed to come clean. The sooner, the better

Maybe it was the clear skies, or the walkways around Rafe's house that were now devoid of snow, or even the fact that the curtains had been pulled back. The dwelling gave off a much more welcoming vibe than it had on her last visit.

It seemed like a positive sign. If Rafe was still scared to death of being charged with murder, he wouldn't have opened the curtains. Maybe.

She took in the scene while she marched to the front door. Next-door neighbor Heather Ewing's car was parked in her driveway. Other than that, there were no vehicles to be seen. Not surprising, since everyone in the neighborhood had garages. That also meant no strange vehicles serving as homes for nosy journalists intent on burrowing into Rafe's life.

As if that had ever happened.

Still, murder was the most serious of criminal offenses. The despicable act happened all too often, in all too many places. If the media had any interest in Rafe, it would manifest itself if he was formally charged.

Darcy pushed the doorbell, then knocked on the door. "Rafe, it's me. Open up before anyone sees me and starts a rumor." That wasn't going to happen, but since the man welcomed her in mere moments later, the threat worked.

"What up, Gaughan." Rafe dropped into his favorite recliner. His eyes were bloodshot. Normally clean-shaven, he looked like he hadn't touched a razor in a week.

"Let me see your hands." She grabbed both of his hands before he had a chance to object and gave his fingernails a close look. They were ragged, and more than half had been chewed down to the quick.

"What gives?" He yanked his hands from her grip and slid them under his legs. "You said you had an update on the case. I'm a busy guy, so get to it."

She bit back a laugh. The man was in too much of a pitiful condition for her to do that to him. At least the false bravado indicated he still had some fight in him. The investigation hadn't crushed Rafe Majors.

Not yet.

"Have it your way." She remained on her feet. The room was a mess with dirty dishes strewn about among too many empty two-liter soda pop bottles to count.

"I've eliminated one suspect-"

"Better be me."

"No such luck, my friend. The suspect, who shall remain nameless, gave me an alibi that I was able to independently confirm. That's something you, for whatever reason, haven't been willing to do."

He shook his head. "I told you. I went for a walk to blow off steam."

"Yeah, I don't think so. I know you, Rafe. Fitness or exercise has never been your thing. Whenever you'd get fed up with Eddie, you'd retreat to your room and play video games. Which is why it's time for a Come to Jesus moment. Unless you want to go to jail, you need to tell me right now where you were and what you were doing after you left The Magic Box the night Angelica Stipe was murdered."

Rafe stared at her, rocking back and forth while he alternated his gaze between the television and his phone. Darcy kept quiet. He was withholding information. Critical information. The kind of information that could make or break the case.

Darcy couldn't force it out of him, though. If he was holding onto a secret, it must be a big one if he was willing to risk prison for it. Nothing could be that bad, though.

Unless he really was the murderer.

If he wasn't, he needed to be the one to save himself. And right now was a good time to start with the saving.

"Come on, Rafe. I can't help you if you won't level with me."

Silence permeated the room as Rafe chewed on a thumbnail. After an eternity, he shook his head.

"Fine. You win. I surrender."

Darcy's heart skipped a beat. "Surrender? Are you saying you murdered Angelica?"

"What? No. I didn't lay a finger on her. I'll tell you everything else, though." He took a beer bottle from a cooler by his chair. "Fire away."

"Where'd you go that night?"

He removed the bottle cap. The beer's fizz was like thunder in the silent household. After taking a drink, he wiped his mouth with his sleeve.

"When I left, I did go for a walk. It was cold, though, so after a couple blocks, I turned around and went back to my car. I drove over to the little amphitheater by the river. And I made a call."

"Who did you call?"

"A crisis hotline." He ran his thumb up and down the bottle. "I talked to a counselor for, I dunno, like an hour."

If true, the information would clear Rafe. Darcy sat as relief flowed over her. Like a warm, gentle wind. The classic Seals and Crofts tune "Summer Breeze" popped into her head. It was a lovely sentiment, but one that needed to be set aside for the moment.

"Can I see your phone log? It'll help verify your story."

Rafe showed it to her without protest. He didn't even complain when she took a photo of the screen, and he hated people touching his things. A sure sign that he was a defeated man.

The log revealed a forty-eight-minute call to 9-8-8, the national crisis and suicide hotline. There was no doubt in Darcy's mind that the police could confirm who had been on the other end of the call. Here was Rafe's alibi.

Instead of showing signs of relief, his eyes took on a vacant look. His current behavior didn't make sense, though. Something else was at play.

"Dude, this is good for you. Why did you keep this to yourself?"

"It makes me look weak, okay?" His chin trembled as he spoke. "I'm a total loser. If my crew found out that I've been talking to a counselor? There goes all my cred."

All too aware of how destructive it was to ignore one's mental health, Darcy was stunned into silence. Rafe's vanity was foolish.

And destructive.

It was a classic case of toxic masculinity at work. Darcy would address that issue with him at another time. What mattered was that Rafe had asked for help that night when he needed it. In doing so, he had proof he wasn't a murderer.

"We'll deal with your crew later. First things first, though. I'm going to call Detective Gerard. Ask him to come over so you can tell him all of this."

"What about my lawyer?"

Darcy shook her head. Even with attorney-client privilege in place, Rafe had been unwilling to admit he asked for help. Which was a shame because, in Darcy's view, asking for help with mental health was pretty darn heroic.

"Get 'em over here. Will save you having to tell the same story twice."

While they waited for the others to arrive, Darcy tidied up around the house and Rafe got himself cleaned up. She was halfway through filling a second trash bag when she noticed the antique mantle clock was missing.

"What happened to the clock," she asked when he returned, freshly showered and in clean clothes.

"Yeah, about that." He refused to make eye contact. "I've been selling some of the old man's stuff. It helps with the cash flow."

"Is that how you paid for those fancy kicks you're wearing?" She pointed toward the Louboutin hi tops he had on.

When he nodded, she gritted her teeth at the man's foolishness. "You need to tell the detective that, too. Make sure he has no reason to think you only robbed Angelica instead of robbing and murdering her."

A bit later, Darcy answered the knock at the door. The police officer was standing there. Rafe's attorney was hurrying up the walkway. While Paul was smiling, the lawyer was frowning.

She ushered them inside and thanked them for their speedy responses. Before anyone could get a word in edgewise, she put up her hands.

"Mr. Majors has information pertaining to the Stipe investigation he wants to tell Detective Gerard." She looked at the lawyer, who had joined Rafe at his side. "It's something that is very personal, so instead of making him tell it to each of you, I suggest we all take a seat and let him say what he has to say once."

"Are you sure about this, Rafe?" The attorney placed her hand on his arm. "Before you say anything, remember that I only have your best interest in mind."

"Nah. I'm good." He shuffled over to his recliner and eased into it like an arthritic old man. The toll his secret had taken on him was heavy.

When everyone was seated, Darcy gave him the go-ahead. She sent a word of thank you to the spirits above that she had enough time to pick up before the detective and lawyer arrived. Maybe it was just her, but having both Rafe and the house in presentable condition would make the upcoming admission more believable. That was the hope.

Unless Rafe blew it and decided to clam up.

"So, um, Detective. I've been thinking about the night Ms. Stipe was murdered. Today, I remembered something and want to tell you about it."

"Remembered something?" Paul raised his eyebrows.

"Just hear him out." Darcy leaned forward. Rafe's introductory statement had her worried. If he dinked around too long, he'd manage to find a way to avoid telling the truth.

The cop opened a notebook and twirled his fingers to get the conversation started while Rafe's attorney pulled out a legal pad.

"When I told you I went for a walk, that's a hundred percent true. There's more to it than that." Rafe ran his hands up and down his thighs. "I made a call, too."

"Who'd you call," Paul asked.

"Nine-eight-eight." Rafe retold his story almost word for word as he'd related it to Darcy. Apparently sensing how hard it was to make the admission, neither of the newcomers interrupted him. When he was finished, he handed his phone to his attorney. "It's there on my call history."

The attorney studied the phone screen for a few moments, then passed it along to the detective.

Paul took a picture of the screen, then wrote down some things in the notepad. "I appreciate you telling me this. Why didn't you tell me before?"

"Because sometimes it's really hard to admit you need help," Darcy said. "Especially when it involves mental health. Believe me, I know firsthand."

"I'm sure you're right, but I'd prefer to let Mr. Majors speak for himself." Paul returned the phone to Rafe. While his tone hadn't been combative, there had also been an unmistakable edge to it. Darcy's commentary was neither necessary nor welcome at the moment.

"You've told the detective where you were, Rafe. You don't have to answer anything else if you don't want to." The attorney glared at the detective, evidently feeling the need to say something to earn the time she'd be billing her client for.

"That's okay. Darcy's right. Didn't want anyone to think I couldn't take care of my own business."

"Given the sensitivity of Mr. Majors' phone call. Can we rely on the

Marysburg Police Department to treat this information, which he has provided willingly, with the sensitivity and confidentiality it deserves?"

"We'll need to verify the phone call with the service provider. But yes, I think we can honor that request, Counselor."

"So, you believe me?" Rafe sat up straight for the first time since Darcy's arrival. It was like he'd been plugged into an electrical socket and was receiving power for the first time in days. "Will you tell my boss at the library?"

At Paul's nod, the former suspect sprang from his chair and shook the detective's hand. Then he exchanged fist bumps with his lawyer and Darcy. Paul and Rafe's attorney had a few things they wanted to discuss, so Darcy made a quiet exit.

She skipped down the walkway to Rusty. Her exuberance wasn't diminished by the fact the murderer was still at large. She'd managed to eliminate another suspect.

With both Rafe and Bethan off the board, that left only Xander and O'Sullivan. The way the shop owner had been singing the blues about the downturn in business, he made a convincing argument in favor of his innocence. That meant Angelica's boyfriend had to be the murderer. Unless, just like Rafe, he miraculously recovered his memory from the night in question and could provide an alibi.

Well, Rafe had done just that. And it had gotten him off the hook. Lightning couldn't strike the same place twice, right?

After giving the Gina picture a knuckle bump, Darcy headed for home. Her in-person sleuth work was done for the day. The drive would be an ideal time to mull over Xander and Todd's status as suspects.

She'd gotten so deep into thought about her remaining suspects that she had to press the brakes hard to come to a complete stop at an intersection halfway home.

"Need to pay more attention to the road, girl, and less on the bad guys." She turned up the volume on the jeep's stereo. The funky pop of Fitz & The Tantrums was the perfect music to sing along to as she continued her drive.

When her gravel driveway came into view, Darcy started debating what special meal to give Ringo in celebration of the day's successes. Maybe some pan-fried chicken. She flipped on her turn signal and let off the gas. Chicken was a solid choice. They both liked it.

A hundred feet from the driveway, Darcy tapped the brake pedal to slow down enough to take the turn. The vehicle didn't slow. She pressed down harder.

Her foot went straight to the floor.

"Frac." The end of the road loomed ahead. The only thing between Rusty and the river was a stand of sycamores and river birches. At her current speed, she'd plow right through the foliage. With the recent snow melt, the water level was high, and the flow was fast. Crashing into the river wasn't an option. She pulled on the emergency brake and yanked the steering wheel hard to the right.

The tires squealed. The jeep veered off the road on two wheels and bounced through a culvert. While the turn reduced her speed, the emergency brake had failed, too. Darcy fought to regain control of the steering wheel, but her efforts were in vain.

The jeep clipped a sugar maple, causing the driver's side headlight to explode. Darcy's torso slammed into the airbag, snapping her head forward and then back. At the same time, the vehicle went into a spin. The front passenger tire caught on a root or a rock, tipping the vehicle up on its side. It came to rest with a deafening crash that knocked her unconscious.

The driver's side wheels remained spinning until they, too, came to a stop.

Inside the jeep, an unresponsive Darcy remained seat belted in place, her arms dangling as if she were a ragdoll. After being tossed around like she'd been caught in a tornado, the only part of her that moved was a stream of blood from a nasty gash to her forehead.

Chapter Twenty

The moment Darcy emerged from a deep, dark state of unconsciousness, she wished she could go right back to that blissful netherworld. Her vision was blurry, the kind of blurry that, in the past, had been caused by massive quantities of alcohol consumed in a short period of time. The only thing she could tell for sure was that the light was dim. A muffled throbbing originated from somewhere inside her head. It was impossible to pin down the exact location because the inside of her skull seemed to be swimming in a sludge lake that had been fouled by an oil slick.

She brought her hand close to her face. Her vision was clear enough to discern that an IV had been inserted into the backside of it. "Holy Mother of…"

"Darcy, thank goodness."

The voice that addressed her was a familiar one. The lyrical, contralto tone was one she'd known all her life.

"Mom?" She turned her head in the direction of the voice. A woman came into view. Despite multiple blinks to clear her vision, the vision of Darcy's mother was like an over-the-air TV broadcast with a lot of interference. "What are you doing here? Where am I?"

"Take it easy, dear." Helen Gaughan came closer and wrapped her hand around Darcy's. "There was an accident. You were injured."

As she emerged further from her stupor, Darcy's surroundings came into focus. She was in a bed with rails on either side. To her right, curtains were drawn over a set of windows. A flat-screen TV hung from the wall opposite her. The last time she was in a room like this, she'd been in restraints.

At least whatever accident she'd been in hadn't included breaking the law. At least, she didn't think that was the case.

"Why am I in a hospital bed?"

A tall man with thinning, gray hair came alongside Helen. It was Darcy's father, Bradley.

"You hit a tree. Your jeep ended up on its side. You got pretty banged up." He put his arm around Darcy's mom. "The neighbor girl heard the crash and called nine-one-one."

"Hallie." Darcy tried to sit up. A wave of nausea knocked her back into a horizontal position. "We have a lesson today. I need to let her know I need to postpone."

Darcy's sister Aisling appeared on the side of the bed opposite their parents. She pressed a button to raise Darcy until she was sitting at a forty-five-degree angle. "Don't worry about that. She knows. It's actually Wednesday morning. You were out all night."

A nurse arrived. Her sky-blue scrubs were cheery enough. When the fact that they featured a cat pattern, Darcy liked her on the spot. After introducing herself, she took Darcy's vitals and asked a few questions about pain levels.

"You had quite a ride. Do you think you're up to eating something?"

"I think so." At the mention of food, Darcy's stomach growled. She started to laugh but stopped with a wince when a searing pain ripped across her ribs. "Can I have something to drink?"

The nurse gave her a sympathetic smile while she poured water into a plastic cup. She dropped a bendy straw into the cup and brought it to Darcy's lips. "You've got bruising from the seatbelt, so don't be surprised if your midsection is sore for a while."

"I guess it's good I was wearing it, huh?"

"You can say that again." A Black gentleman in a lab coat entered the room. "I'm Dr. Freeman. If you don't mind, I'd like to have a look at you."

"Doesn't look like I'm going anywhere. Rock on, Doc."

Darcy was quiet during most of the examination except to answer questions. She had feeling in her extremities. Her reflexes appeared to be normal, as was her hearing. Now that she'd been awake for a bit and had some hydration, her vision was clearing. Well, mostly. If she spent too much time looking at a single item, double vision kicked in.

When he pressed on a muscle while examining her neck, the silence ended.

"Ouch, that hurts." She jerked, which sent spasms rocketing down her spine. "Come to think of it, my back hurts, too. Pretty much everything hurts."

The doctor pressed his lips together. "Uh-huh. How about your head? Any noticeable discomfort around your sinus or at the back of your skull?"

She tried to scratch her nose. It was covered in a thick dressing. An attempt to take a deep breath through her nasal passages failed and left her woozy.

"Mom? Dad? What in the name of Janis Joplin happened to me? I mean, like, what really happened?"

In unison, her parents looked at the doctor. He referred to the tablet in his hand.

"According to the first responders, you appear to have lost control of your vehicle. You crashed into a tree at a significant rate of speed. The airbag deployed. Thank goodness for that. The vehicle ended up on its side. You got knocked around pretty good. The seatbelt and airbags did their job, or your injuries would be much more severe."

"Wow." She scratched her leg. "It's beginning to come back to me. Stuff is still pretty fuzzy, though. How am I?"

"You've got a fair amount of bruising from head to toe, especially across your torso and head. There are lacerations along the bridge of your nose and across your forehead. You also have a concussion, no doubt, due to being banged around during the incident. Lastly, x-rays taken last night didn't reveal any trauma. Don't be surprised if you start experiencing back spasms and similar discomfort due to whiplash."

Darcy chuckled. "Is that all?"

The doctor patted her on the left shoulder, the one that had been free of the seatbelt. "You hit a tree at speed, Ms. Gaughan. Consider yourself fortunate your condition isn't worse."

"You're right, Doc. How soon can I get back to work?" Darcy's brain had turned to the things she needed to do at the record store. And for the investigation.

"The fact that your noggin is in good enough condition for you to have this conversation is a positive sign. You're scheduled for an MRI today. Unless you start experiencing difficulties, you can go home later today."

"Can I have my phone? I need to get in touch with people."

The room was silent as the doctor looked from Darcy's parents to her sister.

He cleared his throat. "I think I've got all I need from you, Ms. Gaughan. You're in good hands. The main thing for you to do is take it easy. Let your body heal."

Once he was gone, Darcy turned her focus on Aisling. "Okay, spill. What's going on?"

"About your phone. It wasn't on you when the paramedics brought you in." The woman glanced toward the door, as if she was considering making a run for it, instead incurring the wrath of her injured sister. "Liam's supposed to be looking for it. He also promised to get in touch with Charlotte."

"Hold on for a second. When did you talk to Liam?"

"Last night. He was here when we arrived. I guess the neighbor girl called him after calling nine-one-one." She lifted a bag that had been sitting on the floor in a corner. "He packed a few of your things and said he'd take care of your cat. Have you proposed to him yet?"

Darcy's cheeks turned hot as her parents laughed. Aisling crossed her arms and shrugged. "Seems like a reasonable question to me. He's a good guy."

Darcy closed her eyes. The pain meds must have been wearing off, as she was beginning to ache all over.

"I swear on Elvis's grave, Ash, if I wasn't in a hospital bed, I would totally take you down for that. We're friends, that's all."

"Good friends, you mean?" Bradley asked.

"Maybe with benefits?" Helen added.

"Mom!" Darcy's horrified shout reverberated around the room, only to be drowned out by the laughter from the other three.

A nurse opened the door. "Everybody okay in here?"

"Help me, please." Darcy held her arms out. "My family is torturing me."

The caregiver held her ground as she began to grin. "Everything looks fine to me. I'll check back later."

"Mom, you should be ashamed of yourself, thinking thoughts like that."

"Well, darling, how do you think you and your sister came into being? Do you really think the stork brought you both?"

Darcy tried glaring at her mother, but her family's continued laughter made it impossible to stay cross.

Then, her vision became cloudy. She tried to wipe away the tears that had formed. Aisling must have thought Darcy was in pain because she was at the bedside in a flash.

"Darc? Are you in pain? Do you need me to call the nurse, like for real?"

"No. I'm okay, all things considered." She sniffed. "That was the first time all four of us were having a laugh together in a long time. Okay, all three of you were having a laugh. At my expense. Still."

The room was silent for a moment. Aisling put her arms around Darcy as Helen did the same from the other side of the bed. Darcy let the tears that came flow freely. Her alcohol use disorder had been the cause of an ocean's worth of tears shed by the Gaughan family. These tears were caused by something completely different.

Happiness.

After a while, the torrent slowed, then came to a stop. A pile of tissues five inches high lay in Darcy's lap. "I didn't use all of those."

"I just didn't want you to cry alone." Aisling dabbed at the corner of her eyes with a tissue, then tossed it on the pile. "Trying to be there for you, sis."

"Same here," Helen and Bradley said in unison.

For a split second, Darcy wanted to call them dorks and toss out a joke to minimize the moment. Too many years had passed since they'd shared a moment like this one. There was no way she was going to do anything other than be appreciative.

"Thank you all for being here. And for looking out for me all those years, especially the ones when I didn't want looking out after. I love you all."

They were in the midst of a family hug when there was another knock at the door. It was Liam. Paul Gerard was at his side.

"Mind if we join the party?"

"As if you need to ask." Darcy waved them in. "To what do I owe the honor of your presence?"

Liam came to Darcy's bedside, taking the spot Aisling vacated. Paul came halfway into the room, then stopped. He scratched his forehead, then tugged at his shirt collar.

"Out with it, Detective." Darcy took a sip of water from the cup Liam offered her. "Whatever you need to say, you can say it in front of my family."

"As you wish." Paul opened a little notebook he always had close at hand. "I'd like to talk to you about your crash yesterday."

Darcy nodded. "I get it. You need to do this for my insurance since I ended up here, right?"

"Not exactly." He cleared his throat. "We have reason to believe the incident wasn't an accident."

The comment sharpened Darcy's dulled senses in the span of a heartbeat. She looked from Paul to Liam. "What do you mean? I was stone sober."

"It's nothing like that." Paul closed eyes while he took a deep breath. "It looks like you missed your driveway. Were you distracted by something?"

"Everything was fine. No, wait. My brakes got squishy, so I missed the driveway. That's why I ended up in the yard."

The detective exchanged a look with Liam, then gave a quick nod.

"Paul called me to have your jeep towed when the crash scene investigation was finished. When I got there, it was still on its side. He asked me to take a look at the undercarriage."

"What for?" Darcy kept her voice level, but she couldn't ignore the icy tendrils of dread that were clawing at her heart.

"One of the officers on the scene is a car woman, a real do-it-yourselfer." Paul glanced at his notebook. "She noticed something odd about your brakes. The emergency brake cable had been severed, and there was a hole in your brake line."

"Are you saying Darcy's jeep was tampered with?" The color drained from Helen's face as she leaned against Bradley.

"That's what they wanted me to assess," Liam said. "At first, I thought maybe both systems were damaged during your cross-country trip. With the jeep's ground clearance, that seemed unlikely, though. I got a close-up look at the spot where the cable was severed. It was a was a clean break. Like someone cut it instead of it separating due to an external force."

"And the brake line?" Darcy gripped the bed rails tight. A gut punch was coming, and there was no way to stop it.

"It was punctured. Your break lines were bone dry. By the time you got home, there was no way you could have stopped."

"I sent an officer to Rafe Majors' house," Paul said. "He found a trail of brake fluid originating at a spot where someone was parked, presumably you. We think it was done while we were meeting with Rafe."

The room was silent as the Gaughan family absorbed the terrifying news. Darcy's been threatened, shot at, and knocked around during her prior investigations. This episode had taken intimidation to an entirely different level.

Unless it was a coincidence. Maybe she ran over a rock and a nail on the way to Rafe's.

Darcy didn't believe in coincidences.

"Thanks for giving me the lowdown. Any suspects?" She picked at the cotton blanket covering her. Focusing on the perpetrator instead of the reason for the crash would keep her from falling apart. There was no time for that. Later, maybe. But not now."

Paul shook his head. "We knocked on doors. Since it was the middle of the day, not many people were home. Among the ones that were, nobody saw anything. Rafe's next-door neighbor, Mrs. Ewing, let us look at the video from her security cam. It didn't reveal anything helpful."

"Well, we know Rafe didn't do it," Liam said with a chuckle.

"Talk to Xander, Angelica's boyfriend." Darcy winced as a wave of nausea rolled through her. "I could totally see that punk doing something like this."

"We'll do that. The thing is, Darcy, whoever did this isn't messing around. They're extremely dangerous." Paul jotted down something in his notebook.

"And? I've crossed paths with dangerous before."

"And." The detective grimaced. "You need to stop investigating."

"Come on, man. You know that's not gonna happen."

"Take a look around you, Darcy. You're in a hospital bed. This is way more serious than getting knocked off your skateboard. Your brakes were tampered with for one reason. To injure you. Or worse. For your own safety, you need to stop. Right this minute."

Darcy drummed her fingers on her thigh. The police officer's demand was one hundred percent reasonable. Most sensible people would agree with the man, go back to their normal life, and be thankful they escaped serious injury. Or death.

Darcy Gaughan never was, nor would she ever be, like most people.

"Paul's right, y'all. Angelica's murderer wants me to stop poking around. The thing is, if I do that, the murderer wins. I can't allow that." She shook her head as a fire of iron resolve bloomed inside her. "They made a mistake coming for me. That makes me even more determined to catch this criminal. You poke the Darcy Gaughan bear. You're gonna get bit."

Chapter Twenty-One

Paul reviewed the details of Darcy's crash once more, then pocketed his notebook. He gave her a long look.

"In law enforcement matters, there's no such thing as a coincidence. Whoever murdered Angelica tried to murder you, too. If you won't back off, promise me you'll take every precaution possible."

"That, I can agree to." Darcy took a sip of her water. The pain medication was making her eyelids heave. "I promise on Elvis's grave to let you know if I learn something important."

Darcy asked him to hold on. "Was the coroner able to guess the height of Angelica's murderer from the bruising on Angelica's neck? I saw them do that once on *The Brokenwood Mysteries*."

"Yes. She gave us an estimation, not a guess. Why?"

"I was wondering if you could tell if the murderer was taller or shorter than Angelica based on the bruising pattern."

"Yes, as a matter of fact." Paul cracked a half-smile, then glanced at the ceiling. "That's not information we can share with the general public, though."

Message received. The murderer was taller than Angelica. That took the Hobbit off the board. Three down. No need to blow Paul's cover, though. She'd thank him for the tip later.

"Okay. Thought it couldn't hurt to ask." She put her fingers to her forehead. "I think I'm going to close my eyes for a while.

When she woke up, her parents and Aisling were the only people in the room with her.

"What happened to Liam?"

"He hung out for a while. Then he had to go to work. You've been asleep for almost three hours, sis." Aisling wheeled a cart into position by the bed. Darcy's lunch was on it, covered by a plastic meal warmer next to a bottle of green tea. "Eat up. We can't spring you if you keep acting all sickly."

"I'm not sickly. Someone tried to kill me yesterday."

"She's fine," Darcy's father took her mother's hand. "Let's go for a walk. Let Darcy Jo eat in peace."

"Really, Dad? Darcy Jo? I asked you to stop calling me that when I was like, ten."

"And you could have died yesterday, dear." Helen shrugged a handbag over her shoulder. "I think that makes it okay for us, as your parents, to refer to you as we wish."

Darcy waited until she was alone with her sister to let out a laugh. "Can you believe them? Not so long ago, they wouldn't speak to me. Now they're razzing me while I'm stuck in a hospital bed."

Aisling shook her head. "I know, right? If you don't like it, I can ask them to go back to giving you the cold shoulder treatment."

"No. I guess I'm still not used to being on good terms with you all again." Darcy lifted the cover off her lunch. It was a grilled cheese sandwich and chicken noodle soup. With a frown, she gave it a sniff. "Not exactly gourmet dining, is it?"

"I was the one who ordered it for you. Wanted something simple to make sure you can keep it down. Concussions can have weird side effects, and I'd rather you not puke up a beef stew or a burrito."

"Good point. Sorry." Darcy's cheeks got hot at the admonishment. She took a bite of the crispy sandwich and let out a sigh. "OMG, this is amazing. Double sorry, Ash."

"No big. While you were asleep, Mom, Dad, and I were talking. About you. Don't get me wrong, your crash scared us all to death. But it was a nice switch to come to your aid because you're trying to do the right thing. It's kind of weird, but does that make sense?"

"Yes, it is kind of weird." She took a slurp of the soup. It was warm without being too hot. Goldilocks would have approved of the temperature. "You know me. I know weird. It also makes perfect sense. While this impromptu family reunion is nice, let's not make meeting under these circumstances a habit. Deal?"

"Seconded." Aisling made a motion with her arm mimicking a gavel being brought down. "There being no objection, motion carried. Now, with that out of the way, who do you think did it?"

"Which one? The murder or the attempted murder?"

"Both. Though, I guess it doesn't have to be the same person. Does it? I mean, you're the expert here."

Darcy chewed on a bit of her sandwich. Now that she'd napped and was getting food into her system, her energy level was rising, which made it easier to think. Her sister had a point. While it was easy to assume the same person was responsible for both acts, it was wise to never assume.

"Expert? About valuing a used record collection, maybe. Solving a murder, not so much. And an attempted murder, even less so. But you're right. It doesn't have to be the same person. This is a small town, though. If the murderer is behind it, seems like it would be a bad move to rope someone else in. Loose lips sink ships, as Brian Johnson liked to say."

Aisling was silent for a moment. Her jaw was working as she stared at the wall. Then she leaned back and looked at the ceiling. "Oh my god, did you really quote from an AC/DC song? That's music Mom listens to."

"Straight-ahead, no-frills rock and roll. Timeless. Both the band and the quote." Darcy took another slurp of her soup.

"Whatever. This thing must influence your thinking about who the murderer is. Why don't we tease it out together? Like when we were in school and placing bets on who was going to hook up with who over summer break."

"Great memories." Darcy let out a satisfied sigh. "Okay, here goes. To start, I'm going to assume the murderer and brake line cutter are the same person. If I'm right about that, then the murderer's getting nervous."

"And cutting the brake line was a shot at scaring you into stopping."

"Yep. That would also confirm that they're local. Not some random person who happened across Angelica and killed her in a crime of opportunity. But they must not know me if they think this is going to stop me."

"Makes sense." Aisling got to her feet. "I'm sure you have a long list of suspects. Does your description fit one of them better than the others?"

"I've got two left." Darcy recounted her suspicions about Xander and Todd. "I don't see Meadows getting his hands dirty. Besides, he was wearing a suit earlier in the day."

"That leaves you with the college kid. If we're still talking about the same person doing both. Do you think he could have messed with your brakes?"

Darcy dropped her spoon into the soup cup. "I don't know. Of course, you can learn just about anything by searching the Internet."

"So, let's recap. He's young, so he might get emotional easily, especially after a drink or two, which would fit with a crime of passion like strangling. He's in college, so it's not like he couldn't blow off a couple of classes to tail you and make his move when the opportunity presented itself. And, if he needed to, he could use someone else's computer or phone to find out how to cut your brake lines. Seems to me he's your murderer."

Aisling was smart. She was thorough and meticulous. She had a great job that paid her six figures. In short, she was everything that Darcy wasn't. Or what Darcy didn't used to be. Her advice was consistently sound. She rarely said something without a decent amount of forethought.

In short, Darcy's younger sister was usually right.

This time, though, she hadn't quite been able to put the whole puzzle together.

"Sounds solid, Ash. I still can't figure out his motive for murder, though. Like, did she want to break up with him, but he didn't want to? Did that lead to a fight that went too far?"

"Sounds plausible. Wouldn't be the first time a dude lost control with a woman when he didn't get what he wanted."

"If it was that, a lover's quarrel gone wrong, why would he take her cell and the cash?" Darcy took a final bite of her sandwich and made a mental note to make grilled cheese more often.

"Maybe he had the presence of mind to try to make it look like a robbery."

Aisling snapped her fingers. "What if there was something on her phone? Like, information about the exam thing. Maybe she had something stored there that could implicate him."

"I see where you're going. It wasn't that she wanted to break up with him. He'd had enough of whatever they were doing and wanted out. She said no. They fought. He strangled her. Whether on purpose or not, that's for another day. Then he took the phone to destroy incriminating evidence and found the cash looking for her phone."

"And what college student is going to turn down a free five hundred bucks?"

The sisters grew silent. While Darcy searched her memory banks for relevant details she may have failed to mention, Aisling started ticking away on her phone.

"Everything okay?"

"Yeah. Got a text from Charlotte at the record store. She was asking how you're doing. I told her you should be going home later today."

"Thanks." Darcy scratched her head, then wiped her hand on the blanket. After everything she'd been through, her hair needed a thorough washing.

"You can thank your dude, Liam. Your employees are pretty freaked out by the crash. I told Charlotte I'd keep her in the loop. She's going to pass the info along to everyone at the store."

"The store." Darcy winced. "I'm a horrible boss. I should call them. Has Liam found my phone?"

"Yeah, about that." Aisling grasped the arms of her chair. "While you were asleep, he gave me the scoop. The cops took it into evidence. Even when you get it back, it's probably done for. He found it but couldn't get it to turn on. I'm sorry. I know you loved that phone."

The device was Darcy's first purchase after leaving the rehab facility. She'd nicknamed it Sammy in a nod to the manufacturer. It had been dropped too many times to count, left on the bar top at Selena's on three occasions, and even survived Ringo hairballing on it.

"Yeah, I did. Sammy was a total boss." She wiped away a tear. "I didn't expect to get so emotional about his death."

Aisling put her arm around Darcy. "He was by your side for, what, like

161

five years? That's a long life in cell phone years. I think I've been through three in that time."

"Thanks, sis." Darcy returned the hug. "I know it's just a thing and that I should be thankful that I didn't get hurt worse. Yeah, he can be replaced, and I back up everything to the cloud, so I won't lose anything. Still, we came a long way together."

"I know. If you want, I can take you someplace to get you a new one when they kick you out of here. With all due respect to Sammy, I'd imagine you'll want a replacement ASAP."

"Yep. I've got a case to solve, and I'll want the notes I've taken."

"Let's do some phone research, then. Move over."

The sisters were still sitting next to each other, hovering over Aisling's phone, when the nurse arrived to take Darcy to her scan. They'd settled on a new phone. Darcy refused to get into the wheelchair until she completed the payment details.

"Is a phone really more important than your health?" the nurse asked.

Darcy smiled. "Some people would say that there's nothing between my two ears so any tests y'all want to run are a waste of time. And I'm feeling a lot better since I ate."

"Better safe than sorry, Darc." Aisling helped her sister into the wheelchair. "I can deal with losing your phone but not losing you."

"Ooh, you got me." Darcy put her hands over her heart. "Sister guilt cannot be overcome."

The next few hours went by in a series of stops and starts. While being wheeled around the hospital wasn't the worst thing ever, waiting for the scan to be taken and then having to hold still during the procedure left Darcy on edge.

Worst of all was waiting for the doctor to show up to discuss the X-rays taken the previous night. While she waited, she spent the lulls in conversation with her family texting back and forth with Charlotte.

Darcy was telling the group about the tournament at The Magic Box when Aisling's phone pinged. The woman let out a snort when she read the message, then handed the phone to her older sister.

"Nope. Not gonna happen." She sent a quick response and returned the phone to its owner.

"What was so funny?" Bradley asked.

"It was Peter. You remember him from Record Store Day, right? Anyway, he wanted to let me know he was happy to volunteer to drive me around while I work on the case. He said he'll be Kato, and I can be the Green Hornet."

Bradley let out a laugh while Helen rolled her eyes. "That boy is one of a kind. I trust you're not going to take him up on his offer."

"No worries, Mom." Darcy looked out the window. A patch of blue sky had appeared among the gray clouds. She took it as a sign. A good one.

"I'd never ask one of my employees to put themselves in a position where they were potentially in harm's way."

"Good."

"I'll ask Liam instead." Darcy scratched her ear. "Instead of Cato and the Green Hornet, we'll be like Hawkeye and the Black Widow. Look out, felons. Justice is on the way."

Chapter Twenty-Two

Darcy and her parents were outside the hospital's main entrance, waiting for Aisling to pull up. She'd been discharged with instructions to rest and take over-the-counter pain medication as needed. The doctor had offered to write a script for something stronger. Darcy declined. She didn't want to risk the temptation of a narcotic. One battle with addiction in her lifetime was enough.

No need to tempt fate.

"Are you sure you're going to be okay?" Helen gave Darcy's hand a squeeze. It was a simple gesture, but one that brought a tear to the tough sleuth's eyes.

"I'll be fine. Ash is going to take me home and hang out until Liam gets there. Y'all have missed enough work already." Everything she said was true. As Darcy hugged her parents, she told herself omitting a few details would leave them less to worry about.

The rock gods knew she'd given them a lifetime's worth of worries in the last decade.

Aisling insisted on buckling her sister into the passenger seat. "One wild ride is enough. Where do you want to go? I assume not home."

Darcy opened her mouth to protest, then clamped it shut. Her sister was right. Besides, the question indicated she wanted to help with the investigation until she had to head back home.

"You know you're gonna get in trouble big time if Mom and Dad find out about this." Darcy grinned as she let out an evil laugh. "Corrupting my little sister once again."

"You wish." Aisling piloted her black Chevy into traffic. "I could tell you some stories that would set your hair on fire. You're not the only Gaughan girl who's taken a few walks on the wild side."

"Lou Reed. Nice." Darcy rubbed the back of her neck. "In honor of that stellar reference, I won't ask for details. How about we get my phone, then head to the record store."

Aisling gave a thumbs up. "Letting your employees know you're okay with a visit. I like that."

"That's totally what I had in mind. Well, that, and I want to take a long look at the suspect board in my office."

"Girl, you are hopeless." Aisling shook her head. "In a good way this time."

A little while later, after picking up the new phone and surprising everyone at work, there was a knock on the door of Darcy's office. Izzy entered, laden with two bulging shopping bags in each hand.

"Provisions have arrived." She set the bags on Darcy's desk with a grunt. In seconds, the room was filled with the aroma of spicy Mexican food from Selena's. Darcy's stomach growled loud enough that Aisling and Izzy exchanged a look.

"Can someone cut a girl some slack? I've only eaten once in the last twenty-four hours." Darcy stuffed two tortilla chips into her mouth. "Good golly, Miss Molly, Selena's never smelled so good. Let's dig in. And y'all can tell me how open mic went last night."

While Aisling and Izzy were laying out the impromptu buffet, Darcy wandered out to the sales floor. Charlotte was counting the cash in the register. Hank was putting merchandise that had been left out back where it belonged. Peter was gathering the trash. There were no customers to be seen.

"For the first time since I've owned this place, I'm glad there are no shoppers. Peeps, Marysburg Music is closed for the day." She nodded in Charlotte's direction. "I take it, you already posted notices on social media?"

"That I did. It's been killing us to stay out here while you've been in the back with your sister." Her hand covered her mouth. "Sorry about that. You know, with everything that went down yesterday."

"No worries. Peter, turn off the sign and lock the door. Hank, the rest of the tidying can wait until tomorrow. Let's eat. And see if we can solve a couple of crimes in the process."

Between her desk chair and the two visitor chairs, Darcy's office could seat three comfortably. On the rare occasion there was an all-team meeting, the group met on the sales floor.

This time, with the mouth-watering spread to be devoured, there were no objections to squeezing in together. There was a determined vibe in the air. One with a sense of purpose. Sure, it was fabulous to share a taco bar with all the fixings, even empanadas.

One of their own had been hurt, though.

When the chips were down, Marysburg Music's little band pulled together. They'd been through a lot together and were almost as much of a family to Darcy as her biological one.

"Aren't we going to talk about what happened to you yesterday?" Hank crossed his arms when Darcy handed him a plate.

"Yes, we will." She poked him in the stomach with it. "First, we eat. I need some positive mojo."

"In that case, Boss," Peter said through a mouthful of black beans, "Izzy's got some news from you. Yesi."

"Out with it, young lady. Good news will help make my aches and pains go away faster."

Izzy's cheeks turned pink. "I wanted to tell you in private, Darcy. You've done so much for me and my dream of playing the bass. It's about my audition for Ball State's music school earlier this week."

The room became silent. Even Peter stopped crunching on tortilla chips. It was only February. Too early for the school to notify prospective students whether they'd been accepted. That usually happened in April. The young woman was bouncing up and down on her toes, though.

"Well, don't keep me hanging. What is it?"

"I got accepted! It's not official, but I got a text from someone who knows someone, and they said it's a done deal."

Darcy let out a whoop and opened her arms wide. "Congratulations, Izzy. Come give me a hug. Just don't squeeze too tight."

With tears in her eyes, Izzy embraced Darcy. The onlookers broke into a round of applause. It was a moment of joy and levity the group needed.

After a round of hugs and toasts in Izzy's honor, Aisling cleared her throat. "Hate to be a party pooper, but I gotta hit the road soon. Is it okay if we get down to business?"

"Yes. Store business first. I can't very well let us go out of business, can I? Char, any news on our surprise concert coming up?"

"Yes. I finalized the details with Pixie Dust's manager yesterday. They'll be here a week from Saturday. The event will start at three. First, there will be a forty-five-minute concert. The band wants to play a couple of songs from their new record; then they want you to play with them for the last half hour or so. After that, there will be a meet-and-greet. We're going to budget an hour for that, which should give them plenty of time to make their soundcheck at Emens. I was going to start posting about it today, but after yesterday, I thought I should hold off on a final decision."

Playing a musical instrument at any level wasn't easy. Performing at the pinnacle of the profession as a touring musician took years of dedication and lots of blood, sweat, and tears spent rehearsing. And that was for someone who was in good physical condition.

Darcy was far from being in the kind of physical condition to play loud, aggressive, and fast Pixie Dust tunes. It didn't matter if she wasn't going to let an attempt on her life stop her from investigating Angelica's murder. There was no way in the world she was going to let bumps, bruises, and soreness keep her from playing with her old bandmates.

"Full steam ahead, Char. The time I spend between now and then practicing will be good physical therapy for these old bones. I'll leave it to you to hammer out the details. Feel free to delegate as you see fit." Darcy rubbed her hands together. "Now, are we ready to find a murderer?"

"Totally," Izzy said. She removed the blanket covering the suspect board. "Nobody comes for our boss and gets away with it."

"Let's rock and roll." Darcy stood while the group ate. She brought them up to speed with new developments.

Charlotte went pale during the portion of the report that covered the brake sabotage. Hank, on the other hand, balled his hands into fists. When Darcy wasn't sure about something, Aisling filled in the blanks. Izzy wrote down new information on the whiteboard. In all, the briefing took fifteen minutes.

"So, who does that leave us with?" Peter asked when Darcy finished.

Izzy tapped on the board with her dry-erase marker. "Xander, Meadows, and a mystery person."

"Why do you think there's a mystery suspect out there somewhere?" Darcy took a bite of a soft taco after asking the question. There was nothing solid that could point the investigation in a different direction, but she couldn't deny the niggling sensation in the back of her brain that Izzy wasn't wrong.

"Whoever murdered Angelica's keeping tabs on you. That's the only way they would have known where you were to mess with your brakes."

Darcy raised an eyebrow as she looked toward Aisling. The two of them agreed with the assessment. Izzy had previously shared that her mom liked to watch mysteries. Sometimes, she'd watch alongside her mother. That time together was paying off in an unexpected but welcome way.

"Okay, why Xander and this mystery person?" Darcy leaned forward in her chair, forcing herself to keep her eagerness in check by not jumping to conclusions.

"If we can find out if he was in class or at his fraternity house when Rusty was messed with, then he would have needed someone else to do the job for him. Maybe one of his frat brothers."

"He's a little too prissy to get his hands dirty, if you ask me." Peter pointed with a chip at the board. "I'd lay money that he talked one of his buddies to do it for him."

Hank shook his head. "That's a tall order, asking a friend to commit a crime like that. We're talking about a manslaughter charge."

"Or attempted murder." Charlotte went to the board. "You make really good points, Peter. Be straight with me, though. If a friend of yours asked you to cut someone's brake lines, what would you do?"

"Depends on whose brake lines I'm cutting." The young man put up his hands. "Just kidding. I'd tell you and Darcy. Doing something like that could totally crash my dreams of playing Carnegie Hall."

CHAPTER TWENTY-TWO

"And it would be wrong," Charlotte said.

"Yeah. That too." Peter nodded. "Of course. That's why I wouldn't do it. I mean, especially in this town. Someone asking me to cut Darcy Gaughan's brake lines? When she's investigating a murder? Might as well be admitting to killing Angelica."

The group discussed the mystery suspect idea for a while. While they did, Darcy sat back and listened. Something that Peter had said was bothering her. In her tired and still-somewhat muddled state, she couldn't put her finger on it, though. Whatever it was could wait until morning when she was fresh from a good night's sleep.

"Okay, peeps, I'm bringing this brainstorming session to a close. Ash has a long drive tonight, and I can't wait to see my cat and give him a hug." Darcy struggled to her feet, grimacing as she did so. She was past due for more pain medication. In the hope of having a clear head during the discussion, she'd put off taking it at the scheduled time.

And was beginning to feel the effects of that decision now.

"Get a good night's sleep, everyone. Tomorrow's gonna be a good day."

Darcy was almost to the door when Hank tapped her on the shoulder. "I know you well enough to know you're planning on coming in. I trust you're not going to try riding your skateboard."

"No. I've made other arrangements. I appreciate you looking out for me, dude." She gave the man a hug and strode into the dark, chill night with her sister on her arm.

"Other arrangements," Aisling asked when they were in her car.

"Yeah. I'm pretty sure Liam will be stopping by the cabin soon. I'll see if I can talk him into giving me a ride."

"Really? Are you going to make this request tonight or in the morning?"

"My dear sister." Darcy patted her on the arm. "A lady doesn't kiss and tell."

Aisling snorted and put the car in gear. "Don't get me wrong, but you're no lady."

"True. Which is why I'll tell you now. I'll ask him tonight." She gave her sister a wink. "After I convince him to stay the night."

Chapter Twenty-Three

"Wakey, wakey. It's time for your meds." Liam gave Darcy's shoulder a gentle shake.

"Go away." She pulled the quilt over her head and rolled the other way. Then she let out a howl as her back protested the abrupt move. After a few deep breaths, the pain subsided enough for her to push the covers from her head.

"Okay, maybe it is time for some pain reliever."

With a laugh, he left the medication on the bedstand. She found him in the kitchen. A mug of steaming tea sat on the table while he hovered over the electric stove, stirring eggs in a cast iron skillet. He paused in mid-stir when two slices of toast popped up. With one hand, he placed the toast on a plate while he added sliced peppers to the eggs. He was humming a tune, the refrain from "123456" by Fitz & The Tantrums.

"Breakfast is almost ready. Take a load off and tell me how your investigation's going."

She took a sip of the tea. The chai spices tickled her tongue. They also helped wake her up. Her stomach growled when he placed her breakfast in front of her.

"Wow. You didn't have to do all this."

"I figure you deserve some TLC after the past couple of days. I can't compete with Selena's, but I like to think I can make a decent omelet."

"You can make an amazing omelet." She bit into a piece of toast the moment he set the plate in front of her. "OMG, this is so good. Thanks for keeping an eye on me last night, by the way."

"Totally my pleasure. I had paperwork I've been needing to catch up on. Besides, your sister texted me three times to make sure you were okay. Being here made it easy to reassure you were, in fact, okay. That's a nice recliner to crash in, by the way. Ringo's a solid sleeping buddy."

"Yeah, sleeping's one of the things he excels at. I take it Ash got home okay?"

"She did." He slid a massive pile of scrambled eggs onto a plate and joined her at the table. "She's really worried about you. I don't blame her. That was some scary business."

"Business." Darcy let out a laugh. "That's a nice word for crashing my beloved Rusty. How is he?"

"He's locked behind a chain-link fence as evidence, so I can't give you a solid answer. Based on what I saw at the crash site, it doesn't look good. I'm sorry."

Darcy took a drink. The thought of having to say goodbye to her unglamorous, but reliable jeep broke her heart. While she took a second drink, her emotions shifted to anger. The vehicle had been a friend to her, a reliable sidekick. It deserved a fate better than being consigned to a junk yard because someone was threatened by her.

"It's not fair. Insurance will probably want to total it and give me a check for, like, a hundred bucks. That's not gonna fly. First, I'm going to figure out who killed Angelica. Then I'm going to rescue Rusty."

They clinked mugs. "About that first part. Ash told me about your meeting at the store. What's this about a mystery suspect?"

She gave him a report while they ate breakfast, even going so far as to use the salt and pepper shaker to represent key pieces of information and suspects.

"The more I think about it, the more it makes sense that there has to be someone else involved. You know me. I'd never be mistaken for a fan of Todd Meadows. But to kill your intern? I don't know."

"What about her boyfriend, then?" Liam got up to give Ringo, who had just wandered into the kitchen, his breakfast.

"He makes more sense to me. If he's got an alibi for when Rusty was sabotaged, then that's where the mystery person comes in."

"Then call Paul." He tore a piece of toast in half. "I know he's not supposed to talk to you about the murder case, but you're the victim of the crash. Seems to me you ought to be able to ask him for an update about that."

"Will do." She looked at the clock on the microwave. "When I'm at the store. I gotta get a shower."

"I'll clean up here while you do that. I don't want your sister thinking I left dirty dishes around when I promised I'd keep an eye on you. That'd be a bad look."

"I don't think you have anything to worry about there, my friend." Darcy gave him a long kiss on the lips, then headed for the bathroom. "Don't forget Ringo's litter box. Forgetting that would definitely make for a bad look. And a bad smell."

Darcy turned the shower setting to the hottest setting and adjusted the flow to the massage setting. The hot water soothed her achy body and relaxed her mind. As she lathered shampoo into her hair, she pondered what her next step in the investigation should be.

Then, as the water pounded her neck and back with rhythmic patterns, a thought came to her.

A bad look.

Or look bad.

What if the murder wasn't a crime of passion? What if the murderer committed the act in a way to make someone else take the fall? Who would stand to lose the most by being framed? And who would gain from that loss?

Darcy went to her original list of suspects. Bethan would lose her job, but the young woman didn't seem to have a lot of material wealth. Not so for Xander. He'd have to leave school. A murder conviction might lead to him being written out of his parents' will, too. From what Darcy had heard, they had serious bucks. That would be a lot for the young man to lose.

If Rafe went to jail, what would he lose? His house was mortgage-free. The building that was home to Marysburg Music wasn't, though. Who stood to gain if Rafe got behind on that mortgage?

Todd Meadows.

Not wanting to jump to conclusions, she let her thoughts drift to the Hobbit while she rinsed her hair. O'Sullivan had complained about business being off following the murder. He was the only tenant in his building. He used the second floor for storage. If he went to jail, the survival of both The Magic Box and The Comic Castle would depend on someone assuming control. If that didn't happen, there was a strong possibility that they'd close. Who benefitted from that unfortunate occurrence?

Once again, Todd Meadows.

Marysburg's preeminent developer would like nothing more than to get his hands on the record store's building. Like water, it had slipped through his fingers once. There was no doubt he'd relish the thought of getting his hands on it for good this time.

His mixed-use condo development had needed the record store's property. The project seemingly died when Rafe decided to keep the property after inheriting it from his stepdad. The project had come to fewer than ten months prior, though. It was entirely possible that the venture could be revived.

And it if couldn't? Then Todd could snap up the property that the Hobbit was renting and redevelop it. It wasn't in a location as desirable as the Marysburg Music location, but the money Todd could make would still be green, even if the pile of it wouldn't be quite as large.

Darcy continued to sift through the idea while she put on a pair of yoga pants and an oversized sweatshirt with an image of Tony Bennett on it. As much as she despised Todd Meadows, she couldn't get around the fact that he had said nothing but good things about Angelica.

They weren't the warmest comments, sure. But they hadn't indicated any animosity toward the deceased. After all, it was one thing to obtain a piece of property by buying it. It was something completely different to get one's hands on it by committing murder.

Where did that leave Darcy?

She found Liam in the kitchen. The hand-washed dishes were on a drying rack. He had a dish towel in his hands and was putting them away after wiping each one down.

"D, it's time to get yourself a dishwasher. You've updated everything else in this place." He draped the damp towel over the sink faucet.

"Yeah, how about we put a pin in that for now. What would you say if I told you I thought Todd Meadows might be the murderer?"

Liam scratched his chin, then ran his hands through his brown hair. "I'd say that I know you don't like the guy and that he's smarmy. But a murderer?"

"Fair enough." She shrugged into her coat. "Let me tell you my thoughts on the drive to the record store. I'll be home early tonight, Ringo, promise. Later, skater."

Typically, the drive wasn't long, fifteen minutes tops if traffic was bad. And that had only happened once, when two cars had collided. Nobody had been injured in the crash, thank goodness, but it had caused a detour through a neighborhood with multiple speed pumps. Darcy never wanted to drive to work that way again.

Currently, there were no traffic back-ups, so Darcy only had ten minutes or so to lay out her case for Todd Meadows being the murderer. When she finished, Liam shrugged.

"I'm not saying he didn't do it. After all, he was in the vicinity not long before she was murdered. I think you need to figure out what kind of coat he had with him that night. If it was one with buttons, maybe you've got something."

"Good point." Darcy made a note in her new phone. She was unlikely to forget Liam's suggestion. It was more of a way to learn her way around the device. "I'll do that. I'll also see if I can find out whether Todd's kind words about Angelica were for real or a big fat lie."

A moment later, they arrived in front of Marysburg Music. Liam parked his truck and went around to the passenger side to help Darcy make her exit. She thanked him for the helping hand by giving him a kiss on the lips, a rarity for her since she wasn't comfortable with public displays of affection beyond high fives and the occasional hug.

She made a silent vow to get better with PDAs with Liam in the future. He'd earned it.

Since Darcy had insisted her team members stop working the previous evening to participate in the dinner meeting, there was still tidying that needed to be done. She started with the restroom. Even though her back protested when she bent over, she didn't quit. She needed the physical activity to work the soreness and stiffness out. It would also help her prep for the upcoming gig.

"Holy Mother of Music, I'm actually going to play a set with Pixie Dust. What in the world was I thinking?"

"That playing with them will help heal some of your wounds that are still open."

Darcy let out a yelp as she almost jumped onto the toilet stool. She wheeled on her visitor, brandishing the toilet bowl brush like a weapon.

"Are you trying to murder me? You almost gave me a heart attack." She braced herself against the vanity as her heart banged away against her ribcage. "I'm in no condition to for surprises like that."

Charlotte stared at her, wide-eyed. The woman held a to-go drink cup in one hand and a paper bag in the other.

"I am so sorry, Darc." She extended her arms toward her friend. "Breakfast?"

Darcy tried to glare at her friend but couldn't stay upset with the woman. Instead, she cracked a smile and let out a shaky laugh. "Sounds amazing."

A second breakfast sounded good. After all, she told herself, she was still down a meal due to missing dinner the night of the crash. She'd gotten adept at rationalizing almost anything for a drink before she got sober. It was pleasing to find out the skill hadn't abandoned her.

And could be put to use in much less destructive ways than in the past.

They chose to sit by the cash register. After the crowded meeting in the office, Charlotte wanted "some elbow room" while they dined. After checking that Darcy was feeling okay and not experiencing any headaches, she moved the conversation to the investigation.

"Any lightbulb moments since last night?"

"Maybe." Darcy took a bite of the blueberry croissant Charlotte had given her. After swallowing, she recounted her idea and conversation with Liam. "What do you think?"

"It's possible. You're right about needing to find a picture of him in a coat that night. You want me to do that?"

"No. Now that I've been thinking about it a while, I ran into him last week outside the Comic Castle. He was wearing a leather coat with a zipper."

"Doesn't mean he wasn't wearing one with buttons the night Angelica was murdered. Wasn't he in a suit and tie during the awards ceremony?"

When Darcy nodded, Charlotte grinned. "Let me do this for you. Spare your bruised brain the pain of wading through gobs of social media posts."

"Just the latest example of why you are the best general manager in the history of general managers." The women exchanged a hug. "I'm going to do some day job work. Give me a shout if you find something."

Fifteen minutes later, there was a knock on the office door. Darcy told Charlotte to come on in. "I need a couple of minutes to finish payroll. What's up?"

With an ear-to-ear smile, Char held her phone out to Darcy. "I think I found the Holy Grail."

"Ooh, gimme." Darcy snatched the device from her General Manager. Her heart skipped a beat as she stared at the screen.

It was a photo of Todd taken the previous December. He and a few other local business luminaries were at the ribbon-cutting ceremony for the new headquarters of Meadows Real Estate & Property Management. He had an oversized pair of scissors in his hands. Angelica and Jasmine were on opposite sides of the building's main entryway, each holding one end of a red ribbon that he was about to cut.

"Good golly, Miss Molly, what do we have here?" Todd, like everyone else in the shot, was wearing a coat. His was a navy peacoat style. With lots of buttons.

"I know, right?" Char made a fist pump. "I was looking at Todd's social media feed from around the time of the tournament. Talk about a total exhibitionist. You'd think the dude lived on the French Riviera, the way he frames his posts. Anyway, I remembered there was a shindig to celebrate his new office. So, I went back in time a few weeks, and there you go."

"This is platinum record material, girl. You are a total rockstar. You want to ask the million-dollar question?"

Charlotte grinned. "Why was Todd wearing a different coat when you saw him last week?"

"Bingo. I'm buying you lunch for all this." She looked at the photo again/ After a moment, she brought it closer to her face. "Huh. That's interesting."

"What is?"

"Everyone in the picture's smiling, except for one. Jasmine." Darcy handed the phone back.

"Hmm. I missed that. What do you think it means?"

"Could be a million things. Maybe she didn't like being out in the cold—"

"Something you can identify with." Char let out a little chuckle.

"Truth. Or maybe she thought the whole ribbon-cutting thing was dumb and couldn't wait for it to be over. Or, and I can't believe I'm saying this, what if she wasn't happy with Angelica being in the picture."

The hair on the back of Darcy's neck stood on end. A sure sign she was on to something.

"Meaning?"

"Everyone knows Todd's with women in his life. It's not a good one. What if Jasmine felt threatened by Angelica? I mean, after years of pursuit, she finally got her man, and then he went and hired this attractive young woman."

"Okay. Let's think this through. You're suggesting that this picture could be an indication that Jasmine was jealous of Angelica and that jealousy drove her to murder?"

Charlotte nodded. "I know how it sounds. Awful gender stereotyping. We women should be lifting each other up, not tearing each other down. But...."

"I don't like the idea, either. You need to follow facts, though. You've said hey, create the narrative. Not the other way around."

"Point taken." Darcy put up her hand. "We've put the needle down. Let the record play. So, what do we know?"

Charlotte held up three fingers. "One, Todd brought Angelica on as an intern. Two, he spoke highly of her. Three, he was at The Magic Box the night of the tournament."

"Good." Darcy wrote the facts on the suspect board. "I saw Todd and

Jasmine at Selena's before the awards ceremony. And then, last week, I saw them at her gallery. Both times, they were arguing. I couldn't tell why they were fighting, though."

The store's phone rang. Charlotte turned to leave. "I'll get it. You keep thinking."

Darcy drummed her fingers on the desktop. She turned the scenario around and around in her head to study it from every direction imaginable. After a while, she threw her hands up in the air. There was no way to avoid the inevitable conclusion.

She was going to have to pay Jasmine Longoria a visit. And ask some pointed and personal questions while there.

It was going to be like going straight into the center of a tiger's lair. With no guarantee of escape.

Chapter Twenty-Four

D arcy was on the sales floor, pricing new merchandise, when Liam entered the store.

"Someone call Simmons' Rideshare Service?" He sauntered toward the cash register as Darcy turned on her heel and made her toward the office.

"Don't look at me." Charlotte pointed at her co-worker. "I'm not the one who's transportationally challenged at the moment. Where are y'all going?"

"He's taking me to get my rental car." She slipped a pink hoodie with a *Barbie, the Movie* logo on it, over her head. Even the snow was gone; the temperature was hanging around in the low forties, a sign that Old Man Winter wasn't finished with Central Indiana just yet.

"Ooh, did you get a Mustang or something cool like that?" Charlotte asked.

"No such luck. Insurance won't cover something beyond the basics. I'm guessing I'm going to be stuck with a boring four-door."

"Beats walking," Liam said. "And nobody will know it's you behind the wheel. You'll be able to surprise your suspects this way."

"That's a very good point." Darcy's mood brightened. The element of surprise was going to come in handy with what she had planned. "I'll bring you up to speed on the way."

Liam let out a low whistle when Darcy finished telling him her new theory. "Let me get this straight. Now, you're thinking Jasmine killed Angelica in a fit of jealousy because she thought Todd and Angelica were getting busy."

Darcy stared straight ahead. The rental agency, situated on the north side of Muncie, was almost in sight. Could she say the same for the young woman's murderer? No. At least, not yet.

"I know it sounds like something straight out of a bad crime novel from the nineteen-fifties. Especially when you put it so bluntly."

Liam brought the truck to a stop as they arrived at a red light. "I'm not saying that. Okay, I guess I kind of am, but it's not a bad idea. Think about it. How long has Jasmine had a thing for Todd?"

She pondered the question. "I remember Jasmine being after Todd back when I was still drinking. That would mean six or seven years. Maybe more."

"Exactly." The rental agency was on the left-hand side of the road. Liam merged into the turn lane. "We know they had an affair going on while he was still married to his second wife. When he got divorced, he claimed Jasmine was the love of his life. What if he never really got over his wandering eye, and it settled on Angelica?"

"That'd be gross." Darcy drummed her fingers on the armrest as Liam pulled into a parking spot. "The guy's old enough to be her father. And he was her boss. It would be a slam-dunk case of sexual harassment. Or worse."

"You're right." Liam put the truck in park but didn't shut off the engine. "I don't want you to think I'm victim blaming because I'm totally not. I just want to make sure you've thought through all the angles before you confront Jasmine."

"Thank you. I appreciate it." Darcy gave his hand a reassuring squeeze. "In your scenario, that would mean Angelica wouldn't have been a harassment victim. She would have been a willing partner."

Liam grimaced. "Man, I don't like the picture this paints of Angelica."

"Right? It also doesn't give us an answer to why the button was at the scene. Unless Jasmine put it there."

"To frame Todd. Kind of like we thought he was trying to frame Rafe and the Hobbit?"

Darcy shivered as she opened the truck's door. "It would make for one cold, calculating she-devil if that's what went down."

"What's your next move? You sure you want to confront Jasmine? Maybe now would be a good time to call Paul Gerard."

"Good idea." She leaned back in to give Liam a kiss. "Doing that will help me figure out my next play. Talk soon."

With a half-dozen scenarios running around in her head, Darcy jogged toward the rental agency office. She'd kept her answer to Liam's questions vague on purpose in the hope he'd think she was, in fact, going to confer with the police.

In fact, as she entered the building, Darcy didn't know what her next move was. That was because there was still a key part of the puzzle song that was missing.

How did the ledger fit into everything?

She set the investigation aside so she could focus on completing the rental agreement. The rock gods must have been smiling on her because she ended up with a gray Kia Soul. While it was no Jeep, it looked like her beloved Rusty enough to satisfy her longing to be reunited with her own wheels.

On the drive back to Marysburg, Darcy called the store. "Wanted to test out the Bluetooth setup in this way cool rental. How are things there?"

"Quiet for now," Charlotte said. "Though my stomach is rumbling, and somebody promised me lunch today."

"On it. I'll stop and get us a pizza. By the way, you're a numbers person, so let me ask you this. Let's suppose for the moment that Angelica and Todd had something personal going on. How do you think the ledger she kept would fit into the picture?"

"I can think of a couple of things. I'll tell you more when you get here. Now get off the phone before you get distracted by all the rental's bells and whistles."

A half-hour later, Darcy and Charlotte were seated behind the sales counter, munching on a supreme pizza, while a handful of shoppers meandered throughout the store. They were studying the photographs of the makeshift ledger Darcy found.

"Gotta hand it to you, Darc. I was never allowed to eat in front of clients at my old gig. Promise you'll let me work here forever?"

"Done." She wiped her hands on a paper napkin. The pie was delicious, but a bit of grease was unavoidable when one had pepperoni and sausage among the ingredients. "What do you make of these figures?"

"I don't think this is a case of money laundering, if that's what you're asking."

Darcy's jaw almost hit the counter. She'd been so focused on murder that financial criminal activity never occurred to her.

"I'm not. Good to know, though."

Charlotte chewed on a bite of crust while she studied the images. "Well, it's definitely tracking income and expenses. My guess is that these are cash transactions."

"Why do you say that?"

"We conduct so many of our financial transactions electronically these days, that there's always a paper trail, even if it's electronic. Even paper checks leave a trail. Why would Angelica need, or even want to, keep track of all this if she didn't have to?"

Darcy nodded. "Unless she had something to hide."

"Exactly. Cash is easy to hide. And even easier to move around." Charlotte pointed at one of the figures. "You can see the money went out almost as fast as it came in. And she spent almost all of it."

"Not exactly building a nest egg, was she? I get that she probably wanted to dress professionally for her internship, which might get expensive if Todd insisted on formal business attire. This seems excessive, doesn't it? I'll admit, I'm not exactly the best person to talk fashion."

"You are if I want to look like a punk rocker." Charlotte gave Darcy a friendly elbow to the ribs, then took a moment to ring up a sale of two Tina Turner records. "Long live the Queen of Rock n Roll."

When the purchaser stepped away with their musical treasure, Char tapped her finger on the image. "Now that I think about it, this reminds me of a backwards expense account. Instead of making a purchase and submitting the expense for reimbursement, someone gave her money to spend."

"I remember when we were on tour and had a per diem. At the beginning, we got by on ten bucks a day. I'd save up my loose change and treat myself to a nice meal at Subway or Chipotle at the end of the week. By the time the band let me go, the situation had gotten a whole lot better."

Darcy closed her eyes. Crossing the country in a beat-up cargo van.

Sleeping among, and sometimes underneath, equipment, brushing her hair and teeth in a travel plaza bathroom. It was a crazy couple of years. And she loved every minute of it.

She didn't miss it, though. Not one bit.

"I never knew that." Charlotte put her arm around Darcy. "I know it's tough for you to talk about those days. Thank you for sharing that."

Darcy returned the hug. "Well, one way to expel ghosts is to confront them. Let them know you aren't afraid of them. With the performance coming up, I need to do some serious ghost expelling."

The women were quiet for a moment as they made the pizza disappear. Then, Charlotte raised her index finger. "Hold on. I think I know what these figures are. You've heard stories of college-aged women looking for sugar daddies, right? They connect with wealthy, older men to provide companionship. Kind of like dating."

"Yeah." Darcy didn't like sugar daddy arrangements. She found them creepy. But, given her past, she was hardly one to judge the choices other women made to make ends meet.

"What if Angelica was someone's sugar baby, and this was the way she kept track of the financial part of the arrangement?"

"Great balls of fire." Darcy rose to attention as a bolt of energy surged through her. "If you're right, you know what that means? There's been one man in her life who fits that profile."

"You mean a certain realtor?" Charlotte glanced at the shoppers. Apparently, she didn't want to drop names in front of people she didn't know. Hank was right. It was possible the customers knew the murderer and would come to their defense by tipping them off to Darcy and Charlotte's suspicions.

"I do." Darcy rubbed her palms back and forth against each other. "Angelica started working for him at the start of the fall semester. What if she turned Todd's wandering eye to her advantage? She supposedly spent a lot of time at the agency. Maybe it wasn't all work. Maybe he paid her off the books to hang out with him."

Charlotte nodded. "And she kept track of the cash he gave her and how she spent it. That's what the ledger was for."

The customers left, giving the women a chance to kick their brainstorming into high gear.

"An under-the-radar relationship would also help explain why Todd sponsored the Magic Box tournament's grand prize. He did it for Angelica. Because he knew she had a good chance of winning."

"Didn't you tell me the reason Rafe got all honked off was because of some new, secret scoring formula?"

"Yes!" Darcy clapped her hands and did a three-hundred and sixty-degree spin. The puzzle was finally coming together. "That was a way to make sure Angelica won."

"Something must have gone wrong, though."

"In the worst kind of way. Maybe Todd actually had a crisis of conscience and decided to break it off."

"Or." Charlotte twirled a pen in her hand. "He wanted to take the relationship to another level, but she turned him down. He's not the kind of guy to take rejection gracefully."

Darcy was typing notes into her phone as fast as her fingers would allow. Both of the scenarios were possible. She asked Charlotte for other suggestions. Now was not the time to bypass an idea for the sake of expediency.

"On the flip side, what if Todd wasn't the decision-maker? What if Angelica decided to call things off."

"Good one." Darcy closed her eyes and took a breath. "How about this? Angelica decides she's done but plays nice long enough to make sure she gets a final score by winning the tournament. Later that night, she tells Todd. They argue. He loses his cool and chokes her. Then he takes the cash—"

"Because he thought it was his to begin with and got rid of her phone as a precaution." Charlotte put her hand up for a high five.

Darcy slapped it with enough gusto that she had to shake her hand out afterward. "Now all I gotta do is figure out how to prove it."

Char's shoulders slumped. "There is that. Todd's no dummy. He'd know to cover his tracks."

"Which makes my next move easy." Darcy moved toward the office. "Do you mind holding down the fort until the kids get here?

"Sure. What are you going to do?"

"I'm going to pay Todd a visit. I'm going to wrangle a confession out of him."

Chapter Twenty-Five

Darcy stopped at the Big Bean coffee shop before she began her manhunt in earnest. Todd Meadows was shrewd. He was confident. He was charismatic. He was wealthy, too. In short, he was the kind of man who wouldn't crumble under pressure. Especially when it came from someone like Darcy, who he didn't respect.

She sipped a green tea at her favorite window table, trying to decide how to confront the man. It was like planning a concert setlist. First, she had to get his attention. Then, she needed to draw him in so she could control the narrative. Last, but not least, she would need to bring the showdown to a close in a way that left no doubt Darcy was the winner.

Anything less than one hundred percent effort and execution would result in Todd escaping through her fingertips. Angelica deserved better than that.

While she stared at the steam rising from her cup, making tiny curlicues in the air, an idea popped into Darcy's head. Maybe the path forward was through Jasmine. If Darcy approached her about "rumors" that Todd was cheating on her with Angelica, how would the woman react?

Jasmine Longoria was as successful an entrepreneur as Todd Meadows. In fact, a strong argument could be made that she was even better. He inherited the family real estate and development company from his father. She built the fine art gallery from the ground up. How had she done it? By applying savvy business principles to every decision she made. In a small town, no less

In short, the woman made decisions based on what her brain told her, not her heart. She wouldn't be surprised by the news of Todd's infidelity. Or would she? If Jasmine truly had feelings for Todd, maybe she would have missed clues about his abhorrent behavior.

Assuming, of course, that Darcy's assumption was correct.

Correct or not, making an emotional appeal to either Todd or Jasmine wasn't likely to work. A different approach might, though. She let her thoughts drift, staying open to other ideas that might form. After a few minutes, a winner coalesced in her mind.

What would Eddie do in a situation like this?

Darcy's mentor had legendary people skills. When one was in the man's presence, it often felt like they were the only person in the world that mattered to Eddie. He knew how to turn on the charm without coming across as smarmy. He also knew how to show respect without appearing subservient.

The man read people better than anyone Darcy had crossed paths with. So, how would he approach Todd and Jasmine? He'd give them what they wanted by appealing to their value to the community, their status, their power.

In short, Eddie would appeal to their vanity.

She would do the same. She hoped. Small talk never had been and never would be her strong suit.

"Forget that negative thinking, girl." She pounded her fist on her thigh. "I'm right. It's time to prove it."

Her phone's ringtone went off when she was walking to her rental. It was Paul Gerard. *Please tell me they caught Angelica's murderer.* It would save her so much energy, both physical and emotional.

No such luck. He was calling to see how she was feeling.

"Headache's gone. Still a little sore, especially where the seatbelt was. Any news on who did the dirty deed?"

"No." He was quiet for a moment, as if debating what to say next. "Look, I know you really want to keep your own investigation on track. Now more than ever, it's time for you to stand down."

"I appreciate it, Paul. I really do." She slipped into the car. It was too cold to carry on a conversation out in the elements. "This isn't about just me, though."

"Darcy, it is. I'm talking about your personal safety."

"And the best way for me to ensure my own safety is to put Angelica's murderer behind bars. Are you close to making an arrest?"

"You know I can't talk about that." He dropped a curse word. It was the first time Darcy had ever heard him use foul language. "Fine, you win. No. We're not. Xander's lawyered up, and with O'Sullivan and Majors both in the clear, we're at a standstill. Have you found anything?"

She started the car's engine. The least she could do was give Paul some help. Without incriminating herself in anything, of course. And without delaying her impending showdown.

"That spreadsheet thing I found. It makes me wonder if it was an expense account for Angelica, like an allowance. Not payments from an exam cheating scheme."

"You're not suggesting she was involved in drug trafficking, are you? That's a serious accusation."

"No, nothing like that." The call was taking too long. She needed to end it without alienating Paul. "More like, I don't know, appearance fees. When I was with Pixie Dust, every now and then, we'd be asked to show up at some big party or event. We got paid for just being there and hanging around for a while. A lot of celebrities make decent bank by being seen at events. I've heard Justin Timberlake can take in a million bucks per appearance."

Darcy crossed her fingers, hoping the suggestion would put Paul on the right track.

"She was a smart and attractive young woman, but there aren't many events around the area that would call for young, beautiful people."

"I don't know. Maybe it was a subtle arrangement, like someone paid her to hang out with them." She let out a sigh. "I gotta go. Thanks for checking in on me. I really appreciate it."

Before Paul could hold her up any longer, Darcy ended the call. She'd gotten him almost all the way there, but he was going to have to come up with the sugar daddy idea on his own.

The conversation helped Darcy in one way she hadn't anticipated. As she put the car into gear, her path was clear.

Next stop, the Todd Meadows residence.

With that decision made, Darcy drove past Jasmine's gallery. It wasn't quite six, so the woman should still be there. It couldn't hurt to make sure. Facing Todd alone would be easier than with Jasmine by his side.

As she slowed down the car to get a look in the window, a knot formed in Darcy's stomach.

Todd was there.

"Frac." Darcy turned into a parking spot. "Fine. I'll take them both on. Try to play one off against the other."

Todd and Jasmine were in the midst of yet another argument when Darcy entered the gallery. The two of them were standing in the middle of the room, practically nose to nose. A ceramic object lay at their feet, smashed to bits. Images of Angelica's trophy crossed Darcy's mind. Todd's hand was resting on an empty pedestal, presumably the former home of the piece of artwork. A stream of blood was trickling down one cheek.

Jasmine's arm was raised. Her phone was in her hand. Whether it was to take a picture of the damage Todd had apparently created or to bash him over the head, Darcy was uncertain. Well, they were all in the same room. Might as well dive on in like she was on stage and a mosh pit was awaiting her.

"Hey, y'all. Everyone okay?" Darcy put her hands up to signal she was no threat to them.

"The gallery is *closed*. Please leave. Right now." With her free hand, Jasmine pointed toward the door. The tip of her index finger was covered in red. While it might have been nail polish, the possibility seemed good that it was Todd's blood.

Darcy stepped backward until she reached the door. Without taking her eyes off the fighting couple, she flipped the lock and turned the OPEN sign around on its gold chain so it read CLOSED to passersby.

"I'm sorry for arriving at a bad moment, but this can't wait. You see—"

Todd took a step toward Darcy. His hands were balled into fists. A vein in his neck was pulsing against the collar of his dress shirt. His hair, which was normally a picture of perfection, was askew.

"Get out. Now!" His shout reverberated around the room.

The volume, and venom, caused Darcy to lean back. She was not going to be intimidated by this man, though. She'd faced down other equally monstrous villains in the past.

She took a step toward him. "As I was saying, I need your help with something, Todd. You see, I've learned that in the months leading up to her death, Angelica was being paid by someone off the books, in cash. The payments stopped not long before she was murdered. Before someone put their hands around her neck and strangled the life out of her."

"What are you talking about?" Jasmine backed toward the sales kiosk. It was as if she knew something and was preparing to make a break for it. In her form-fitting dress and five-inch stilettos, she wasn't going to get far before Darcy caught up to her, though.

Todd ran his fingers through his hair. "What could this absurd story have anything to do with me?"

Given the agitated state of the man, Darcy debated cutting to the chase. Accusing him of murder might send him into a rage, though. Perhaps like one involving Angelica. Diplomacy for now.

"You were her mentor. I was wondering if she might have confided in you. In case she was being coerced into something. Did she ever say anything to you about it?"

He was silent for a moment, his lips in a thin, straight line. He glanced at Jasmine, then returned his gaze to Darcy.

"No. She never said anything to me."

"Wait a minute." Jasmine marched right back toward him. "I know that look. You're hiding something. That's it, isn't it? You were carrying on with Angelica, weren't you?"

"Of course not." Todd's cheeks pinked up. "You're the only woman in my life."

"Now, maybe." Jasmine turned to Darcy. "I can't believe I was so blind. I gave him a new coat for his birthday last fall. He went on and on about how much he liked it until a couple of weeks ago. Then, all of a sudden, he couldn't seem to find it, and he'd gone back to wearing that awful leather one."

Darcy's pulse quickened. She searched her phone until she found an important photo that had suddenly become critical to the investigation.

"Look at this." She pointed at the image on the screen. It was the one from the ribbon-cutting ceremony. "Is that the coat you're talking about?"

The art dealer stared at the photo for a second before nodding. "That's it. Now that I think about it, he had it the night that young woman was murdered."

"I told you, darling, something must have happened to it." Todd held out his hands to Jasmine in a pleading fashion. "I thought I simply misplaced it. Somebody must have stolen it when I was at The Magic Box."

Unable to stop herself, Darcy barked out a laugh. "Seriously, dude? I saw you and Jasmine at Selena's that night. You were arguing. What were you fighting about?"

"None of your bus—"

"He'd been canceling plans, showing up late to things," Jasmine said, cutting Todd off. "I told him I'd had enough of it."

Darcy glanced over her shoulder to make sure she was blocking the entrance. If either of them made a move, she was going to make sure they didn't escape before answering her questions. To her satisfaction.

"The holidays are a busy time for me. If I don't take care of my clients, I'll be out of business."

When Todd kept droning on with another excuse, Darcy tuned him out. Instead, she showed another picture to Jasmine. "Does this button look like the one on his missing coat?"

"Yes, absolutely. I recognize the anchor logo on it. Todd's grandfather was in the Navy. I thought the buttons would be a nice tribute to the man's memory."

"This is a waste of time." Todd reached for Jasmine's hand. "Come on, Jazz. You know this woman's history with mental issues. I think it's time to call the police."

"This button was found at the crime scene," Darcy said in a rush. "I know because I found it."

While Todd shrugged, Jasmine left his hand grasping for air. She shuffled toward Darcy. Did that indicate Jasmine thought Todd was the murderer? Maybe. It could be a clever ploy, though.

In response to her move, he snapped his fingers and pointed at Jasmine. "She's the killer. She got me that coat. Then she murdered Angelica and dropped that button there to frame me."

"How dare you." Jasmine slapped Todd across the face, then wrenched his phone from him. "You're not calling anybody with that phone. Darcy, you call the police. You must have them on speed dial by now."

Darcy did, in fact, have Paul Gerard among her favorites. It wasn't time to call him quite yet, though. Todd's accusation might seem outlandish, but there was enough truth in it to give Darcy pause.

"What about it, Jasmine? Any truth to what your dude said?"

"Absolutely not. I got him that coat because I cared about him. Yes, I didn't appreciate that he spent so much time with that little tart. I won't deny that. I'd never resort to murder, though. If I wanted to retaliate, I'd do it in a much more artful way." She swept one arm to the side, as if indicating a clue to her cryptic words could be found somewhere in the gallery.

Todd barked out a laugh. There was a waver to it, though. The man's veneer was beginning to crack.

"Do you hear yourself, Jazz? I'm sorry, but you're sounding as unhinged as Ms. Gaughan here."

"Oh, really? I'll show you unhinged." Her high-pitched shout as she dashed to the sales kiosk made Darcy wince. A moment later, the woman lunged at Todd. She had a box-cutter in her hand.

The metal blade shone in the light cast by the overhead light fixtures. With each slash at Todd, Jasmine forced him backward until his back was against the wall.

"Let's all take a breath." Throwing caution and her own safety to the wind, Darcy inserted herself between the feuding parties. She turned her gaze to the woman wielding the weapon. "What do you mean by retaliating in an artful way?"

"Fine." Jasmine raised her chin but backed away. "I had a growing suspicion that he was cheating on me. A leopard can't change its spots, apparently. I didn't know who the other woman was until that night."

"What happened?" Even though Jasmine still had the box cutter in her hand, the tension in the room had dropped a bit. If Darcy could keep the woman talking, maybe she could resolve the situation without anyone getting hurt.

"When he left for the awards ceremony, I stayed at Selena's for another drink. Then, as I was leaving, I ran into the tart's boyfriend, Xander."

Darcy took in a breath at the bombshell revelation.

"The poor thing looked like his pet dog had just died. It only took a second to put two and two together. I invited him back to my place so we could...commiserate."

"How long did he stay?" Darcy's stomach turned itself into a knot as she uttered the words. She needed to know, though. The woman and Xander must have left Selena's before the time Darcy started reviewing the CCTV footage.

"All night." Her lip curled when she looked at Todd. "It was a welcome change to spend the night with someone who knew how to show a little gratitude. If you know what I mean."

"No!" Todd made a break for the back of the gallery.

Darcy had been ready for someone to attempt a runner. She was on Todd before he made it ten feet. He may have had a height and weight advantage, but he was no fighter. In no time, he was face down on the floor with Darcy straddling him.

"Get me some packing tape, Jasmine. Then call the police. Tell them we have Angelica Stipe's murderer under control."

Chapter Twenty-Six

Paul Gerard and Darcy were standing in a quiet corner of the art gallery. Uniformed police officers and EMS responders milled about the room, focused on their duties. In the opposite corner, Todd Meadows stood next to a uniformed Marysburg police officer while an EMT tended to his cut. His tie was askew, his head was bowed, and his hands were behind him. In cuffs.

Meanwhile, Jasmine was seated at her sales kiosk, typing away on a tablet.

"Let's go through this again." Paul tapped a notebook in his hand with a blue pen. "Meadows murdered Angelica. You know this how?"

"Process of elimination. Once Jasmine gave Xander an alibi, that eliminated them both as suspects. Based on the available evidence, only one person could have done it. Todd had the motive, the means, and the opportunity."

"Care to elaborate?"

"He was Angelica's sugar daddy. That's what I was talking about earlier. She kept the ledger to track her income and expenses from the arrangement. Since he was involved with Jasmine, it gave Angelica leverage over him so when things ended between them, they'd end on her terms."

Paul made a circular motion with a hand for Darcy to continue.

"When the awards ceremony was over, he approached her in the parking lot. Since he'd argued with Jasmine earlier, I don't think he wanted to go home. Instead, he wanted to spend the rest of the evening with Angelica. She turned him down. He didn't like that." Darcy wasn't one hundred percent certain of this part of the story, but she wanted to show confidence in her theory. Paul wouldn't appreciate guesswork.

"Are you saying that's all there was to this? She'd been up for over twenty-four hours. I'd say no to a night out, too. She turned down an invitation, so he murdered her?" He raised an eyebrow.

"That was just the straw that broke the camel's back. She said no because she wanted more money from him. When he rejected that, she probably said they were done and made some threats. Her missing phone? I'd bet one of my Pixie Dust gold records that she had incriminating information on it. Pictures, text messages, maybe voicemail messages. That's why it's missing. She threatened him with it, so he took it after strangling her. I'm sure she had things backed up to a cloud account. You get access to that; you'll find at least some of what she had to hang over his head."

"Assuming you're right about all of this."

"Oh, I'm right. I wouldn't risk taking someone like that guy down if I wasn't sure." That was a bit of an exaggeration. Still, she couldn't bear the thought of Paul releasing Todd due to a lack of confidence in Darcy's story.

"And the missing money?"

"He pocketed it. He was taking back what he must have thought was rightfully his." She shrugged. "In the heat of the moment, people don't always think clearly. Believe me, I know. Todd freaked out when Angelica turned him down. I mean, he'd set things up to make sure Angelica won the five hundred bucks as the overall winner."

"He did what? I thought O'Sullivan took care of the scoring. That's what he said when I talked to him."

"True, with Todd's input, though. I think the Hobbit didn't realize what he got himself into when he agreed to let Todd work with him on the secret scoring formula."

"He must have really wanted Angelica to win the big prize."

"Exactly. When has he ever done something without having strings attached? There's no way he agreed to put up the grand prize money unless he could guarantee Angelica she'd win it. It was his ultimate sugar daddy move."

"I'll have to talk to O'Sullivan again. He won't be happy to find out Meadows manipulated him." Paul jotted down something in his notebook.

"Twice, actually. First, with the scoring formula. Second, leaving the body for the Hobbit to find. The poor guy had nobody to verify his story. That led to a downturn in business at his stores. It's good for him that the bruises on Angelica's neck were positioned in a way that ruled him out. Thanks for that, by the way. Meanwhile, Todd decided to hang back and wait for you to make an arrest."

"I have no idea what you're talking about." Paul scratched his chin as he looked at the ceiling. "I'll give it to you. It sounds good except for one thing. Got any proof?"

"The coat that goes with the button. It's a navy peacoat. You'll find it at his house. I'd check the attic. You'll want to get a look at his and his company's bank accounts, too. You'll find money that matches the figures in Angelica's ledger."

Paul nodded and turned toward Todd. He'd only taken a few steps when the realtor pointed at Darcy.

"I want to press charges against that woman. I sprained my wrist when she tackled me and wrenched my shoulder when she hog-tied me." To complete the pathetic picture, he rolled his allegedly injured shoulder while he massaged the wrist he claimed to be hurt.

"Oh, give it a rest, Todd." Jasmine tapped a few keys on his phone, then started scrolling through something. After a few moments, she stopped. Then she slapped him across the face. Twice. "You son of a…"

Paul was at Jasmine's side in a flash. He put his hand around the woman's wrist to prevent any further violence. And prevent Todd from demanding that Jasmine be charged along with Darcy.

Before the detective could say anything, Jasmine shoved the phone in his face. "See? Darcy was right. Here's a text thread between that rat and the tart. The idiot deleted it but obviously didn't know it could be retrieved."

She gave the phone to Paul, then grabbed a set of keys from the kiosk. "I'm going to have a drink in my office, Darcy. You can join me while the police finish up out here."

A little while later, Darcy strolled through the front door at Marysburg Music. She stopped to take in the scene. A handful of shoppers were perusing

196

the aisles. Peter was talking to a customer while moving his shoulders to the rhythm of a bubbly reggae tune by Shaggy.

Izzy was ringing up a sale. At her side, Charlotte deposited the purchase in a canvas Marysburg Music bag. Hank was at home, enjoying a day off.

All was right with the world.

"Sorry I'm back so late." She nudged herself between Charlotte and Izzy. "I got this, Iz. Why don't you take five? Go put your feet up in the office."

"Oh, no. Not by a long shot." Izzy put her hands on her hips. "Charlotte told me what you've been up to while we've been working our fingers to the bone. Spill it, Boss."

Darcy held her tongue about the day's development until Peter locked the door at closing time.

"Must be good news, Boss," Peter said. "You've been smiling from ear to ear ever since you got here."

"I didn't know it was that obvious." She chuckled. It was like a five-hundred-pound weight had been lifted from her shoulders. Once again, it was accomplished.

"Todd Meadows is in custody for the murder of Angelica Stipe."

In the stunned silence, Izzy checked her phone. "The cops are keeping mum. What's the deal?"

After taking a deep breath, Darcy recounted the tumultuous events at the art gallery.

"It was crazy. Once Jasmine showed Paul the recovered the text messages that Todd thought he'd deleted, it was game over. I mean, I had it practically sewn up, but that totally sealed the deal."

"It's a good thing she knew the phone's password." Charlotte started counting the cash in the register. "I'm no fan of hers, but that was a pretty boss move."

"What's the old saying?" Izzy held up her index finger. "Hell hath no fury like a woman scorned."

Darcy sprayed the sales counter with glass cleaner. "That's true. Personally, I think her move on Xander was totally inappropriate, but I can't deny it got him off the hook."

"Two points for our friendly neighborhood art dealer." Peter mimicked taking a basketball shot. "Any idea if Todd's the one who messed with your brakes?"

"No, but Paul told me he'd look into Todd's whereabouts on Tuesday. With Xander cleared, he either did it himself or hired someone to do it. My guess is he's got some flunky on his payroll who he talked into doing it."

"Heaven forbid the man get his hands dirty." Charlotte practically spit the words out. "Do you think he really kept the coat? That seems like a dumb move to me."

In unison, the teenagers commented on their agreement with the observation.

"You're right. It was dumb." Darcy picked a piece of lint from her shirt while she formulated what she wanted to say next. She really wanted to get the words right.

"It was also classic Todd Meadows. Arrogant to a fault. I think he held onto the coat for two reasons. First, he was convinced that nobody would ever suspect him, such an important member of the community, of murder. Second, once someone else was arrested, he'd get the button replaced, probably in Indianapolis, where nobody would be the wiser, and start wearing it again. That way, he could use it to get back in Jasmine's good graces."

Peter let out a low whistle. "That is some cold as ice calculating."

"But he didn't get away with it. Thanks to you, Darcy Gaughan, P.I." Izzy put up her hand. "High fives all around."

After hands were slapped, Charlotte asked what was next.

"Detective Gerard wants to see me tomorrow to go over my statement, ask more questions, update me on the crash investigation. You know, the usual." She put her hand over her mouth for a moment, then let out a laugh. "I can't believe I just called talking to a cop about a murder investigation the usual. What has happened to me?"

"You're Marysburg's own superhero, Boss. The Dynamic Drummer." Peter pretended to perform a drum roll."

"Not bad. I think I like Record Store Ranger more," Izzy said. "Got a nickname for our crime fighter here, Charlotte?"

Charlotte put her hands together while she mulled over the question. "What about the Manic Musician?"

The group broke out in laughter, with Darcy laughing the hardest of all. She wasn't certain whether her Marysburg Music teammates were being serious or were yanking her chain. It didn't matter.

What did matter was that, with Angelica's murderer in custody, she and her merry band of mischief makers could spend their time joking about silly nicknames instead of worrying about a killer who was on the loose.

The next morning, Darcy was in her recliner, sipping a cup of green tea with Ringo on her lap, when there was a knock on her door.

"Sorry, dude. We both know I was going to have to move you sometime." She picked the old tomcat up, then placed him back on the recliner. "Enjoy the warmth."

Wary of having an unannounced visitor so early in the morning, Darcy grabbed her canister of pepper spray as she made her move to the back door. Liam had given the self-defense item to her the previous evening. Along with a spaghetti and meatballs dinner.

She'd thanked him for it, then asked the reason for the gift. He told her that despite everyone's advice, she'd carried on with her investigation. Since her family and friends couldn't stop her from putting herself in harm's way, the least he could do was make sure she had some extra protection on her at all times.

The thoughtful gesture brought tears to her eyes. Yeah, Liam was a great guy. Approaching the door, she thanked the rock gods that her boyfriend was so amazing.

She pulled back the curtain covering the window in the door. Her visitor was none other than Paul Gerard.

Darcy opened the door, breathing a sigh of relief. "Hey, Paul. What brings you by this fine, peaceful morning?"

"I thought we could conduct my follow-up interview here." He raised a hand that was holding a brown paper bag. "Got some of Jenna's finest pastries."

"Come on in." While Paul laid out the bakery delicacies, Darcy brewed him some coffee. "What's the occasion? Detective Rosengarten always made me come see her at the station to follow up."

Paul took a bit of his chocolate chip muffin. While he chewed, he seemed to debate how to answer the question. After a sip of coffee, he shook his head.

"That was a power move by Kaitlin. She wanted you to know she was the boss."

"Even though I solved two murders on her watch."

He raised his coffee cup to her. "True enough. The way I see it, you helped the department out. The least I can do is make this meeting a little more convenient for you. Especially since we're still working on the brake sabotage case."

"Then hit me with your best shot. With all respect due to the legend herself, Pat Benatar."

They spent the next ninety minutes going over Darcy's story from the previous day. Paul covered every angle, from the peacoat appearing in the ribbon-cutting photo to the ledger to the confrontation in the art gallery. When he was satisfied that she'd answered all his questions, he said he had one more.

"I gotta know. What was the moment when you knew really Meadows was the murderer?"

It was Darcy's turn to chew while she thought it over. "I guess my gut told me he did it when I realized he'd benefit from either Rafe or the Hobbit going to jail by getting his hands on their real estate. To be fair, though, I didn't know for sure until Jasmine admitted to spending the night with Xander."

"Yeah, I didn't see that coming. I talked to him last night. At first, he tried to stick to the loss of memory story. He finally came clean when I threatened to charge him with interfering with an official police investigation."

"Look at you, bringing the hammer down." Darcy let out a laugh. "Though, I suppose if he would have been honest from the start, you'd have been able to make an arrest a whole lot sooner."

"The poor kid, once he started, it was like a water faucet on full blast. He told me Jasmine put a full-court press on him to keep his mouth shut. She supposedly told him that 'Nobody would believe the Midwest's preeminent art dealers would have a tryst with a run-of-the-mill frat boy.' That was after they got busy, of course."

"Wow, that's messed up. I suppose it shouldn't be a surprise to see how quickly she turned on Todd when she realized he'd been Angelica's sugar daddy."

Paul shrugged. "What's the old saying? All's fair in love and war. Anyway, I'm surprised you haven't asked me the million-dollar question."

Darcy knew exactly what question he wanted her to ask. Throughout the conversation, she'd been so tempted, but didn't want to jinx anything. On the other hand, she'd served the case to Paul on a silver platter.

"Did Todd confess?"

The detective smiled. "Yes, he did. It took a while, but he finally did when we told him we had a warrant to search his house and his financial records. You should be proud of yourself, Darcy. You did it again."

A warm feeling engulfed her. She'd completed the deal and got justice for Angelica. The young woman might have had a soul as black as a vinyl record, but that didn't make it okay for Meadows to take her life. Not only had he murdered her, but he'd also prevented any chance of her making changes in her life.

Unlike Darcy, Angelica would never get to make amends for her poor choices. She'd never have the opportunity to learn from her mistakes and grow from them.

A tear ran down Darcy's cheek. It was heartbreaking. The fact that the murderer was in custody provided solace, though.

"Thanks, Paul. Between you and me, let's hope this is the last time Darcy Gaughan, P.I.'s skills are called upon."

Chapter Twenty-Seven

Nine days had passed since Todd Meadows's arrest for taking the life of Angelica Stipe. Initially, the town had been in an uproar. News that one of their leading citizens had been implicated in such a horrific crime was unfathomable to the good folks of Marysburg, Indiana.

The initial protests over the real estate developer's incarceration gave way to begrudging acceptance, then vocal approval as information about the case became available. In some circles, Darcy was hailed as a hero. Especially after the maintenance man for Todd's rental properties admitted to cutting Rusty's brake line. He only did it after his boss offered him ten thousand dollars while promising nobody would get hurt. The guy wasn't the sharpest tool in the shed and had worked for Todd for years. His loyalty to the local real estate mogul was understandable, if obviously misguided.

In other circles, she was criticized as a troublemaker who shouldn't get involved in the affairs of others. Those comments were mostly coming from people with business interests tied to Todd Meadows and his real estate empire.

The man's father was among those defending Todd, even though he was only doing it via social media from his winter home in Arizona. The man's former girlfriend, Jasmine Longoria, was not in the defender camp and was now leading a campaign to have a street named after Angelica.

"Is your new BFF coming?" Jenna gave Darcy a playful jab to the upper arm. They were in the rental car on their way to Marysburg Music to prepare for the Pixie Dust event that afternoon.

Darcy inhaled the mouthwatering aroma of fresh scones, muffins, and cookies emanating from the back seat. Jenna's teasing was no match for the yummy aromas.

"If you're referring to Jasmine, I don't know." She slowed the car as a stop sign came into view. "And she'd not my BFF. You are. At least you were until you started giving me grief about her the last few days."

Jenna laughed. "Let me see if I remember what the note said. 'My deepest thanks for saving me from untold days of pain, both emotional and financial. Best, Jasmine.' That's what came with that to-die-for painting she sent to you, isn't it?"

" The woman wanted to show her appreciation. That's all." She accelerated through the intersection once traffic cleared. "I don't think you'll ever see me hanging out at wine bars and going to art exhibits with her. I'd rather spend my time with you, listening to ABBA records and watching *Mama Mia*, any day of the week."

"Aww, you're the best. And look how far you've come, from outcast to people lining up to be your friend."

"No, you're the best for sticking by me when I was at rock bottom." It was true. Darcy would never be able to adequately repay Jenna for giving her a place to stay when she had none and being a steady shoulder, along with Eddie, when Darcy had nobody else to lean on.

The duo grew quiet for a few moments until the record store came into view. When they rolled to a stop in Darcy's parking place in back, Jenna put her hand on Darcy's arm.

"Are you sure you're ready for this? I have no problem telling people you got sick. Shoot, half the people I know are walking around with an extra supply of tissues and cold medicine."

"Gotta love cold and flu season in Indiana." Darcy shook her head. "I'm good, I think. My rehearsals have gone well. It's been fun having Hallie Birch coaching me, making sure I'm not cutting any corners."

"You've taught her well. What about meeting the band and the manager? This is the first time you'll all be face to face since you went separate ways, isn't it?"

It was. There was no denying seeing the man who had fired her and the two band members who went along with it was going to be emotional. This was something she wanted to do, though. After all, at the time she was fired, Darcy couldn't play. Now, even though she was sober, the injury made it impossible for her to perform at the level Pixie Dust deserved.

She'd given the issue a lot of thought over the last week. One thing Darcy had realized was that Pixie Dust continued to thrive in her absence. They still made new music, still played live gigs, and above all, kept Darcy's dream from all those years ago alive and well.

The quarterly royalty checks she continued to receive from Dust's early albums helped ease the pain, too. And grow her retirement account.

"It's gonna be okay. I had a video chat with them all a few days ago. There were some tears, but they were mostly happy ones. Does it still hurt? A little. I'm at peace with the situation, though. Finally."

Jenna wiped a tear from her cheek, then took Darcy in a tight hug. "I love you so much, girl. And I'm so proud of you. I'll be close by the whole time if you need anything. Let's do this."

By the time the band arrived, Pixie Dust fans had already formed a line that stretched two blocks long. While the manager, tour manager, and technician came inside, the musicians socialized with those in the queue, shaking hands and taking selfies.

"Welcome to Marysburg Music." Darcy strode up to the band's manager, Kyle Powers. They shook hands. "Hope the tour's going well."

"It is. Thanks for asking. And thank you for agreeing to host this event." He opened his mouth, as if to say something else, then shuffled his feet. "I'm glad to see you're doing so well. Music store owner and detective. You're keeping busy."

"I have. Let me show you around." Darcy gave him a smile as she gestured toward the Pixie Dust display Izzy and Peter had set up.

Kyle had apologized during the Zoom call for the lies he told Darcy in the weeks leading up to her being let go. It had been a sincere one. Darcy could sense it. In return, she accepted the apology with gratitude. In retrospect, he'd done what he needed to do at the time. All was forgiven.

CHAPTER TWENTY-SEVEN

It was time to move forward.

Actually, it already had been. For a long time. Among the things Darcy learned in her almost six years of sobriety was that healing came at its own pace. Some of the damage her alcohol dependence and elbow injury caused got better quickly, in the matter of months or a couple of years. Others might not ever completely heal. That was okay.

Those injuries, both physical and emotional, played their roles in making Darcy Gaughan the woman she was now. It was a woman who had a great job, was respected in her community, and had the love of family and friends. While she didn't always love herself, she accepted who she was. And was proud to be that person.

At the moment, she was a retired punk rock drummer about to put a period on a segment of her life.

After wandering the aisles, Darcy and Kyle arrived at the platform at the back of the store.

"Oh, wow. Is that your kit from back in the day?" When Darcy nodded, he pulled out his phone. "Do you mind if I take a picture? The fans would love to see it."

It was a simple, five-piece setup, the kind Ringo Starr, the world-famous musician, not the cat, would approve of. There was the bass, snare, and three tom drums. Ride, crash, and hi-hat cymbals completed the layout.

If one got close, they'd see a few chips in the glossy, black finish of the drums. Scars from life on the road. Darcy didn't mind the blemishes. They were an apt metaphor for her own unconventional story.

"Click away. I'm going to say hi to the band."

Darcy had only taken a few steps when the current drummer of the band, Yvonne Schmidt, let out a little squeal and wrapped her up in a bear hug.

After a moment, the drummer took a step back and ran her fingers through her spiky, cobalt-blue hair. "OMG, I'm so sorry about that. The girls in the band told me you're not super touchy-feely. It's just that I've been so stoked to actually get to meet you in person. The woman who founded Pixie Dust. Wow."

"Nice to meet you." Darcy opened her arms wide. "I've been working on that hugging thing, so come here."

While the two women embraced, the other founding members of Pixie Dust, singer and guitarist Kate Crash and bassist Sandy Goldberg, approached.

"What's up, D," Kate said as she gave Darcy a little wave.

"Long time no see," Sandy added as she removed a pair of round sunglasses. "Cool place you got."

Darcy's Marysburg Music team members kept their distance. Every single one of them-Hank, Charlotte, Izzy, and Peter-would walk through fire for their boss. If things didn't go well during this initial greeting, they were prepared to usher the band and their staff right back out the door.

There was no need for them to worry. Without saying a word, Darcy gave Kate, then Sandy their own hugs.

"I missed you knuckleheads." Darcy wiped tears from her cheeks with her thumb. "It's great to have you back in your old stomping grounds."

After a few minutes of chatting, Jenna directed the visitors toward a table where she'd set laid-out pastries with some drinks. While starstruck Izzy and Peter served the refreshments, Charlotte and Hank reviewed the details of the meet & greet with Kyle.

The session was almost finished when Darcy's phone buzzed. She laughed, then wiped away another tear as she stared at the screen.

"You okay, young lady?" Hank put his arm on her shoulder. The man was such a steadying force in her life, from keeping the store spotless to words of wisdom whenever they were needed.

"Yep." She sniffed, then turned the phone screen toward Hank. "It's from Liam. He and a friend who runs a body shop in Muncie have gotten together. They're going to repair Rusty. He promises that when they're done, he'll be as good as new."

The older gentleman clapped his hands. "How about that? This is turning into quite the momentous day, isn't it."

"Got that right. One I'm sure I'll never forget."

A little while later, Charlotte raised her hand and asked the group for their attention. "The meet and greet starts in a few minutes. If the members of

Pixie Dust could take a seat and the Marysburg Music folks could take their positions, we'll get started."

Despite the entire Pixie Dust group encouraging her to join the band at the autograph table, Darcy kept to her assigned position behind the cash register. "People are here to see a real band, not a has-been drummer who's more of a cat lady than a performer these days."

The comment elicited a round of laughter.

"I don't know about you all, but I can't wait to see you prove yourself wrong." Yvonne twirled a drumstick in her fingers and took a little bow as the group applauded her statement.

At Charlotte's signal, Hank opened the door. Fans and friends streamed inside, and an excited buzz soon filled the store. Among the first to enter were Rafe and the Hobbit. Both men had large canvas bags that looked to be laden down with memorabilia. While they waited in line, they looked toward Darcy. In unison, as if they'd practiced the move, they saluted her.

She laughed and gave them a thumbs-up. It was remarkable to think how, in such a short period of time, both men had gone from antagonists to, if not friends, allies. The development would have made Eddie proud.

And brought a tear to her eye.

Darcy kept herself busy ringing up sale after sale. If she didn't have something to keep her occupied, she would have lost the battle, keeping a flood of happy tears at bay. That was okay. All things considered, tears of joy were pretty decent things to contend with.

At one point, while she was chatting with a customer, Aisling arrived. Instead of remaining in line, Darcy's sister made a beeline to the sales counter.

"There was no way in the world I was going to miss this." She leaned across the counter to hug her big sister. While they were embracing, Aisling asked Darcy how she was doing.

"I'm good. This is good. I need to stay here, but there's Paul Gerard. You should go chat him up. He's single. And a good guy."

Aisling looked where Darcy was pointing. She smiled and pushed a lock of hair behind her ear. "I thought he was a looker when we were at the hospital. Good to see I wasn't wrong. See ya, sis."

In what seemed like the blink of an eye, the meet-and-greet session ended, and the band prepared to take the stage. While they were setting up, Liam joined Darcy behind the cash register. He didn't say anything, just took her hand in his and gave it a gentle squeeze.

She returned the gesture. Yes, indeed, she was good.

The plan was for the band to play four songs from their new album, *Kiss This*. After that, Darcy would slide behind the drums for a twenty-minute session of Dust music from when Darcy was still with the band.

Once Yvonne kicked off the show with an aggressive drum fill, Darcy found herself snapping he fingers and tapping her toes to the music. As evidenced by the roars of approval from the shoulder-to-shoulder gathering, the Princesses of Punk hadn't lost their edge or the ability to please a crowd.

Fifteen minutes later, Yvonne got to her feet. Kate took her mic in both hands. Sandy draped an arm around Yvonne as the drummer joined the other two at the front of the stage.

"Fourteen years ago, I was a Theater major at Ball State when I met this tough-as-nails music student. She played the drums with an aggressive style that left me breathless. The woman wanted to put a band together that was going to give a one-finger salute to the status quo. When she told me it was going to be an all-girl band, I was totally in."

Kate handed the microphone to Sandy.

"The same woman tracked me down after I performed at an open mic night at the campus coffee shop. Her vision for changing the world of rock and roll, and her passion and belief that we could do it made me a believer from day one. That woman is right over there." Sandy pointed to Darcy. "She's gone on to bigger and better things, but she's agreed to sit in with us today for a few songs. People, please join me in welcoming our founder, our friend, and one whale of a record store owner, Darcy Gaughan, to the stage."

A window-rattling roar from the crowd accompanied an equally deafening round of applause. On legs that were a bit unsteady, Darcy worked her way through the assemblage.

She was almost at the stage when Yvonne leaned toward the mic. "I've heard Darcy's a pretty good private eye, too. If I ever get in trouble, I know who I'm calling."

The joke got the crowd laughing and calmed the butterflies flitting about in Darcy's belly as she took her seat behind the drum kit. Her drum kit, which Yvonne had said would be an honor to play. The butterflies in her stomach settled down the moment she grasped her drumsticks.

She could do this. She'd figured out who murdered Angelica Stipe and brought the young woman's family justice. After that, playing songs she wrote and had played hundreds of times would be as easy as putting a vinyl record on a turntable.

As the image of a record album spinning round and round flashed before Darcy's eyes, it hit home how her life had taken a wandering path that somehow brought her back to where she started. After starting out as a drummer in a college band, Darcy Gaughan had gone on to become a key member of the punk music scene, lost her dream gig due to alcohol dependency and injury, got sober, and became the owner of a thriving music-related business.

She'd even solved three murders along the way.

And now she was back behind the drum kit. Darcy counted off the start to Pixie Dust's most popular song, "Let's Ride," with a grin. This chapter of her life had indeed come full circle. She couldn't wait to find out what the next chapter had in store for her. Because life was good, indeed. And was only going to get better.

Acknowledgements

I would like to thank my editor, Shawn Reilly Simmons, and the entire team at Level Best Books for everything they've done in bringing Magic Box Murder and the entire Darcy Gaughan Mysteries series to life. You rock!

About the Author

J.C. Kenney is the bestselling author of mysteries full of oddball characters in unusual settings. He's also the co-host of The Bookish Hour and The Bookish Moment webcasts. When he's not writing, you can find him following IndyCar racing or listening to music. He has two grown children and lives in Indianapolis with his wife and a cat. You can find him at www.jckenney.com.

SOCIAL MEDIA HANDLES:
   Facebook: https://www.facebook.com/JCKenney1
   Instagram: https://www.instagram.com/j.c.kenney/
   Threads: https://www.threads.net/@j.c.kenney

AUTHOR WEBSITE:
   www.jckenney.com

Also by J.C. Kenney

The Darcy Gaughan Mysteries
  Record Store Reckoning
  Concert Hall Hit

The Allie Cobb Mysteries
  A Literal Mess
  A Genuine Fix
  A Mysterious Mix Up
  A Deadly Discovery
  The Dead of Winter
  A Parting Shot